She wanted to show Trevor they had something in common, a bond.

She wanted the guy from the bar back.

Somewhere in that stuffy package Trevor presented was the guy who'd helped her get through New Year's Eve. He'd made her laugh, made her feel seen and appreciated. She had no idea where that guy had gone, or why.

For that one afternoon, Trevor had made her feel attractive and witty. He'd talked to her about things she loved.

But whoever he had been that afternoon, he didn't feel the same way about her now that he knew more about her. And yes, that was a depressing thought. But it would be better for her to shove that afternoon away and forget about it, because there wasn't going to be a repeat.

Was staying in Cupid's Crossing even worth it?

Dear Reader,

Thanks for coming on this journey with me as Carter's Crossing transforms into Cupid's Crossing. This third book in the series was an additional challenge, as it starts before *A Valentine's Proposal* and continues past the events of *A Fourth of July Proposal*. The transformation of the mill that happens in this book was the major event to make the town the romance center it aspired to be, so this was an important part of the series.

The story idea began as I imagined an architect who'd had problems with a crooked contractor on his last job coming to Carter's Crossing and meeting a female contractor who'd had it up to here with mansplaining and people questioning her fitness for a traditionally male job. From there, I just needed to get them to see that they needed each other. No problem!

Over the course of construction, they learn to trust each other, but of course, it's not an easy journey. I hope you enjoy Trevor and Andie's story. Maybe something has happened to you that damaged your confidence in others and yourself. Or maybe you have had to adjust your dreams or found your dreams have changed over time. But always, we want to find our special someone.

Thank you for taking this journey with me.

Kim

HEARTWARMING

A New Year's Eve Proposal

—

Kim Findlay

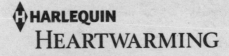

HARLEQUIN®
HEARTWARMING™

ISBN-13: 978-1-335-42657-4

A New Year's Eve Proposal

Recycling programs
for this product may
not exist in your area.

Harlequin Enterprises ULC
22 Adelaide St. West, 40th Floor
Toronto, Ontario M5H 4E3, Canada
www.Harlequin.com

Printed in U.S.A.

Kim Findlay is a Canadian who fled the cold to live on a sailboat in the Caribbean and write romance novels. She shares the boat with her husband and the world's cutest spaniel. Bucket list accomplished! Her first Harlequin Heartwarming novel, *Crossing the Goal Line*, came about from the Heartwarming Blitz, and she's never looked back. Keep up with Kim, including her sailing adventures, at kimfindlay.ca.

Books by Kim Findlay

Harlequin Heartwarming

A Hockey Romance

Crossing the Goal Line
Her Family's Defender

Cupid's Crossing

A Valentine's Proposal
A Fourth of July Proposal

Visit the Author Profile page
at Harlequin.com for more titles.

To Lara, Ritchard and Grant,

who all helped with technical things I know nothing about,

with my apologies for my mistakes in the Cupid books.

CHAPTER ONE

SHE'D BEEN STARING at the glass of soda and ignoring the people in the pub around her for fifteen minutes. At least. Arms crossed and leaning on the bar countertop, she watched the glass like it held the secrets of the universe.

He knew it had been that long because he'd arrived fifteen minutes ago, and she'd already been deep in her staredown with the fizzy liquid. The stool beside her had been the only empty seat in the place when he came in, so he'd sat down and ordered a beer for himself. He tried not to watch her, but it was hard, because she was right *there*. Staring at her soda.

He hadn't planned on this stop at the Goat and Barley, but he'd needed to clean up after helping a senior citizen change her tire. Changing the tire hadn't made a mess, but her Great Dane had managed to lick his face and hands, and he preferred to not wear a layer of dog saliva. It seemed only right to order a drink in return for use of their restroom.

Now he thought he might stay for a bit. It

was better than spending the afternoon on his own, and it *was* New Year's Eve.

Something about his barstool neighbor pricked his attention. She looked sad. That was obviously not his problem, but it seemed wrong to ignore her distress.

Something jammed into his ribs, and he turned as cold liquid dripped onto his pant leg. He looked up and met the shocked gaze of an older man.

"My apologies. I lost my balance and…"

From the smell, it was Scotch now dripping over his thigh. The man reached forward to rescue the glass from the bar top, and Trevor got a blast of more Scotch.

He wiped at his leg, but it was no use. The whiskey had soaked into his pants.

"I'm sorry. Let me buy you another, um, whatever…"

Trevor's beer was only half gone. He didn't want to drink another, since he still had to drive. He shook his head and forced a smile.

"No problem. Accidents happen."

The man blinked at him for a moment, then his phone buzzed, and he moved a shaky hand to his pocket.

"Rachel? What? I can't hear—"

The man wandered away, weaving through

the crowd, people moving out of his way as he blundered into them.

"Are you okay?"

Trevor turned his attention to the bartender wiping the bar top. He'd taken the spilled glass and was watching for Trevor's reaction.

"I'm fine." Trevor glanced over his shoulder. "Is he alright?"

The bartender glanced toward the door, with a frown. "I called someone for him. He'll be good for now."

Trevor reminded himself he didn't know these people, and they could undoubtedly take care of themselves.

The bartender moved away, and Trevor turned to the woman on the stool next to him. She hadn't moved. She'd ignored the whole incident.

He should just leave her alone, but he was in a strange place on this day of celebration, and he was tired of fixating on his own problems. Some variety would be a distraction, if nothing else.

The only thing that had changed with the woman since he'd arrived was her soda was less fizzy. It would soon be flat.

He was rusty at this, no longer at ease in social interactions. But tonight was about ending the old and starting anew. He could start a conversation. If he could think of something to say.

"Are you breaking up?"

Had he actually said that? He wouldn't normally do anything like this, but that unwavering stare at the flattening pop was...eerie.

She blinked and looked at him for the first time since he'd sat down next to her.

While she'd been leaning over, a curtain of brown hair had hidden most of her face, and he hadn't gotten a good look at her. Now frowning hazel-green eyes met his. She had a straight nose, strong jaw and pink lips without makeup.

She raised her eyebrows, and he felt his cheeks warm. He should have kept silent.

"What?"

She'd had to lean toward him to respond, and a whiff of some clean scent, soap perhaps, tickled his nostrils and gave him courage to continue.

He nodded at the drink.

"Are you two breaking up?"

She looked back at the drink, as if it might have changed in the last thirty seconds.

"Am I breaking up?"

This was awkward. He was out of practice and was making a fool of himself. No one could say he didn't follow through, though.

"With your drink. You've been frowning at it since I sat down here."

A reluctant grin pulled up the corner of her mouth. It added a sparkle to her eyes, and he realized with a jolt that she was pretty. And that maybe he hadn't completely embarrassed himself.

She turned her gaze back to the glass.

"No, it's not a breakup. It's more of…an anniversary."

It obviously wasn't a happy anniversary, but he didn't know her and didn't want her story. He wasn't sure why he'd felt the need to break into her reverie, but he wasn't going to pry.

"What about you two?" she asked, looking at the half-empty glass of draft beer in front of him.

She was interested in talking, in spite of what was going on with her and her beverage. He was surprised he wanted to talk to her, as well.

He cocked his head, considering his response, thinking of something light, easy.

"This is what I'd call a blind date."

Her smile grew, and he felt good. Like he'd accomplished a challenging task.

She lowered her voice to a whisper.

"How's it going?"

He leaned in, playing the game with her. "Nice, but I don't think this is the one."

She nodded, solemnly. "Well, you have to drink a lot of toads before you find your princess."

A laugh snorted out of him. He hadn't made a sound like that in…forever.

"You did not just say that. That is the grossest—" he said, shaking his head.

Her lips were pulled between her teeth to prevent her own laugh, but the eyes dancing above them gave her away. "I have three brothers. *Gross* is their forte."

Brothers. The smile slipped away from his face.

He didn't want to talk about family, not now. He felt her gaze on him, but he kept his face turned to his beer.

"You're not from around here."

She changed the subject, and he appreciated it. He made sure he had a polite expression on his face when he turned back to her.

"What gave me away?"

He thought he looked like most of the other customers. Sweater and jeans, warm jacket hanging on the back of his seat. Utility boots, whether for working or simply for keeping warm. Once he'd left the outskirts of New York

City, the temperature had dropped and kept dropping as he'd driven for hours to get here.

Here being a small town named Carter's Crossing. He'd signed on for a yearlong project in the hopes of keeping his firm alive so he wouldn't have to go back to working for someone else.

"I grew up here. Lived in Carter's Crossing all my life. I know all the locals."

That must be what it was like in a small town. No anonymity. Presumably, most of the people in this bar were locals, but none of them had come over to see if she was okay. Interesting.

"I'm from New York. The city. I'm not familiar with this part of the state." He considered his next question. He could call this research. "What's this place like?"

She seemed to think for a while and then come to some decision. There was a trace of a smile on her face, so he thought the decision was in his favor, and that warmed him. Maybe he hadn't lost all his social skills over the past two years.

"Do you know anything about small towns?"

He shook his head. He'd been born and raised in New York City. He was accustomed to crowds and lights and the sounds of people all the time. A feeling of hustle even when sitting still.

Her lip quirked on one side, and he found his gaze hooked there. He noticed her lips, their shape and color, and he wondered what it would be like to kiss them.

Whoa. He gave himself a mental slap, met her gaze again and listened to the words coming from that mouth.

"It's small, which means there are no strangers. It's great when you want people or when you need help, because everyone gathers around, but it's more difficult when you want to be alone. And it's hard to keep secrets."

Trevor was suddenly aware this woman was on her own by choice, and that the people in this bar, who would all know her, had left her alone because that's what she wanted. He was intruding. He *was* still missing some of those social skills.

He leaned back slowly, reluctantly. He felt himself flushing as he realized he was one of those guys convinced a woman on her own needed his company.

"I'm sorry. I didn't mean to intrude."

She made an abrupt movement with her hand, as if she was reaching out to touch him, to keep him there beside her. But she stopped it, and her face reddened.

"No, it's okay. As you might have guessed, this isn't a happy day. I'm bracing myself to get through it. I appreciate the distraction of talking to someone who doesn't know and isn't anxiously asking me how I'm doing."

He could relate to that. She had no idea how tired he was of the same. Enough that he'd driven out to Carter's Crossing on New Year's Eve to take one more look at the place he'd agreed to work, just to be out of the city and away from those sympathetic eyes.

He held her gaze, letting her know he understood. Empathized. Was avoiding his own stuff.

"I'll promise not to ask you about your business if you promise the same."

She gave a slight nod and then continued the conversation as if there hadn't been that break. "Carter's. It's a pretty town, for the most part."

He'd noticed as he'd driven through.

"It was a lumber town until just a couple of years ago. The better-off people lived around the park in their nice Victorian homes. When you cross the train tracks, heading to the mill, you have the places where the workers lived. As the mill had to lay people off, those homes got a little more run-down."

The buildings in a town said a lot about a

place, and he'd been reading Carter's story on his visits.

"There's a literal wrong side of the tracks?" He meant it as a joke, but all sign of humor left her face.

"If you judge by money, then yes. And maybe people were a little more likely to break the rules on the poorer side, but it's only because not having money is one of the things that can limit your choices. I know good people on both sides."

For some reason, he was upset that he'd been put into the group of people that judged by money. The kind who would consider the worker side of the railroad to be the wrong side. He was mortified he'd leaped to those conclusions and that she'd seen that.

"I'm sorry." He shrugged. "I've been fortunate enough that even though I've never exactly been rich, I've had choices."

Until his choices had been taken away. He would guard against that in future. He suspected she might not have had many choices, and that maybe limits had been imposed on her by others.

He didn't think poverty was her problem. Even though she'd ordered a soft drink and then simply sat looking at it, her clothes were clean, almost new, and good quality. Her skin was clear, and her eyes weren't shadowed from lack of sleep. There were lines at the corners of her eyes, but her mouth was still positioned for smiling, not pulled down at the corners by endless struggle.

It was something else, and he'd guess it was connected to the anniversary drink in front of her, but he'd promised not to ask. He hadn't thought he'd want to.

She closed her eyes for a moment. "I didn't mean to be judgmental. Most of my people live in that part of town, so I may be a little protective of them."

She had people? "Which side do you live on?"

It was a little pushy. They had an unspoken agreement not to probe too closely, didn't they?

"Neither, really. My family's place is just outside of town, so you could say we have a foot on both sides."

We? Family *we* or partner *we*? He hadn't thought she was with someone. No ring on the fourth finger, no mention of someone before this. It had been a while since he'd been curious about someone else, but talking to this woman kept him from feeling sorry for himself or second-guessing his decision to come to Carter's Crossing. Knowing about the town and its people would help.

"You've never wanted to leave?"

She narrowed her eyes, and he realized he'd touched on something.

"I did once. Maybe I will again someday, but for now, this is where I am."

He glanced over at the glass of soda and wondered if that was connected to her reason for staying, but again, they weren't allowed to dig deep.

She talked about leaving, without someone with her. That pleased him. He wanted to keep talking with her.

"Tell me more about Carter's Crossing. I promise I'll withhold judgment."

Her lips twisted as she considered his request.

"Okay, if you'll tell me about living in the city."

He held out his hand. "Deal."

She lifted her hand to shake his, and he noticed hers was rough and calloused, the nails short. This was a woman who worked with her hands. He was so curious, but he ignored the impulse to ask her any questions, as well as the jolt of awareness that skin-on-skin contact provided. Instead, he took his hand back and had another sip of his beer.

He'd promised not to pry.

She sat back in her seat, a smile playing on

the corners of her lips. "This reminds me of the city mouse and the country mouse. You know, that kids story? Only, I can't remember the ending. Did the city mouse move to the country or the country mouse to the city?"

He might come to a town like this to work, but his home was in the city, and that wasn't going to change.

He shrugged. "The country mouse probably stayed in the country and the city mouse in the city."

She shook her head. "In real life, the country mice tend to end up in the city. Only a few of us stay in the country."

ANDIE WASN'T SURE what it was about this guy, but talking to him was fun. She wasn't Andie, business owner, responsible for her family and her employees. She wasn't poor Andie, reliving the worst day of her life. She was just a woman in a bar, talking to an interesting man.

He was interesting and not just because he was from somewhere else. Not just because she liked his rangy build and the way a lock of dark hair fell over those deep brown eyes framed by tortoiseshell glasses. She felt a connection with him.

He had secrets, wounds he didn't want to share. She could tell by the way he respected hers. He knew the burden of sympathy, and how it refused to let you forget.

He listened as she told him about Carter's Crossing, the mill town now trying to reinvent itself as a romance destination. He talked about his experiences in New York. Nothing personal, nothing too revealing, but even those bits did expose glimpses of who he was.

He had respect for people. He had a sense of humor. He didn't mention friends, and she wondered if he was lonely.

He didn't mention his family, either. He'd flinched when she'd mentioned her brothers, so she suspected he had family issues. On the other hand, who had a family without some kind of issue? When he described New York City, he often described the buildings as if they were residents, part of the population that made up the city, and she found that fascinating.

Her phone pinged with a text message, and that was the first she became aware of how much time had passed. The pale winter sunlight was gone, leaving the windows dark. It was almost dinnertime, and her mother would be worried about where she was. Of course she would be, on today of all days.

Andie picked up the phone and quickly responded, assuring her mother she was at the Goat and Barley, wasn't drinking and would leave now. She knew her mother wouldn't relax until she pulled into the driveway.

She sighed.

She was dreading tonight. She looked up at the man beside her, who was watching her with raised brows. Had he thought of asking her to eat with him? To stay for the evening and see in the New Year?

Andie didn't do that. New Year's wasn't a time to party or celebrate. It hadn't been for a long time. And she had to leave, now.

"I'm sorry. I have to go."

That was disappointment she saw in his eyes, wasn't it? She told herself it was. That would be her comfort for the rest of the night.

"Thanks for the chat. This is a bad day, and you helped me get through some of it. I hope this new year is good to you."

He stood as she pulled her coat on and grabbed her bag.

"Thank you. I've enjoyed talking to you, too."

She wondered if he was going to ask her name? Her number? Was there any point, when he was traveling through and she was stuck here?

Her phone rang, this time a call from her brother. She answered it, already edgy as she anticipated his reason for calling. His excuses soon filled her ears.

"Joey, that was your responsibility," she said, interrupting him. "Can you not do anything I ask you to? I'm supposed to be your boss, not just your sister. Mom is already freaking that I'm late."

More excuses, more dragging her back to her regular life. The man with the soothing voice had sat down and tactfully turned away to give her privacy.

It was probably for the best anyhow. She had no time for interesting men, even if they were staying in the area. She had responsibilities and decisions and ties, and until she was free of those, she couldn't be distracted. Maybe one day she'd be able to leave.

She smiled at the stranger who was almost a friend, and he nodded at her before she headed for the exit, winding her way through the people who knew her, cared for her, and who watched her with sympathy and pity.

It had been nice to talk to someone who didn't know what today was about, but her family needed her now. This night, above all others in the year.

Her brother was supposed to check out all the sites they were working on before he went home, but he'd already had a few to drink and couldn't drive. Andie was going to need to check out those sites while her mother sat at home worrying about losing another family member.

If only she had someone to help her deal with Joey, some way to get him to grow up and be responsible. She wished there was someone to reassure her mother, to take charge of the company and worry about finances if these romance initiatives didn't keep Carter's Crossing alive.

She wished she could be the kind of woman who could meet a strange man in a bar and exchange names and go for dinner and visit New York City.

For now, she just wanted this night over. Maybe some of her wishes would come true this year.

CHAPTER TWO

HE'D ALMOST ASKED her what her name was after that text when it became apparent she was going to leave. He'd even thought of asking for her number, but then her phone rang again and broke whatever there was happening between them.

It was a reprieve. He didn't need to know her name or talk to her again. She walked out the door, and it was not disappointment he felt. Impossible.

He wasn't here to make friends or find dates. He wasn't going to stay in this town after his year was done. He planned to restore his reputation and get his life back on track. In New York.

He was here in Carter's Crossing on New Year's Eve because he'd decided to take one more look at the place and try to get a feel for it. When his new client, Abigail Carter, owner of the mill wasn't around to curate his impressions. A year was a long commitment, and if this went badly… Stomach acid roiled in his belly.

He'd chosen New Year's Eve to accomplish several goals simultaneously. He didn't want to spend the holiday with his family or his former friends. They couldn't hide their pity, and he'd had to deal with too much of that this past couple of years to handle that, as well. Not today.

He found his hand rubbing over his leg reflexively. The one with the prosthetic.

He'd thought New Year's Eve would provide him an opportunity to drive in, check out the building again and head out without attracting any attention or arousing any suspicion.

He'd been successful at the mill. He'd taken pictures, imagining the final building once he'd finished. Abigail Carter had asked him to keep the project quiet until everything was ready to go, so he'd been aware every minute that he might be discovered by someone wanting to know his business.

Once he left the mill undetected, he'd decided against driving back to the city. There was no reason to rush back. He'd find some place nearby to take a break, grab a beer and maybe spend the night.

He'd driven by a woman standing outside her car, frowning at a flat tire. She'd looked about eighty and slight enough for the wind to blow her over. He hadn't seen the dog until he'd already stopped, and it was too late to escape. He wasn't sure how he'd missed the Great Dane.

After putting on her spare and refusing offers of food, money or recognition, he'd needed a place to wash off the dog spit. He'd pulled into the Goat and Barley on a whim. That whim had led him to the woman contemplating her glass of soda.

She was gone now, and the pub was filling up, the stool beside him already taken. Newcomers were looking for a seat, and it was time to leave. He paid for his beer, leaving a good tip, and made his way cautiously through the crowd to the cold air outside.

According to his phone and the internet, there was a slightly larger town about a forty-minute drive away. It had a couple of chain motels, something Carter's Crossing was lacking. He made a reservation through an app, not needing to interact with an actual person, and got into his car.

The hotel room was bland and surprisingly quiet. He'd intended on spending his New Year's Eve reviewing his designs and ideas for the mill, but he was restless and edgy.

Meeting that woman in the bar had brought up feelings and memories that he'd ignored for a long time. Something about her had drawn him in. Then she'd made that comment about having problems with her employee. It reminded him of the disaster of his last job and how that had led to his prosthetic, the end of his engagement to Violet and almost the end of his career.

The woman in the bar was lucky she wasn't in his shoes. He couldn't afford another mistake. He needed to talk to someone tonight. It was three hours later in California. Howard had probably not gone out yet.

Howard was someone who'd been in his corner after the whole debacle of his last job. He was in graphic design and had moved to the West Coast, so they weren't able to see each other often, but they kept in touch, and Trevor counted him as one of his friends.

He threw himself down on the bed and called the familiar number.

After three rings, he thought Howard must be out or be with someone. He was about to hang up when he heard, "Hello, Trev!"

No one else called him Trev.

"I hope I didn't disturb you."

"Nah. It's fine. Just getting ready to head out later. Are you back from Cowlick Cove yet?"

Trevor shook his head. "Carter's Crossing. And no, I stopped at the next town and got a room. I didn't want to drive back tonight."

There was a pause. Trevor closed his eyes, waiting for Howard to chastise him.

"You can't keep hiding. You gotta move on. Unless you got an invite in Redneck Woods for a party tonight?"

Trevor opened his eyes, a smile crossing his face. He knew Howard worried about him. Trevor worried about himself, too.

"No, I'm not going out. But I did talk to someone."

"A female someone?"

"Definitely."

"That sounds promising. Pretty? Young? Single?"

"I think so. I mean, she was pretty, near our age, and she wasn't wearing a ring." He frowned. She hadn't acted like she was with anyone.

"Who is she?"

"I don't know. She got called away before I could ask her name." He didn't know how to explain their unspoken agreement to keep it light.

"Maybe you'll see her again while you're stuck in Boonieville."

"Maybe you should insult this place less since you're the reason I'm here, Howard."

Howard laughed. "I know. This year will be

great, though. You'll get back on track, and life will return to what you want."

"Will it?" Trevor hated that he felt the need to ask. It wasn't as if Howard had a crystal ball. But Howard had heard about this job through his channels—he'd kept up with everyone even after he'd left New York for LA—and he'd asked Trevor if he would consider working in a small town on an intriguing project to get his career kick-started again. Something to keep his business going.

Trevor had appreciated the lead, and Howard's support.

"Trevor, you're great at what you do. Don't let one setback ruin architecture for you. You love it, you're great at it, and you deserve to have your career back. Just be careful."

Yes, that was the problem.

"I will be."

He'd learned the hard way that not everyone was trustworthy. That people might smile and joke with you, spend time with you as if they were your friends, and still stick a knife in your back. It had been an expensive lesson in many ways, but he had definitely learned.

"This time, I'm going to make sure everything on this job is done right."

"Good," Howard encouraged.

"This time, I'll check on everything. I can't

trust people to do their jobs and risk another accident. It's a local contractor, and I don't know if they've done anything this big before."

"That's a reasonable concern. Don't go overboard, though, Trev. Not every contractor is crooked."

"Well, Compton's was supposed to be good."

"And it was, until his son took over. There's no way you could've known that the kid was going to cut corners."

No, but he was prepared for it now. Just in case.

"I hope nepotism isn't a thing out here. People should be hired based on their abilities, not who their parents are."

Howard grunted.

Neither of them was familiar with how things worked in a small town, but Trevor suspected nepotism would be possible here, as well. He thought of the woman at the bar, with a brother working for her who didn't listen. She'd also talked about her mom. Maybe she had a family business like Compton's, where family didn't do what they were supposed to.

Real damage could be done if someone wasn't in control and let things slip. He hoped the woman in the bar managed something simple, like a gift shop. He hoped the local contractor he'd be working with was good—

knowledgeable and skilled and organized. He'd micromanage as necessary if they weren't.

Once this job was done, and done correctly and safely, he could return to New York City and restart his firm. He'd get his do-over.

He could supervise the contractor, but he wondered about the owner of the mill.

"Mrs. Carter has a good reputation, correct?"

"I'd never have given her your name if she didn't. She's apparently tight with Gerald Van Dalton, so if she's happy with you, you might get some work from his companies back in the city. I promise, Trev, I checked this out for you. Besides, you met with her. She was good, right?"

"Yes, she was. Sorry, I'm just nervous. It will be fine. I can keep an eye on the contractor, and if they can't do the job, I'll make sure Mrs. Carter knows about it. And if she won't do the right thing, I'll have to walk away."

"It's not going to come to that, Trev. This is going to work. Hey, maybe you'll meet the pretty woman and have some fun while you're in Sticksville Station."

Trevor thought of the woman from the bar. It would be nice to see her again.

But this job was important. Too important. He couldn't afford distractions. He remembered those hazel eyes, and the laughter in them as she looked at him.

She could definitely be a distraction, especially if she was having trouble with managing her own business. He didn't have bandwidth for that.

"No, no fun till this project is done. This time next year, maybe."

"I'm gonna hold you to that. If you can't find a New Year's party on the East Coast, you'll have to come out here. Are you sure you don't want to move west? I could hook you up with some people."

It was a generous offer, one Howard had made before. But Trevor wasn't running away. He was going to work his way back to where he'd been.

All that stood between him and a triumphal return to New York City was this project, and he was going to make sure it was done right.

He wished Howard a happy New Year and finished his call. Then he pulled out his laptop, opened up the 3D BIM model, and checked and rechecked his work to make sure he was confident about every aspect of the project. That was all he was going to focus on while he was here, but somehow, his mind kept drifting to the woman in the bar.

IT WAS LATE when Andie turned into the drive beside the Kozak Construction sign. She saw her mother pull the curtains aside. She must've been listening for the truck. That meant there was no time for Andie to bring her irritation under control.

She shoved open the truck door and faced the evening chill. She drew in a lungful of cold, sharp air, reminding herself that her brother, Joey, was the baby. Her mother spoiled him, and when Andie came down on him, he sulked.

Her mother asked her to be more patient with him, and Andie did try to bite her tongue. But when their world blew up, Andie didn't get more patience. She hadn't in the years since, either.

Andie let the cold air, now warmed by her lungs, cloud into the dark sky. Her mother opened the door, as if needing to see her daughter in person, whole, before she could relax.

Another irritation. Andie forced a smile.

She was more than thirty years old. She didn't want her mother checking on her all the time, like someone fifteen years younger. Part of the dream of leaving Carter's Crossing was just to win her own independence.

When she'd first taken over the company after her dad's death, she'd hated how people had wanted to check and double-check her work. But she'd been new, young and untested then. Some people still did it, new people she worked with who assumed she didn't know what she was doing because she was female and had taken over her father's company. Those people were in the minority now, and she didn't allow them to get away with it.

She didn't micromanage her crew—except maybe for Joey, but she had good reason for that—and she didn't want anyone micromanaging her, either. Not at work or at home.

Andie had established herself with the people of Carter's Crossing as the head of Kozak Construction, one of the biggest employers in the county. She was competent, trustworthy, someone they came to when they had questions or wanted advice, but she still lived like a high school kid in her mother's home.

She'd contemplated moving out. Several times. When she'd had her first serious boyfriend, she'd considered it every day.

Part of the problem was the expense. With four siblings in school incurring tuition and boarding costs and the need to ensure there was a financial buffer for the business downturns that happened, spending money on a place here in Carter's seemed pointless. Decadent. Definitely not practical.

Moving out into her own place in Carter's Crossing also signaled that she'd given up on her dream of leaving. That she was settling in, ready to stay for the rest of her life. No more school. No more dreams.

She refused to do that.

Another reason not to move out was that her mother worried. All. The. Time.

Somehow, her mom wasn't as worried about the three kids who'd moved away. All the fear that resulted from her dad's accident was focused on Andie, because Andie was the one who'd been with him that afternoon before the accident.

Andie waved to her mom, breathing the cold air in and out again, hoping her irritation would dissipate with it. It would be cruel to contribute to her mother's anxiety. Especially today.

Andie couldn't do it. She walked into the house, closed the door behind her and hung up her coat in the same closet, just as she had her whole life. She pulled off her boots and set them on the boot tray at the side of the door, where it had always been. She tossed her hat and gloves into the basket that had held jumbles of mittens and scarves for as long as she could remember.

"Smells good, Mom." She kept the irritation out of her voice. Her mom was a good cook. She tended to prepare meals for the family that used to live here, not the three of them still here now in the house. Andie took leftovers to work for lunch almost every day.

She didn't get to eat out like her siblings did,

because that would be wasteful. She shoved the thought away, not sure why she was more on edge today. She could only blame some of it on the anniversary.

Her brother came down the hallway when her mother called them for dinner.

"Joey, you were supposed to check the sites today."

She did her best to keep her voice level. She couldn't let him slide on every responsibility.

"My friends are all going out to parties tonight. I just wanted to see them before they left," he said as he slid into his usual chair and reached for the salad. Andie sat down, as well.

People came back to Carter's Crossing to visit family for the holidays and then returned to their real lives. Andie's siblings had left over the last few days—back to their work commitments, families, etcetera. They didn't want to be here, in this house, tonight. And she couldn't blame them.

Still, since she had to be here, it would be nice if they'd have helped share the burden.

"You could have gone to see them after you did your job." Andie bit her tongue so she didn't say more.

"Oh, Andie, he deserves some time off." Her mother was always defending him, always treating him like a child, not a twenty-two-year-old man.

"So do I."

The silence was louder than any words. Andie didn't usually say things like that, but tonight, she wasn't able to keep the peace.

Joey didn't read the room. "You're the one afraid something is gonna happen. Nothing does. Ever. So if you're worried, you check it out."

Andie opened her mouth to tell him that the reason nothing ever happened was because she always checked things out, but her mother was watching her, expression pleading.

Not tonight.

Andie bit back the words and asked her mom to pass the rolls.

The meal was mostly silent and awkward. Her mother asked Joey about his friends, and he answered sulkily.

He didn't like being stuck in Carter's Crossing, but he had no idea what else he wanted to do. He didn't want to leave without money, and Andie refused to give him her college savings or her mother's retirement fund to go and explore his interests, which changed frequently.

Their siblings had found their passions on their own initiative, and with their own money. Joey wanted a shortcut.

After the mostly silent meal, Andie offered to clean up the kitchen. Joey didn't feel any need to help, and she was happy to have him keep her mom company anyway.

Fourteen years ago tonight, their dad died. He'd had a heart attack while driving home after checking the work sites. For years after, her mother had made New Year's Eve a memorial for him, but as her siblings began to find reasons not to be around, it had changed to a family night. They'd watch a movie, watch the ball drop and her mother would cry.

It was draining, but she couldn't leave her mother alone. Not on New Year's Eve.

It was Andie's least favorite night of the year.

It was a relief when her phone rang, and she saw the familiar name.

"It's Denise."

Her mother nodded, eyes welling with tears.

Andie escaped to her room. "I'm so happy to hear your voice," she said.

"How's it going, Andie?"

Andie didn't need to keep up the fake cheer with Denise. Her best friend had been here that night. She'd been here every New Year's since, until her husband was transferred to Florida.

Andie flopped down on her bed. "It's... Well, it's what it is, but Joey is doing his best to make it worse."

"What did he do?"

"He was supposed to check the sites before he called it a day. He didn't, so I had to do it after I was at the Goat."

Denise knew Andie went to the pub every New Year's Eve.

"Did you tell him off?"

"I tried. Mom got upset, and I can't do that to her, not today."

Denise gusted a sigh. "You've got to do something, Andie. He's gotta grow up."

"I know. He's good at some of the job. He just doesn't like to be the boss. And I don't know how to push him without riding him all the time. I can't do that."

Not only would it make home life impossible, it wasn't how she operated. She had faith in the people she hired, and she trusted them to do their jobs.

It helped that in a small town, no one was a stranger, so she knew who she could count on.

"He's gotta step up, Andie. If you're leaving this fall—"

"I'm not."

Silence.

"What? Andie—"

"I know, I know. I'm just putting it off one more year. We've got this new project with the mill. Abigail Carter has big plans for the town, and if we get the mill done, there's going to be a lot of work. I'll use this job to push Joey, to get him ready to take over, and then I can go."

More silence. Andie knew Denise wouldn't like this plan.

"Andie, it wasn't your fault."

Andie closed her eyes. "But—"

"No, Andie. We've been through this. What happened to your dad?"

"A heart attack."

"Exactly. It was nothing to do with the fact that you and he stopped at the Goat and that you went to a party. That didn't make him have a heart attack."

Andie swallowed.

"But if I'd been with him—"

"Andie! What would've happened if you'd skipped the party and driven with him?"

Andie couldn't form the words, even though they'd talked this over so many times.

"Andie, he'd still have hit the tree. The roads were slick. You couldn't have stopped it. And you might have been hurt, and then what would've happened to your family?"

Denise waited, letting her work it through again. She knew Denise was right, but on New Year's Eve, with her mother still weighed down by grief, she couldn't help playing the what-if game. What if she'd done this differently, or that?

No matter how many times she played, though, she couldn't what-if away the heart attack that had caused her dad's death.

"Thanks, Denise. I'm sorry I'm such a pain."

"You're not a pain. You're a good person who's had a lot of crap to deal with. I just wish I could be there."

"I know. But you're not. So tell me what you two are doing tonight."

By the time Denise hung up to get ready for her own evening, Andie was back in control of herself and ready to spend the rest of the evening with her mother and Joey.

She was ready to say goodbye to another year. She didn't know if New Year's Eve would ever be something to enjoy again.

CHAPTER THREE

TREVOR LOOKED AROUND the house he would be living in here in Carter's Crossing for the next year.

It was nice. It had the conveniences he required. What claimed his attention, though, was the knowledge that tomorrow he would meet with the contractor and Abigail Carter, and after that the mill project would begin.

He had concerns about the contractor, but he reminded himself he'd had the same concerns the first time he met Abigail, at the restaurant in New York City.

It had been his most promising lead since the accident. Trevor had recovered physically but found returning to his place in the building industry to be a challenge. He could go to another firm and work for someone else, but his dream had always been to have his own business. So instead of approaching others, he'd looked for new work.

The offers he'd been presented with were from clients looking for someone crooked or stupid. Trevor was neither. What he was, was cynical.

Trevor had agreed to meet with Abigail Carter, but his expectations were low. It wasn't a surprise that Abigail had exceeded them, but he'd still been surprised that she'd asked him to come to the prospective site to check out the project.

That had been in September, on-site in Carter's Crossing. Trevor had driven up, a mixture of excitement, hope and suspicion churning inside him the whole way. He'd met Abigail in the parking lot of the building.

"Thank you for taking the time to come, Mr. Emerson."

"I can't start planning a project until I know what it is."

Abigail turned to the building, and Trevor took a look at what was a functional, seemingly well-built, ugly mill.

"As I mentioned, I admire your work, and I think you can do a good job here, but I'm sure you want to examine the place. Would you like to look inside first?"

He nodded, inspecting her as well as the building. He'd done his own research into Abigail Carter. She'd been widowed young and took over running the family business while raising her children. Generations back, her family had been among the first to settle in Carter's Crossing, and they'd built the first mill structure. The current mill had closed recently, but there was no indication that the Carter family didn't have money.

Abigail herself was tall with silver hair. She was dressed in expensive clothing and was composed. Whether they could work together was still up in the air, but she would not be a pushover. This was someone who would want to understand what was happening. Would she give him room to work?

He was going to need space to check things out in detail. He planned on being more involved than many expected an architect to be. Abigail pulled out keys and opened the door. He followed her into the building. He stopped, surprised at what he saw.

He'd expected a dusty, crowded space. She'd told him the mill had been closed for two years. She hadn't mentioned that it had been emptied of all equipment and was being maintained, based on the lack of dust or dirt.

He examined the ceiling and let his gaze run down the walls to the floor.

"You've done some work here. The old equipment is gone, and the place has been kept up. That wasn't done just for this meeting, was it?"

He fought to keep any notes of suspicion out of his voice.

She shook her head. "The equipment was sold for salvage value so we could maintain the retirement fund. I've been hoping to make use of this space again, to find a way to keep the town alive. It was only sensible to keep it up.

"I've got a wedding planner coming to Carter's Crossing to show us what we need to make this a wedding destination. The mill will be at the heart of that. And that's where you come in."

Trevor nodded. *If* he came in.

"You mentioned you want a commercial kitchen for catering and space for large events. Anything else?"

She considered him for a moment. "Why don't you look around and get your own impressions? Then we can discuss options."

He nodded again. He had to be cautious, but he was also curious. He had come up with a few ideas after their initial meeting, but now he could see what he had to work with and make actual plans.

The space where they'd first entered was large, at least two stories high. It was empty. He examined the walls, looked over the beams and crossed to the far wall. There were a couple of windows, but this was the side that faced the river. He wanted to see what was there. Adding windows here would open up the view and offer a lot of possibilities.

The newer parts of the building were set back from the water, leaving a space between the building and the riverbank. There was enough room to create a patio. The view across the water showed trees and a gentle hillside. There was no sign of the town from here. They needed to take advantage of that. This side of the building should be opened up.

He turned from the windows and the possibilities he saw out there and headed to the back of the building. In this rear section, the height of the building had been split into two stories. There was a metal stairway leading upstairs. He bypassed that to see what was on the main floor behind the doors and the partition that separated it from the main space.

A hallway led to storage, washrooms and what must have been a small kitchen and lunchroom at one point. At the far end was an exterior door. The windows in the back of the lunchroom showed a parking lot.

He did a quick check of the plumbing and the electrical, then he returned to the main room and climbed the stairs to the second floor. Abigail Carter was where he'd left her, reading something on her phone, giving him space and time to check the place over.

He appreciated that. He was going to need to change the way he usually interacted with a contractor to monitor the job more carefully, and that would be unsettling enough. He didn't want to have to change how he dealt with his client, as well.

Upstairs were the former offices. The largest one in the back corner overlooked the river and had good-sized windows to bring in the view. There were additional washrooms, and while the construction wasn't innovative, it was functional and well-built.

He returned to the open space and Abigail. "I'll look around outside, if you don't mind. You don't need to come with me."

She nodded.

The mill was outside the town, and no other homes or businesses were visible. Across the river was a sloping hillside where leaves were starting to change on deciduous trees. There were hints of the vibrant reds and oranges that would light up the view shortly. This was what he wanted to bring into the mill.

The parking lot needed to be redone. The outside of the mill was…functional. That was the best word to describe it. The setting was incredible, and a facelift to the exterior, just enough so that it didn't compete with the beautiful setting, should be sufficient.

He took photos as he walked around, barely feeling his prosthetic leg, noticing the lack of noise and crowd. He wasn't used to that, but it was soothing. He heard a few birdcalls and the gurgle of the water. A car went by, but that was the only sound of civilization.

If they did this right, people would love to get married here. Violet had been looking for something like this. He forced those memories out of his head. They were no longer engaged, and there were no wedding plans. He hadn't seen her in months.

He opened the door to return to Abigail, blinking as his eyes adjusted to the dimmer light inside the mill. She put away her phone and gave him her full attention.

"The place has definite possibilities, but I need to know what your budget is and how much you want to do here."

Trevor had lost his ability to charm and schmooze. He wanted to get to the point and know what he was dealing with before he got excited about the project.

Which he might not even get.

"I have neither the time, budget nor inclination to tear this building down and create a new one."

"I assumed as much, or you wouldn't have asked me to tour through the building."

There was a half smile on her lips. "You're not going to try to talk me into that?"

He shook his head. He didn't know if she was testing him or if other architects she'd talked to had tried to sell her on a new building, but it was her project and her bank account. He didn't think it was his place to try to change her plans.

If the building had been decrepit or impossible to bring up to code, that would have been a different discussion.

"However, I also don't want to simply move a couple of walls and paint the building to try to make this work."

He'd barely knew Abigail Carter, but he already understood she wouldn't want something cheap and superficial. That was good. Cheap often meant shortcuts.

"As for the rest, I can be somewhat flexible on budget if I'm convinced it has long-term benefit. I'm not a fool."

No kidding.

"I don't know exactly what all has to be done or how much it will cost, but I have an upper limit. I will spend up to that amount, if necessary, to make this space what it needs to be," she added.

He wondered if people had tried to take advantage of her in the past, if they'd assumed because of her gender and her looks that she could be fooled.

He was quite confident that she'd taken care of those people, and that they hadn't had a second chance. She could probably teach him a lot.

He pointed at the wall facing the river.

"If you want this space to be beautiful, we need to open that up. This is where I think you should spend most of the money."

"I agree." She nodded.

"Also, the outside of the building needs a change. You can't make this a place people come to get married with the way it looks now. It needs to fit with its surroundings, but the changes we can make depends on your budget and timeline."

"The building has never been known for its appearance. Obviously, we need to deal with that. What else?"

"Inside, we can put your commercial kitchen on the main floor, where the kitchen and workrooms are now. Upstairs can be offices, if you want them, or storage." He decided to test her limits. "I'd also want to install an elevator."

Abigail's brows lifted. "I hadn't considered that, but we should. The building should be fully accessible."

"There aren't any stairs from the parking lot to the main doors, so that will make entrance from the exterior easily accessible. I'd also like to put in a patio outside by the water, and maybe around back, as well."

Abigail looked around the space, evaluating what he'd said, or maybe remembering what the place had been.

She turned back to Trevor. "I appreciate you driving all the way to Carter's Crossing. I went through the recommendations I was given carefully, and I only asked two people to come out here to see the space. I saw examples of your work and liked your vision."

Trevor felt something moving inside him in gentle ripples. It might be hope. Was he one of only two candidates? Were his odds that good? Could he get his career and his business back on track? His life?

"Your vision is the closest to mine, which means you're the front-runner."

The ripples inside him were getting bigger and starting to interfere with his breathing.

"I'd like you to take the initial steps. Survey the building and do some drawings for me. I will of course pay you, but if they come out as well as I expect, I'll offer you the job of renovating the mill. Also, as I mentioned, this town needs some more pedestrian work from an architect. We don't have anyone local. There are a lot of beautiful homes here that we're hoping to open as bed-and-breakfasts, and they'll need to be adapted. If this project takes off the way I hope it will, this town will be rejuvenated, and there will be jobs and opportunities for everyone who wants them."

Redesigning an older home to add some bathrooms was far from glamorous work. But Trevor could show his vision and his talent here at the mill. The home renos would feed his bank account, even if they didn't feed his soul.

"I guess the project will take approximately a year. I'd like you to consider relocating for that amount of time."

A year. Leaving New York City for a year. He hadn't anticipated that.

"You wouldn't need me on-site every day."

"You would know that better than me. But I'm anxious for this to be done as soon as possible. I don't want delays because the roads are in bad condition or you have other commitments and can't get to Carter's Crossing from New York."

"A year?"

"I think so. Does that seem reasonable?"

Trevor ran through potential problems in his head. "I can't promise the project will be finished in that timeline. There are things out of my control. I don't do the inspections and approvals."

Abigail nodded. "I have enough clout to make sure that we don't lose our place in line when it comes to those things."

She must have read the concern on his face.

"I'm not talking about taking shortcuts or paying bribes. Just that if someone in my town overbooks, they won't cancel on me. I've earned that, and I will take advantage of it.

"The mill bears my family's name, and I don't want my reputation damaged. If I thought you were at fault for the accident last year, I wouldn't be speaking to you."

It sounded good, but Trevor had learned to be cautious.

"I'd like time to think it over. And I need to know everything will be done by the book."

Abigail took a moment to study him. She must know why he'd stipulated that.

"Some things will be different here since we're dealing with a small town. There's only one contracting firm who can handle this kind of work, but we will do everything as it should be done. You have my word."

"I'll want to monitor things closely."

"That's fair. But I don't want to wait too long. If I don't hear from you within the week, I'll speak to the other candidate."

She knew he wanted this. She was intelligent and observant, and he'd probably showed his excitement on his face. But *she* also wanted *him*. She needed someone who could do this. Getting this project and finishing it, doing the job well and without problems would give him a chance to get back on his feet and back on track.

He could make this big, hulking building into a beautiful place for people to celebrate.

Sure, life in a small town might be a little dull for a year, but he could survive that.

He'd agreed to her terms. And now he was committed, living in Carter's Crossing, ready to start. And ready to meet the local contractor, Kozak Construction.

ANDIE PARKED HER truck in the mill parking lot.

It was still cold here near the end of February, but soon March would bring warmer temperatures, and her life would get busier.

There were no other vehicles around, so she was the first one here for the meeting. That was how she'd planned it. She'd come half an hour early, just so she could have time on her own to check the place over.

Abigail Carter had given her a set of keys, and Andie walked around the building, her footprints leaving marks in the fresh snow.

She'd grown up in Carter's Crossing, but she'd never been inside the mill. While it was open, the mill had had its own employees to take care of its maintenance, and she couldn't remember Kozak Construction ever coming in to work on the building during her lifetime.

It wasn't an attractive building. She'd forgotten just how functional it looked, but it had been constructed well. She liked to think one or more of her ancestors had been involved in the original construction, but it was long done before her grandfather opened their company, and she didn't know if there were records to show who'd built the original structure or the later additions.

Abigail had said she maintained the building, and Andie saw no signs of worrisome neglect. Still, no one would want to get married here, not with the way the building looked now.

She'd circled the exterior and was now back at the main door. She pulled out the keys she'd been given and slid one into the lock. It turned with a soft click. She pushed the door open and stared.

It was a huge space. Clean and empty, ready for whatever work was needed. Andie moved over, eager to check out this space where some demolition would undoubtedly be needed first. She walked toward the back of the building, noting the rooms and condition of the various sections. She made notes on her phone, taking photos to match, until she heard voices from the entry and made her way there.

"Andie? Is that you?"

Andie pushed open the door to bring her back into the main part of the mill. She saw Abigail looking as polished and at home in this empty space as she did at town events, and her mouth curved up in a smile.

There was someone with Abigail, the architect, presumably. Abigail had asked Andie here to meet him so that they could start to plan the renovations. Andie had been impressed by the drawings Abigail had shared and was looking forward to this project.

She was excited about tackling something new and challenging, and it was a chance to work closely with an architect from New York, someone with a vision she admired. On small jobs, she'd see the architect only at the beginning and end.

This would be Kozak's biggest project yet. That should mean more meetings, more time with the person who'd draw up the plans. She hoped they could talk and maybe she could get some advice for her own aspirations after this job.

At first, she saw only his back. He was a little taller than she was, and dark hair touched his collar. He was wearing a warm jacket and sturdy boots and had a large computer bag slung over his shoulder. She saw the frame of a pair of glasses resting on his ear. Then he turned.

She did a double take. The man standing with Abigail stared back at her in equal shock. It was the man from the bar.

She recognized the dark brows, the straight nose, the lines fanning out from his eyes. She'd stared at those while they'd talked at the Goat.

She'd hoped to see him again, but she'd no idea it would ever happen. Her smile widened.

She'd regretted the calls from her mother and Joey that had interrupted them at the bar. She'd thought he'd been about to ask what her name was. She'd wanted to thank him for making that horrible day a little better, at least for a while.

One major drawback of a small town was that you knew everyone in your potential dating pool, and most of the men in hers had either left town or found someone. Andie was out of pool buddies, and she'd liked the man at the bar.

She crossed to where Abigail was standing ready to introduce them. She'd finally know his name.

"Andie, this is Trevor Emerson, our architect. Trevor, this is Andie Kozak, of Kozak Construction, the firm that will be undertaking the work here."

Andie was close now, almost close enough to shake hands. Close enough to see the expression on the man's face. Trevor's face. She knew his name now.

He knew hers, as well. And he looked stunned.

Andie's smile faded. She had no idea why, but he didn't look happy to see her. In fact, he looked upset.

What was his problem?

CHAPTER FOUR

ANDIE SHOVED HER hands in her pockets while she tried to make sense of this. He'd been friendly, fun, attentive in the bar. What had changed?

She glanced at his hands, but his left was hidden in his pocket. There hadn't been anything on his ring finger on New Year's Eve, but she'd bet there was now.

Her face stiffened. Great. She worked with mostly men, mostly married, but they didn't try anything with her, not after the first time. She shut that down immediately.

Guess Mr. Emerson was worried what she might say. She nodded at the man, irritated that he didn't start to look as distasteful as he acted.

"Mr. Emerson."

His lips were pressed tightly together, and he nodded back. "Ms. Kozak."

Abigail's glance flickered between them. "Have you two met before?"

Andie wasn't about to lie to Abigail Carter.

Kozak Construction did a lot of work on projects Abigail was connected with.

"I ran into Mr. Emerson at the Goat and Barley on New Year's Eve, but we didn't exchange names."

She heard Trevor suck in a breath. Too bad for him. She wasn't jeopardizing her working relationship with Abigail for a cheating scumbag.

She'd fantasized about this job at the mill, about meeting with an established architect from New York and getting advice, mentoring, perhaps a future reference.

She'd also had fantasies about running into the man from the bar again and spending more time with him.

Apparently, those fantasies were closer to nightmares now that they'd coalesced into one. She just needed to concentrate on her job.

Abigail's expression softened for a moment. She knew what New Year's meant for the Kozak family.

Abigail's glance shot back to Trevor, who still looked shocked. Trevor didn't say anything, and Andie wasn't explaining.

"I've had the heat on so we can work and for the Valentine's Day planning. I brought in a table and chairs to my old office. Shall we talk there?"

Abigail headed to the metal stairs, and Andie followed, Trevor somewhere behind her. Abigail's heels clicked on the metal treads, while Andie's boots thudded. She didn't hear Trevor over her own treads. Her boots were heavy and steel toed. Work boots.

Maybe that was part of his problem. Maybe he didn't like women in traditionally male roles. Too bad. She'd dealt with that before, a lot more than she should've.

Men.

Between Joey and Trevor Emerson, she was ready to be done with them.

ABIGAIL HAD ARRANGED to have a folding table and some chairs set up. She sat down at one end, and Andie sat beside her. Trevor sat across from them, and Andie kept her attention on Abigail.

Abigail took the lead. Andie imagined she'd chaired many meetings in this room.

"I've looked at your drawings, Trevor, and your budget. I'd like to focus initially on the interior, and if we run behind, the patio and driveway can be done after the snow clears in about fifteen months. I've shown Andie the drawings so we can go over them together."

Andie saw the frown cross Trevor's face from the corner of her eye.

Trevor reached into his bag and pulled out a laptop as well as some papers. Andie restrained herself from reaching for them. She had copies she could access as needed. Instead, she pulled out her tablet and stylus, ready to take notes. She set it on the table, raised her gaze and caught Trevor staring at her, still frowning.

His hands were on the table now, not hidden in his pocket. Andie noticed the ring finger was still bare. She took the few extra seconds to look for a white circle at the base, where a ring would normally be. Nothing.

So maybe he was the kind of married man who didn't wear a ring. No matter, she was still keeping her distance. She wasn't interested in a cheater.

Abigail looked at Trevor, waiting for him to begin.

He cleared his throat. "I'm used to dealing with the contractor himself. I'm sure Ms. Kozak takes excellent notes, but…"

Andie felt the familiar bile rising. Chauvinist. She'd dealt with many of them, had finally established herself in this community. It had taken years. She was so tired of it.

She didn't appreciate that she would need to convince this man that she was capable of doing her job.

She stared at him, waiting till he met her

gaze. Abigail Carter let the silence hang, trusting Andie to deal with this.

Abigail was her idol.

"Mr. Emerson. Kozak Construction is *my* company." At least, it would be until Joey was ready to take over and she could finally leave for school.

"I *am* the contractor. I sign the checks. I choose the jobs. I oversee every subcontractor and employee who works on a Kozak Construction site. I have the license, and the buck stops with me. While you might be more comfortable dealing with someone with a Y chromosome, my brother is ten years younger than me and has minimal experience, so it would probably be best if we don't wait until he's up to speed."

Andie waited for his response. Her arms were crossed, her chin raised. Would there ever come a time when she wouldn't have to deal with this crap?

Trevor glanced at Abigail, as if for help. Was he that bad at reading the room? Did he not realize Abigail had dealt with this same attitude while managing the mill?

The older woman's expression was no longer pleasant. "Kozak Construction is the best firm in ten counties, and we're fortunate that they are local and available for this project. Do you have a problem working with them?"

Andie relaxed, a little, knowing that Abigail was backing her up. Andie had been looking forward to this project, and now part of her wanted to throw up her hands and say they could find someone else. But she couldn't dwell on hurt feelings. She was a business-woman, and this was her job.

She shot a glance at Trevor. His cheeks were red, and he was looking down at his papers.

"I apologize. I didn't mean any disrespect. Most of the contractors I've dealt with have been older, and I made a poor assumption. I've worked with women before, and that has not been an issue. I have no problem working with Kozak Construction if they have no problem working with me." He glanced over at Andie before settling his gaze on Abigail.

Andie didn't buy his apology. She wasn't any happier with someone negging her for her age than she was for them doing it for her being female. Too often, the one was an excuse for the other.

She held her tongue.

There'd be more meetings with the man than on a usual job, since this was a big project. He might want to be around for inspections. But she would do her best to make any interactions short and infrequent. Her idea of spending additional time with the architect on this project was obviously not happening, and she was sure he wouldn't want to spend any more time with her than necessary. If she was lucky, she shouldn't need to see him more than once a week. This project would raise the profile of Kozak Construction, and she'd leave a successful and sound company in her brother's hands to provide a safety net for her mother and siblings.

Then she could finally pursue her own dream. Surely there were architects out there who didn't specialize in being chauvinistic jerks.

Abigail considered the two of them for a moment. "I like your drawings, Mr. Emerson, and I know Kozak's work, which is impeccable. Together, we can make this mill what it needs to be to keep the town alive. Let's start now."

Andie waited till Trevor looked back at her and then gave him a big smile. Totally fake, and she didn't try to hide that.

"I do take excellent notes, by the way."

She thought she heard what sounded like a well-covered snort from Abigail's direction.

Trevor held her gaze and nodded. "I'll keep that in mind."

Andie would like to think she'd come out on

top in the encounter, but she had her doubts. She'd show him, though. She'd done nothing but immerse herself in this business for the last fourteen years, and before they were done, he'd have to acknowledge he'd been wrong about her.

She looked up and caught those brown eyes staring at her. A shiver ran down her spine.

Trevor opened his computer and started to talk about the job. Andie kept her mind on his words, taking notes of the things she needed to know. She did her best to focus on the equipment and outside contractors she'd need to arrange, anything new she'd have to do some research on, the kind of timeline they'd be following.

She'd show him what a woman could do.

TREVOR SLAMMED THE door of his rented house behind him. He kicked off his boots, venting his irritation on them. He dropped his bag on the dining table and pulled off his scarf and coat.

Then he took a deep breath and swore.

This was supposed to be an easy job. It was too important for him to mess up, and he'd almost done that at the first meeting with Abigail Carter and her.

The woman from the pub.

He'd spent too much time since New Year's Eve remembering his conversation with her. That night he'd laughed like he hadn't since the accident, and he liked to think he'd brightened the sadness from her expression.

But then there had been the problems with her employee, a relative, making this another job with a contractor with family issues.

When Abigail Carter told him he had the job, he'd been excited. It was his chance to get his career back on track. To show everyone that he really was good at his profession. To get his confidence back. His business back.

Part of that excitement had been the memory of the woman in the bar, and that maybe he'd have the chance to get to know her while he was in town. She'd said she was a local, and it was a small place. He'd hoped he'd see her again. He just hadn't expected it would be as the contractor on his job.

His plan had been to get the mill project set up and established and then maybe try to find her again, but only once he was comfortable with how the mill was going. No distractions until then.

Now he was second-guessing that encounter in the bar. What if Abigail had told Andie about her plans and about the architect she'd hired? What if she'd known who he was?

If the town was so small that people recognized every stranger, Andie might have deliberately tried to soften him up, get on his good side in the hopes of keeping him from checking up on her.

Wasn't that almost the playbook Geoff Compton had used on Trevor's last job? Had Andie known who he was? Was that meetup a setup?

He sat in a chair, huffing a frustrated breath. Was he paranoid? Probably. Didn't mean he was wrong.

He couldn't have something like that happen again. It would destroy his reputation. Permanently. He'd been approached by people he knew were shady, after the Compton job. If anything like that happened again, it was either his fault or his judgment was far off.

He scrubbed his face with his hands.

He'd liked Andie and was horrified when he found she was someone he had to work with, someone he couldn't be involved with. He'd hoped she just worked for the company, then they might have been able to see each other.

But no. She was the contractor. How experienced was she? He needed to know, since she was the person essential to getting this job done, to getting his life and career back on track.

How in the world could he trust that she was a capable contractor? She was young. He'd heard her on the phone and knew she was having problems.

This was such a big job. Could she handle it? And would she try to use anything from their first meeting to take advantage?

Abigail Carter had hired the two of them, but she knew and trusted Kozak Construction. Unless he had a better reason than anything he had come up with so far, she was going to trust Andie if it came down to a choice between them.

Abigail Carter said that the company was good. Maybe it was, for this tiny town and whatever jobs they had around here. That didn't mean Andie and her company were capable of doing what he'd envisioned for the mill.

The mill was why he was here. He was going to take that functional, ugly building and make it a place people came for their dream weddings. He was going to make it a thing of beauty. It was going to take a lot of work. Work that Kozak Construction had to carry out. Carry out to his specifications. No shortcuts. No mistakes. No crew making their own decisions without his approval.

He had to make sure of that.

He was good at his job. He'd been doing well

until that last project, the first he'd done solo. And though he'd done everything right, he'd been blamed when it had gone wrong. Since he'd been in the hospital, he hadn't been able to defend himself.

He'd been exonerated later, but no one remembered that. They remembered the immediate aftermath, when his contractor and the owner had placed all the blame on him. That couldn't happen again. He wasn't going to be blamed for something he didn't do. And no one was going to take any shortcuts on his project.

That meant he was going to have to be involved, to be really hands-on, checking and double-checking everything.

Abigail Carter had mentioned there would be other work here in Carter's Crossing. Buildings being renovated, new businesses, things that would keep him busy and pay the bills.

During the day, he was going to be at the mill. Every time someone was working on the structure, he'd be there. He'd make sure this job went perfectly.

It would mean spending a lot of time with Andie. Maybe he could show her how to keep control of her crew. It would mean they'd have to keep a professional relationship. No laughing over stupid jokes at the pub. No noticing hazel eyes or the way she bit her lip. No discovering whatever had her staring at a drink on the bar on New Year's Eve.

Not now.

He stood up, restless, his leg bothering him as he moved to the kitchen. He'd brought food with him and stocked up the empty cupboards. Tonight, he planned to go over his drawings and specifications with a careful eye, checking what his contractor would be starting on.

Waiting for his food to heat up, his brain conjured up a pleasant daydream. One where Andie wasn't someone he'd be in conflict with. Where she did some other innocuous job here in Carter's Crossing. Like being the town dentist. He'd run into her once the mill project was well under way and no longer requiring constant supervision. Maybe they'd bump into each other on the sidewalk somewhere, and her face would light up to see him. Like it had in the mill, before she'd lost that sparkle. After he'd probably looked as shocked as he felt.

He needed to stop thinking about the woman from the pub, to put those thoughts well behind him. Now she wasn't the woman from the bar. She was Andie Kozak, the contractor who could ruin his job and his future with just a small amount of incompetence.

He urged his brain to get on board. He opened his laptop, plugged it in, and with a plate of food in front of him, went through his work one more time, carefully focusing on what was on the screen and not remembering the hazel eyes that had stared at him with dislike.

"HOW CAN ANYONE in this day and age possibly think I can't do my job because of my age or gender? Really? I mean, he's supposed to be from New York City, not redneck central."

Denise laughed over the phone. "You don't think there are misogynists in New York?"

Andie huffed a breath. "I know, but to try something like that in front of Abigail Carter? I thought she might fire him on the spot. I hoped she would."

Andie could still hear the laughter in Denise's voice. "That does take nerve. Why do you think she didn't?"

Andie squirmed against the pillows on her bed, getting herself comfortable.

She missed Denise. They'd been friends since high school, and Andie didn't have a lot of time to make new friends. She wished there was an app for that, but in Carter's Crossing, it wasn't likely that she'd find anyone with or without an app. It was as difficult as finding someone to date here.

"I hate to admit this, but his work is good.

Really good. That mill is the least appealing building I can imagine, the way it looks now, but in his drawings, it's...totally romantic."

"Can buildings be romantic?"

Andie thought they could. Buildings weren't just wood and concrete. Andie had always found the variety in them appealing, intriguing. It was why she'd always wanted to be an architect.

Working on building sites with her dad, growing up, she'd had a close-up look at structures and the variety of things that could be done with them. There were the basic bones of something, like the mill. The things needed for functionality. If you left it at that, you had... well, the mill. It stuck out against its setting, against the beauty of nature that surrounded it. It was nothing but functionality.

With some imagination and a plan like Trevor had designed, you could bring in beauty and warmth. You could make people feel better. They could *be* better in a home or workplace that did more than just provide the necessities.

"When we get done with the mill, you'll see how romantic a building can be. I'm going to make it beautiful."

"I know you will."

Andie relaxed against her headboard. That

was Denise. Always supportive, always on her side.

"But enough about me. How are things in Florida?"

"Oh, no. I can tell you about Florida after we're done with this."

"What do you mean, done with this? We're done. I vented, and you agreed Mr. Emerson is a jerk, and now we're moving on."

"Uh-uh. Not till you tell me about him."

"I did."

"No, what does he look like? How old is he?"

Andie paused.

She hadn't told Denise about the New Year's Eve encounter at the Goat and Barley. She wasn't sure exactly why she hadn't.

It hadn't really been anything, of course. Two people talking. It was just that New Year's Eve was a bad day for her, so being distracted had been a good thing. It had obviously colored her impression of Mr. Emerson.

Denise was too good at seeing through her. She hoped she could describe Trevor without giving anything away.

"Well, he's a little older than us."

"Thirty-five? Forty? Fifty?"

"Stop it! You think fifty is just a little older than us? How old are you? I'm only thirty-two, thank you."

"Okay, so he's more like thirty-five." Andie brought up his face. "Yeah, probably something like that. If he's got his own firm now, he has to be at least that old."

"And ugly, right?" The amusement was back in Denise's voice.

If only. If he had been, she'd still have enjoyed their conversation on New Year's Eve but probably not thought about it again. Somehow, she'd started imagining meeting up again, talking more. Maybe more than talking...

"Andie? You there?"

Andie brought herself back to her phone call. "Yes, I'm here. Where else would I be?"

"Tell me how good-looking this guy is."

"Who said he was good-looking?"

Andie could imagine her friend's eyes rolling.

"I said he was ugly, and you disappeared, at least mentally. That tells me he's the opposite of ugly."

Yeah, that's what happened when someone knew you so well.

"No, he's not ugly. His hair is brown, a little long. His eyes are brown, too."

They were brown with flecks of gold near the pupils. And there were streaks of gray at his temples when he brushed that slightly too long hair back behind his ears.

"Well, that sounds…boring? Tall, short, fit, beard…"

"Tallish."

When he'd stood up, he'd been taller than her, and she was tall for a woman.

"And?"

"Lean." He'd looked like a runner, or a swimmer. Not a guy who lifted weights in a gym or beers in a bar. "No beard."

Or moustache. But there'd been a bit of stubble…

"Andie!"

She'd drifted off again. "Sorry, Denise. I'm here."

There was a pause.

"He's good-looking, isn't he?"

Andie sighed. "Yes, he is."

"Why do the good-looking ones have to be jerks?"

There was a grumble in the background.

"You're the exception to the rule, darling." Andie could hear Denise talking to her husband despite the hand she must have placed over her phone.

Denise and her husband were stupidly in love. Andie would agree Don wasn't ugly, but he wasn't her idea of a great-looking guy. Which was good, since he was married to her best friend.

"Hey, Denise, tell him needy isn't a good look on a guy."

Denise gurgled a laugh. "I know. But there are a limited number of non-jerks, so I take what I can get."

Andie smiled, her grin broadening as she heard the muffled "I'm joking!"

"Sorry, dealing with Mr. Needy. So you have to work with the good-looking jerk for a while. Will it be worth it? Maybe, I don't know. Is Joey ready to step up a bit?"

Andie shuddered. "No, he's not ready yet. But I can handle Mr. Jerky. I doubt he'll be around much. If he does his job and leaves me to mine, we'll be fine. Fine-ish."

"Andie, you did an incredible job taking over that company after your dad died, and you are great at it," Denise said, her tone growing serious. "You've earned the respect of the guys who work for you, and this guy will learn to respect you, as well. I believe in you."

Andie swallowed a lump. She'd needed this call. She'd needed Denise.

"Can't you talk Mr. Needy into moving back up here? I miss you."

"I miss you, too. But we're doing really well down here."

"Don't mind me. I know you're doing well. Tell me about it."

Andie would be fine. Denise was just a phone call away. Andie was normally much stronger on her own, but something about this thing with Trevor had unsettled her.

She *would* be fine, though. She was good at what she did. She just had to do a good job on this project. Like she always did.

CHAPTER FIVE

TREVOR RUBBED A HAND over his face. Things were not going well. He needed to fix this relationship with his contractor. Andie.

They'd had a few emails back and forth, and he'd sent through an article on dealing with employees. It wasn't just the cold New York winter giving him frostbite.

He should reach out, try to build a bridge. He'd injured her pride, and that wasn't the man he normally was.

At least, it wasn't who he'd been before. The individual he was now was still a work in progress. There'd been a lot of changes to adapt to, and he had yet to feel settled in his own skin. He didn't want this new person to be a jerk.

He pulled up his laptop and opened his email.

Ms. Kozak
I think we should meet in person and talk. I apologize that our first meeting did not go well and would like to clear things up.
Trevor Emerson

He considered it for a moment and, with a shrug, hit Send. Then he realized that, actually, their first meeting had been great. It was the second meeting that had blown everything up.

It seemed he was doomed to keep messing up with her. He considered sending a second email to clarify but figured it wouldn't help. He'd just have to wait and see how she responded.

ANDIE DID RESPOND, and that was how Trevor found himself in the town diner on a cold Monday evening. He was early. Driving on his own on a regular basis was an adjustment, and so was being able to get anywhere in town in a matter of minutes. In New York, he took cabs and allowed an ample time buffer for traffic.

He supposed a nonexistent commute time was an advantage to a small town. He didn't think it really offset the limited offerings of places to meet. He couldn't suggest the Goat and Barley again, and the only other sit-down restaurant in town was a place called Moonstone's, which appeared to aspire to fine dining. He didn't want to imply this meetup was a date, so he'd picked the diner.

The place was warm, and there was a buzz of chatter. After a pause near the door, he realized there was no one to seat him, so he made his way to an empty booth. He wanted this to be a private conversation, and the booth offered the most in the way of privacy. A waitress came over with a coffee carafe. She stood for a moment at the end of the table, waiting, so he turned over his coffee cup, and she poured.

"Creamer? Sugar?"

He forced a smile. "No, thank you."

She turned and left him dubiously assessing the coffee.

"Andie! How are you doing?"

Trevor looked up and saw Andie in the doorway being greeted by the waitress with a lot more warmth than she'd shown him. More people called out to his contractor, and he managed to rotate the handle on his cup around three times before she got to the table.

Not that he was nervous.

Andie took off her parka and hung it by the hood on a hook at the end of the booth seat before sliding in across from him. He didn't have time to greet her before the waitress was back, flipping over Andie's cup and filling it. She dropped a creamer beside the cup and asked if they were going to order food.

Andie looked at him for the first time.

"I haven't eaten, so I hope you don't mind

if I do. I wasn't sure what you intended, and I was out late on a site."

Trevor stiffened. This was supposed to be a business meeting. He hoped Andie realized that and didn't consider this a potential date. He'd been clear in his email, hadn't he? Their first meeting had been...unprofessional, but he had no plans to revisit that easy camaraderie they'd enjoyed. He was not going to let any personal entanglements interfere with business. He was here to work and had already eaten. If only he had an office or there was a coffee shop in town.

She was watching him, her face a polite mask. She'd lost the warmth she'd had in her friendly greetings to the other diner customers. *That's good*, he reminded himself. They needed to be professional. He couldn't allow any attraction to her to affect his performance on his job or the way he planned to scrutinize everything.

He didn't want to think about why it felt like he was missing out on something. It wasn't the first time he'd felt it, but he had to swallow before answering.

"I've eaten, but please, go ahead."

She narrowed her eyes, but with a flash of something on her face, she turned to the waitress.

"Guess it's just me, Jean. Burger and fries, the usual."

The waitress looked at him and sniffed before leaving.

Andie added the creamer and sugar to her cup and took a sip. She set it back down and met his gaze, head slightly tilted.

Right. He'd asked her to come here to talk. "Since we're working together on the mill, I wanted to discuss your processes."

She let the silence sit for a minute. "My processes."

He nodded. "I've worked exclusively in the city so far, so I'm not sure how your tendering process worked, and I wanted to see the bids."

She was still looking at him. He couldn't read her expression. He slid his glasses up his nose with one finger, pointlessly, since they were still sitting exactly where they should.

Then she sighed. "Mr. Emerson, I'm going to guess you've never worked in a small town."

He stiffened. "I grew up in New York City. Went to school there, and that's where I've worked."

Her lips twisted. "Yeah, I remember you saying that, and even if you hadn't, I would have guessed. I don't think you understand what life is like here."

He didn't need to understand anything. He

had no interest in moving to a small town. His singular goal was to do a good job here and get back to the city where he could do the work he really wanted to do. With a blemish-free project on his resume to prove he was back to being the same architect he'd been before the accident.

Andie waved a hand around at the diner. "We have this diner. We have Moonstone's, which is as close to fine dining as we get."

Trevor nodded. He'd done the research. He knew this was all there was.

"So when you wanted to meet, you had two choices. That's all."

He wasn't sure where she was going with this. If they weren't going to meet in whatever places they each called home, those were the only two options. He had definitely noticed the limits of the town.

"So how many tenders do you think we can get for a job here?"

A chill ran up his spine.

He didn't care if this was a small town that had limited options. If this woman intended to use that as an excuse for not following specifications or for using inferior materials or not keeping to a timeline...

He sat up, crossing his arms. "This project

isn't someone's basement renovation. This is a big job that needs to be done properly."

He recognized the expression on her face now. She was angry. Her cheeks were flushed, and she was sitting equally at attention.

"You do realize you're questioning both my ethics and skills? With absolutely no reason? We may not have a lot of options here—"

Their waitress arriving with Andie's burger and French fries stopped her rebuke. She placed the plate before Andie, along with a wooden rack containing condiments.

"Cook added some extra cheese for you."

Andie's expression was a lot happier as she turned to their server. "Thanks, Jean. I appreciate it."

"Need more coffee?"

The three of them looked at the level of creamy brown in Andie's cup. "I'm good, thanks. Maybe some water when you have a chance."

"Sure thing, Andie."

Jean flicked Trevor another glance but didn't offer him more to drink. His cup was almost empty. The coffee was better than he'd expected.

He hoped Jean not offering him more coffee was an oversight and not intentional, because he felt that more coffee might be needed to finish up this conversation. However, he suspected it had been deliberate.

Andie took a bite of her burger, moaned and wiped a napkin on her lips. The food smelled really good. She swallowed and set the burger down. Then she speared a fry.

"The burgers here are excellent. And the fries. You should try one."

Trevor opened his mouth to refuse. He was here to discuss the work on the mill, and he'd eaten already. They'd been arguing, so he didn't know why she wanted to be nice to him. He had been...rude.

The food did smell good, and it wouldn't hurt to bend a little. They weren't on the clock now. It would be beneficial to know what the quality of the food in the diner was like. He might want to eat out at some point, and this place was convenient.

"Thank you." He reached over and grabbed one of the golden sticks. It was still on the verge of being hot, but it didn't burn his fingers.

He took a bite and almost moaned himself. He didn't often allow himself fried food, but this... This was temptation in a deep-fried bit of potato.

If the rest of the food here was of the same quality, he could occasionally indulge himself.

He would check the menu to see if there was anything healthier for more regular visits.

Andie had taken another bite of her hamburger, and he suddenly wished he hadn't eaten before arriving here.

She set the burger down again. Her expression was more relaxed, and the tension in her jaw gone. If the burger was as tasty as the fries, he could understand why.

"Good, isn't it?"

"Very good." He might be a little regimented when it came to his diet, but he was also honest.

She smiled at him. Apparently, the burger had really improved her mood.

"The diner here is convenient. Locals come here because it's not worth driving too far for a cup of coffee. But they couldn't survive selling only coffee. If the food wasn't good, people would go to the Goat and Barley for meals."

Trevor held his expression still when Andie mentioned the pub where they'd met.

"Just because this is a small town with limited choices, doesn't mean those choices are rubbish. We might not have sophisticated palates, but we're not without standards."

Trevor understood where she was going now.

"My company might be the only one in this area, but if all we did was shoddy work on basement renovations, we'd have gone bankrupt or closed our doors a while ago.

"Over and above those considerations, I'm a craftsperson. I take pride in my work. I may work in a small town, but I need to know I've done my best. If someone is unhappy with the results, it bothers me. I wouldn't be able to face people around town if I did a bad job on their homes."

Andie leaned forward, holding his gaze with the passion behind her words.

"We did the renovation for Benny Gifford's place. He's in a wheelchair. I went to school with Benny, and I would never cut corners when it could result in another injury.

"We don't always have a lot of options, or alternate suppliers and workers. But I know my customers, and I protect them. I know my workers, and if they don't do their jobs properly, they don't work for me again."

He leaned forward now. "But you don't have to limit yourself to locals. You could ask for bids from firms elsewhere in the state."

Andie pointed a fry at him before she took a bite of it. "And where would they stay? We're about to start demolition, and it's still winter. We don't have hotels in Carter's Crossing. We won't have functioning B and Bs until some of these old homes have work done on them.

"The mill might be the biggest job we've had here for a while, but it's still not big enough for someone to pay for hotels and crews to commute from Oak Hill or farther."

Trevor leaned back, away from the tempting fries. Andie was making a convincing argument. He could believe that *she* believed her words. She wanted to do a good job for the people she knew. He just wasn't sure of her competence. By her own admission, this was going to be her biggest job. It might be beyond her skill set. And her crew's.

She had sat up again and was eating her burger. She shot a glance at him, waiting for his response to a very pointed argument.

He wasn't unreasonable. He appreciated her points about the inherent problems in bringing in crews from farther away, even if they were more competent. He understood budgets and had every intention of bringing this job in on time and on budget.

She'd made her case. Unless Abigail Carter wanted to increase her spending to include vendors and workers from farther away, he was working with Kozak Construction and the local people they had relationships with.

That meant *he* was going to have to make sure the project was a success. He'd have to be on-site every day. He'd check over who was working, what they were working on and how well they did their work.

He had a lot riding on this. If this job was messed up, he'd never get more clients. He'd have to beg for a position with another firm and would be stuck working on someone else's projects.

Besides his reputation and future being at stake, he also had to be vigilant so that no one would be hurt again...

"You won't mind if I check the work, will you?"

The burger was gone, and Andie pulled the plate of fries closer to her edge of the table.

"I've worked with architects before. I'm accustomed to the process. Unless you mean something more by that?"

"You said this is going to be the biggest job you've done."

"You do realize we've done a lot more than basement renovations, right?"

He shrugged.

"Does 'check the work' mean oversee? Do my job? Micromanage the project?"

There was fury in the tone of her voice and in the snap in her eyes.

He shrugged. "Unless you have something to hide?"

"Check what you want. I don't 'hide' anything."

Jean returned with a glass of water and the coffeepot. As Trevor glanced around the diner, he realized people were watching their...argument? Discussion? Andie had a lot more fans around here than he did.

He stood, keeping his distance from the pot of hot coffee. From the look on Jean's face, she was tempted to pour it on him.

He reached into his pocket to grab his wallet. He took out a five-dollar bill, more than enough to cover his coffee, and tossed it on the table and grabbed his jacket.

"I'll see you tomorrow morning at the mill."

Andie's arms were crossed, and the glare she had focused on him made him uncomfortable. She gave him a short nod, and he walked out of the diner as quickly as dignity allowed.

Outside, he took a deep breath, and the cold air burned his lungs.

He'd hoped to reach a rapprochement with his contractor. That hadn't happened. It wasn't a problem, though, not really. He was here to do a job, not make friends. This wasn't his town, and he had no desire to stay here.

He just wished the woman at the bar, the one he'd liked talking to so much, wasn't the one he was going to be checking on for the duration of this project.

It might have been nice to have one friend here.

CHAPTER SIX

ANDIE WAITED AT the door. It was still dark out, but it was time to go. She tapped her foot while she watched her brother fill a coffee travel cup.

Joey was hard to get moving in the morning. Andie, on the other hand, made it a personal mission to be the first one on-site each day. Normally, they took two vehicles, but Joey's was in the shop for repairs, so they were traveling together in Andie's truck.

It was the first day working on the mill, and she needed to be there before Trevor. Andie was determined that Mr. Emerson would have nothing to complain about. *Nothing.*

She was used to misogyny and guys who thought women couldn't do this job. After her dad died, it had been a struggle to keep the company afloat. There were nights she'd cried herself to sleep, but she'd done it when no one could hear her.

Now her crew respected her, or at least they kept their opinions to themselves if they didn't. It hadn't been easy.

She knew these guys and did her best to be fair. She wouldn't tolerate shortcuts or shoddy work, but if someone worked hard for her, she worked hard for them. Construction slowed during the winter, but she did her best to keep her crew employed as much as possible.

Even though it was still winter, they could start demolition and renovations inside the mill, in the section that wasn't having drastic external changes. Now that the Valentine's Day events the town had arranged to kick-start the romance initiative were wrapped up, the mill was available to them. One event that had included most of the town had been held there, an appropriate beginning to what everyone hoped would be a successful and prosperous transformation.

Andie had enjoyed Dave and Jaycee's engagement party. There'd been skating on the river next to the mill, music and lights, and everyone had warmed up with hot chocolate. It had been beautiful and fun, and it had given everyone a sense of optimism.

If Abigail Carter could make this town a tourist destination for people wanting romance, engagements and weddings, it would breathe in new life. And would keep Kozak Construction busy for a long time.

Andie tried to hang on to that feeling of optimism as her brother slowly pulled on his boots and hat. It was as if he was moving through molasses.

"Come on, Joey. This is a big day, It's the start of our biggest project to date. Let's get on it."

"Jeez, Andie, it's still dark out."

Andie counted in her head. Ten wasn't enough. Neither was twenty. She let out a careful breath. "It's the first day. I have to be there to get things started. It's expected when you're the boss."

"When I'm the boss, we'll start an hour later."

Andie shook her head. "I wish that was possible."

Andie was tired, too. She'd spent too much time last night thinking of what could go wrong in front of Mr. Emerson before she'd finally fallen asleep.

She hustled Joey out the door and jogged over to the truck, breath frosting in the air. The seats were stiff and cold under her as she turned the truck engine on and started blasting air through the vents.

Joey turned down the fan. "Wait till it's warmed up."

Andie resisted the temptation to dial the fan back up. It was her truck, after all, but Joey had been struggling this year. It wouldn't hurt her to concede on the little things.

The truck moved stiffly as they left the yard, towing a trailer full of tools. Andie checked the road for traffic out of habit, but things were dark and still at this hour.

In spite of her gloomy brother and the grouchy architect, there were bubbles of excitement working through her veins. The first day on a new site was like the first day of school. There would be challenges, but right now, it was all possibilities.

She was going to turn the empty space into something beautiful and functional. She might not be the architect in charge of creating the vision, but she would implement it, make it real. And that was enough for now.

The excitement bubbles took a hit when she finally got to the mill. There was a car already there.

She knew that car. The day they went through the mill, there'd been Abigail's Lincoln, her truck and this car.

Trevor Emerson's car.

She'd really wanted to be here before him. She checked the time. Five minutes later than she'd planned. She might have beat him if Joey hadn't been dragging his feet.

Andie backed her truck in carefully, leaving the doors of the trailer accessible, then she headed in to see Trevor. Mr. Emerson. Trouble.

He was standing near the side of the building with the kitchen and bathrooms. This would be where they would focus most of their efforts until the weather warmed up.

The people staging last week's skating party had left the space heaters behind, as arranged. The right side of the main space also had some tables, chairs and boxes waiting to be picked up, but they were in the far corner and wouldn't be in the way. Joey had followed Andie inside, and she nodded at a space heater. They'd need them blowing warm air toward the back where the crew would be working.

Andie picked up one, as well, and started carrying it toward the spot where Trevor was standing. He turned, and a frown creased his forehead.

If she hadn't met him at the Goat, she'd never believe he knew how to smile.

"Should you be carrying that?"

Andie heard Joey snort behind her.

"Are you asking whether I'm incapable or stupid?"

She slid the heater to the ground with a bit more force than normal.

Trevor's gaze moved to Joey, following behind her.

"Is that your equipment? I thought they were from the party."

Andie crossed her arms, and Joey went back for another heater.

"Did you think we just commandeered them? They belong to Kozak. We loaned them out for the skating party. They were left behind because they're ours."

Trevor swallowed and seemed to regain control. "I see. Are you planning to set up an office in one of these rooms?"

Joey was back with another heater. He answered for her. "I ordered the trailer for the office to be delivered first thing, sis. Want me to check on it?"

Andie gave her brother a smile, both for the support and for getting his task done.

"Sure, Joey. Once it's here, Sid will get it hooked up. Want to check on those gennies that are coming, as well?"

Joey nodded and headed toward the door.

Trevor put his hands in his pockets, but they didn't fit well with his thick gloves. He took them back out and crossed his arms.

"So we'll have a trailer to work in."

Andie kept a level gaze on him. "Yes, since we're planning to do a lot of demo in here, we'll keep the paperwork and electronics in a trailer to keep them safe."

"Good, good."

Andie had had enough. She wasn't an idiot, and she knew how to do her job, but this man seemed determined to think her deficient in some way.

"I hear my crew arriving." She turned and headed to the door, happy to be with people who respected her and valued her.

As she opened the door, she looked back at Trevor. He was staring at the floor, looking... sad.

She felt a twinge but reminded herself that she wasn't the one double-checking to see if he was able to perform his job. He'd apparently come into town determined to think the worst of them and the work they'd do.

That was all on him.

THE CREW FELL into a familiar first-day rhythm. They got the office set up and the gennies and other rented gear in place. Andie gathered the crew, mostly men but with two other women— who were also working on breaking the concrete ceiling in the industry—and ran over the expected schedule and the order in which the work would be completed.

The team had questions, and she answered them. She introduced Trevor, though everyone already knew who he was.

This was a small town.

There was a rumble of welcomes for the newcomer and a lot of curiosity on their faces. They asked if he was finding everything he needed, and he nodded.

Then Sid blurted out the million-dollar question. "Will we be seeing much of you?"

Most of their jobs were smaller, and they didn't see the architect that often. Sometimes, Andie was the only one who interacted with them. She'd get the plans and discuss the work they'd do, and then they'd look at the completed job.

Trevor nodded. "Yes, I hope to be here every day."

Silence.

Andie turned to him. "Every day?"

What would he possibly do here every day? She might not have worked on a lot of major construction projects, but she knew the architect wasn't normally on-site every day unless it was a very big project. Something bigger than would ever be built in Carter's Crossing.

His arms were crossed again, his feet spread. "Yes, I think it's going to be very interesting."

The crew were watching her, waiting to see her response. She'd like to tell him she didn't need a babysitter. She'd like to tell him what he could do with his 'every day' and his 'interesting'. She'd like to tell him a lot of things, but she wasn't going to do that, because she was a professional.

She also wasn't going to tell him that it was fine or that she was looking forward to it. She wasn't going to lie. Instead, she turned back to her people.

"Let's get started on the kitchen. We're gutting it. We've got a bin arriving here in ten minutes. I want to have it filled by lunchtime. Bathrooms are next.

"Are the porta potties here yet, Joey?"

Joey cocked his head. "I think I hear them now."

Andie walked with her brother back to the big door. She wondered how Mr. Emerson was going to enjoy using porta potties *every day*.

THE TRAILER WAS too small.

It was a standard trailer for a job like this. There was room for a desk for him and one for Andie and a table. It would soon be covered with a confusing litter of odds and ends as the work went on. There was a water cooler and a small fridge with a coffee maker on top. Somehow, it felt too small on this project.

As Trevor sat with his laptop on the desk in front of him, he swore he could feel Andie breathing. The first day was winding down.

So far, things were going well. The site was organized, and the work had started and was progressing as expected. Andie was going over paperwork on her end, and he could hear the muted sounds of the work site through the walls.

There was a knock on the door, and Joey appeared, reminding him yet again that this was a family firm.

"We're wrapping for today, sis. I can get a lift home with Badger, so take whatever time you need."

Andie looked at the watch on her wrist and nodded. "Everything's cleaned up for the night?"

"Yes, boss."

Trevor tried to decipher Joey's tone. Was he upset? Did he mind working for his sister?

"Tell Mom I'll call when I'm on my way."

Joey closed the door, and Trevor heard truck and car doors slamming, voices crossing over each other, and the sounds of vehicles pulling away. Andie's head was back down, her fingers clicking on the keyboard as she worked away.

How late did she work? Was she always the last to go? Was it a first-day thing? Or was she doing this to assure him she was capable? To impress him, make him trust her?

She rubbed a finger up and down the middle

of her forehead and then moved it back to the keyboard. Her hair was pulled back in a tie but ruffled from being in a hard hat while she'd been on site. She'd taken off her parka and a flannel shirt was peeking out over the neckline of her sweater.

No makeup, no jewelry. Her feet were still in work boots, crossed under the desk. Her gaze moved upward and caught his. He felt his cheeks heating and concentrated on his screen again.

"Is there anything you want to say?"

He looked back up. She was staring at him, mouth in a tight line. He couldn't tell her he'd been wondering if she was staying in the trailer to impress him or if she wanted to spend more time with him. That would be epically bad.

She wouldn't like him to ask how much nepotism played in her company's operations, either.

"Not really."

She nodded. "If you have any questions, any problems on-site, I'd appreciate it if you speak to me in private first."

He frowned, considering her words. She huffed a breath.

"If I don't deal with the issue, then you can take it further, but I can usually handle it. That's my job."

"You don't want me talking to your crew?"

Her lips thinned. They'd soon disappear.

"You can talk to anyone you like. But if you see a problem, please talk to me first. If someone isn't doing their job, that's my responsibility. If anything goes wrong, the buck stops here."

Her fingertip tapped on the tabletop in front of her. "I'd like a chance to explain to you if the problem isn't what you think it is. I don't want my crew thinking you're here to critique them. Tell *me* first."

Her phone rang, and she answered it, leaving him dismissed.

"Okay, Mom, I'll head out now. Give me fifteen minutes to pack up here and check the site."

She shoved her phone in her pocket and closed her laptop. "I can trust you to lock up the trailer?"

"Yes."

She shoved her laptop in a bag and straightened some papers. Pulling on her coat, she tossed him a key.

"I'm gone after I do this walk-through. You have my number if you need me."

Her coat was zipped, and a hat was pulled over her ears. She left the trailer without any further words. He stared at the door for a long time before he shook his head and focused on his computer. He finished up his notes for the day and looked over at Andie's desk. She'd taken her laptop but left a pile of papers weighed down with a rock on top of the desk. He was curious about those papers.

He remembered Geoff Compton shoving papers in his briefcase, laughing that details like this were the bane of his life, and that Trevor was lucky not to have to deal with them.

That paperwork had later showed Geoff had been making substitutions. Ones that had led to the accident.

He shouldn't look at Andie's paperwork. It really wasn't part of his job.

He opened up an email from Abigail Carter. She wanted to meet with him and some of the locals about renovations to their homes to set up B and Bs. He agreed to meet her tomorrow afternoon, and then his gaze wandered to Andie's desk again.

It wasn't like she was even at the stage where any substitutions could be made. And she probably wasn't making any mistakes. She was on the level and capable enough to do this job.

It was just the memories were returning, over and over again, making him anxious and tense. The story on TV and in the papers, where his picture was captioned with words like *suspected* and *at fault*. The interviews with the owner and contractor looking so earnest and concerned, blaming him for the accident.

His hand rubbed his leg.

He hadn't been able to tell his side, not at first. He'd been in hospital. Some had called it karmic justice that he'd been hurt.

It hadn't been karma. It had been his contractor in collaboration with the building owner, cutting corners, ignoring safety issues to save money, bribing inspectors. When that had led to the accident that brought the south wall down, a good portion of it on his leg, they'd been quick to blame him.

Maybe they'd hoped he wouldn't recover. But he had. And he'd fought back. He'd been exonerated, but not in the court of public opinion. That court had closed up session long before he'd been able to participate.

It had been his first major project since going out on his own, and it had almost crushed his dreams along with his leg.

This project here in Carter's Crossing was his chance to show what he could do on his own, without someone else's company to back him up. He couldn't risk a contractor cutting corners. Not again.

He stood, went to the trailer door and opened it. He looked and listened, but the winter sun was long gone and the place quiet and dark. He closed and locked the door.

He went over to Andie's desk, picked up her paperweight rock and set it aside. Then he scanned the pages. Invoices for the trailer and generators. Deal memos with the crew. Nothing looked out of the ordinary.

He set the papers down and carefully replaced the rock. Then, since he'd already crossed the line, he looked through the file cabinet under her desk, finding nothing but empty folders. Was that suspicious? Or was there just nothing to file because it was the first day?

There was a notepad at the side of the desk. She'd written down a name, a supplier of hardware. He took note of that. He'd check what other companies competed with them, make sure there wasn't too cozy a connection between them and his contractor.

He felt...dirty. Dishonest.

He didn't really know Andie. He'd done some research, and Kozak Construction had no red flags online that he could find. He wished he could believe that was enough proof, but his previous contractor had had a good reputation, as well.

He rubbed his leg again. The cold was making it ache. As his hands ran across the hard plastic of his prosthetic device, his resolve hardened.

He'd lost too much to a shady contractor and conspiring owner. It didn't matter what Andie thought of him or if he was snooping. It might not be nice, but next time, it might be worse than someone losing a limb. Someone could lose their life.

CHAPTER SEVEN

ANDIE CHECKED THE time and made her way through the debris of the former kitchen to find her brother.

"I need to head out now. Sure you don't want to come?"

Joey shook his head. "Nah, I'd rather be here working than sitting in Abigail Carter's parlor while she talks with the old ladies about bathrooms."

Andie shook her head.

"We'll talk about *bedrooms*, too. And you're going to have to learn to do the customer side, as well."

Joey shrugged. "You're staying for a while yet, right? So no rush."

Andie checked her brother's expression. "Would you rather I'd planned to go to school this fall?"

He rolled his eyes at her.

She was the oldest of the family, and Joey was the youngest, so they had the biggest gap in age, and in relationship, as well. Andie felt she understood him least, even though they were the only two still living at home.

Andie had been the de facto boss of the family company after her father died. That responsibility, added to her status as the oldest child, meant that she and Joey didn't have a normal sibling relationship.

Each of her siblings in turn had left to go to school and found the careers they wanted somewhere other than Carter's Crossing. Andie had been sad to see them go but had encouraged them to follow their dreams.

Abigail Carter was hoping to rejuvenate the town so that people could pursue their ambitions here in Carter's Crossing. It was too late for her siblings, but Andie supported the initiative and hoped there would be more opportunities for other kids growing up in town to stay if they wanted.

There were worse places to live.

Joey had gone away to school, but he hadn't found what he wanted. Like all the Kozak kids, he'd worked for the company on weekends and during the summer. He seemed happy to continue working here, waiting to take over. Was he tired of waiting?

Andie had been trying to get him more involved with the company and to take more of a leadership role. When she was off-site, he was the guy in charge. If they split between two sites, he managed the second one. But she didn't think he was ready to take over, not yet. So far, he'd shown no interest in meeting with clients or handling the paperwork that seemed to grow with every job.

Was it her fault? Had she prevented him from being more of a leader because she didn't know how to step back?

"Hey, Joey. Sure you don't want to take this meeting? I could stay here."

Joey gave her a puzzled look. "Why would I do that? I don't know the right things to ask anyway. Go. I can take over here."

He turned back to his work, and Andie, untypically uncertain, turned and headed to the office to get her bag.

Trevor was there putting his laptop in his computer bag. He'd been quiet this morning. He'd walked through the site first thing and then again before lunch. No one had complained, but none of them were used to being watched like this.

She knew he was going to the same meeting as she was, and despite their conflicts, they did need to work together. So far, she'd smiled and let the crew think she was fine with what Trevor was doing. She wasn't. She hated feeling like she needed to prove her competency, but if it would help them get along, she'd do it. Maybe if they spent time not talking about work, he'd feel like he could trust her?

"Want to share a ride to Abigail's?"

Trevor looked up, startled.

"Abigail's? You're going, too?"

The dismay in his voice irritated her. What was with this guy?

"Yes, I am. Since Kozak Construction will be doing a lot of the work, it only makes sense that I'm there to help with scheduling."

Trevor frowned.

Andie didn't have to ask what his problem was with her being there. Her very existence was a problem for him. She just didn't know why. This had never happened before or, at least, not since the early days when she'd taken over after her father died. She hadn't liked it then, and she liked it less now.

"You know, I might prefer to have more choice in architects around here, as well, but here we are. It's supposed to snow soon, so I'm offering to give you a ride since you don't have snow tires on your vehicle. That's all. I'm fine on my own. See you there."

She shoved her computer in her own bag, grabbed her jacket, and prepared to head out while doing her best to pretend Trevor was invisible.

"I would appreciate a ride, thank you."

Andie's head snapped up. Trevor stood in front of her, wearing clothes that looked a heck of a lot nicer than her work wear, ready to go and without a frown. He'd flipped in the few moments she was getting her coat on. Talk about Jekyll and Hyde.

Andie wanted to ask if he really trusted her to drive, but if he could pretend to be polite, so could she.

"Okay. Joey has a key to the trailer if anyone needs something, so we can lock up."

Trevor raised his brows, but he merely waited while she turned the key in the door, and followed her to her truck.

Bertha was big and functional and not pretty. She could drive through almost anything, and she could carry a lot while she did so. Trevor's car was fancier, but Andie could be sure of arriving almost anywhere, in almost any conditions. She wasn't apologizing for Bertha. She hated that she'd been tempted to do so.

She beeped open the locks, climbed in and turned the ignition on to get some heat going. There was a bag of assorted hardware on the passenger seat. Trevor had opened the door but paused. Andie glanced over and picked up the bag.

"Sorry, leftovers from our last job. I need to return it or get Joey to."

"Mind?" he asked, gloved hand hovering over the button to warm his seat.

"Go for it."

He hit the button for her seat, as well. Andie stayed quiet, putting the truck in Drive and heading out from the parking lot to the road. The first few flakes started to fall as they turned onto the asphalt.

It took only a few minutes to make their way to Abigail's home. She assumed it was Trevor's first chance to see the place, and she watched for his reaction. She saw appreciation in his stare and felt vicariously proud. There were several cars parked in front of the house and lining the drive. Andie didn't bother trying to squeeze Bertha in. She stopped at the end of the driveway.

"If you get out here, I'll pull up just ahead."

There wouldn't be any room for Trevor to get out of the vehicle without falling into the ditch once she'd done that.

He paused for a moment before thanking her and opening the door.

He puzzled her. The man she'd met in the bar had been warm and had exhibited a strong sense of humor. The architect she was trying to work with was prickly and suspicious. And he had these exasperating pauses, as if he considered everything before he spoke or acted.

She was curious about what those pauses meant. She wished she wasn't. And while she was at it, she wished she was working with the man from the bar instead of the architect she saw on-site.

It had been a long time since she'd felt just like Andie, a woman someone found interesting, instead of Andie, head of Kozak Construction. But she was Andie the contractor now, as far as Trevor was concerned. And he didn't like his contractor.

Shaking her head, she parked the truck as close to the side of the road as she could and climbed down.

Trevor had waited on the drive for her instead of rushing ahead to get in first. She wasn't sure if it was manners or some kind of power play, but she walked beside him and went first up the steps. With some guys, she might suspect he was checking her out, but not with this one.

Mavis Grisham opened the door. She acted as Abigail's second in command. Andie was glad to see she hadn't brought her dog, Tiny, with her. The Great Dane wasn't good at remembering his manners, and she had no desire to shove his nose out of her crotch in front of Trevor.

"Andie! So nice to see you. How's your mother?"

Andie returned the embrace, careful of Mavis's tiny form.

"We're all good, thanks. How are you? Have you met Mr. Emerson?"

Mavis held a hand to her chest. "You're the lovely young man who helped me with my flat tire on New Year's Eve! That was very sweet of you. I don't think I properly thanked you before you rushed away. But I'll be sure to bake you a cake to show my gratitude, now that I've tracked you down."

Really? Andie wouldn't have guessed that about him. But Mavis kept on.

"I wondered if you were the architect. Abigail told us a bit about you. I'm Mavis Grisham, but you can call me Mavis. I'm so looking forward to you working for me. So handsome."

Andie shot him a glance out of the corner of her eye. Trevor looked startled, but he responded appropriately, falling somewhere on a scale between the man she'd first met and the guy she knew now.

Andie pulled off her coat and added it to the pile already on the chair in the entry.

"You all got here early?" Andie jerked her chin at the coats.

They were dry, so their owners had arrived before the snow started.

Mavis nodded. "Oh, yes. We've been having a committee meeting. We'll just roll that over into talking to you two. Mariah's in charge of the romance iniative, and she's been going on about us setting up websites and getting the B and Bs going. It's really happening!"

Mavis had a huge smile on her face. She was right. It was happening. With every wall coming down at the mill, with the orders Andie was making for new materials, Carter's Crossing was becoming something new. That bubble of excitement was returning, despite Mr. Emerson beside her.

This was all going to be worth it in the end.

TREVOR HAD MADE a lot of notes by the time the meeting was done.

It had been difficult to keep things straight. The women in the meeting tended to start telling him about their homes and the work they needed done to adapt them, and then they'd divert into stories about people he'd never heard of, many who appeared to no longer be part of the town. Then someone else would start, and after two more stories, the original speaker would add something else to her list.

Andie was making notes, as well, but it was easier for her. She had the advantage of knowing these people she was talking to and also the ones in the stories. She wouldn't start noting something that George had done to a home, only to discover George had left town or died more than twenty years ago and then his house had burned down or had been sold to Harold.

It was enough to give him a headache. Except, it didn't. The stories were rambling, but he itched to see these homes. He expected some of the work that had been done in the past would probably not meet current codes, and some had undoubtedly marred the beauty of the original structures. But he loved buildings and the stories they told. The homes in this town, especially the ones in the more prosperous downtown area, had decades and sometimes more than a century of stories to their brick and mortar and wood. He wanted to read the stories.

The ladies finally began to trickle away, leaving Trevor and Andie and Abigail to evaluate their notes and plans.

Abigail looked at him with a smile at the corners of her lips.

"I hope you were able to keep up, Trevor. Sometimes we older people can ramble a bit."

"A bit" was an understatement. But Abigail wasn't one to ramble.

"I'll need to see the homes, but today gave me an introduction."

"That's a nice way to express it. Honestly, I've been in Eloise's house at least once a month for as long as I can remember, and I couldn't keep what she was talking about straight."

Trevor allowed a smile in response to her comment. He thought Eloise was the one with the white Victorian with green shutters, but George might have painted them blue.

Abigail closed her own notebook. "I'd suggest Andie set up a schedule for going over the homes."

Trevor stilled. Was he going to be able to do anything without involving Andie?

"It will take an hour to get Eloise to settle on a start time. At least Andie will know what she means when she talks about the day before the bazaar meeting. Also, these women know her and will be more comfortable settling things with her. In a small town, you're a stranger for a long time."

Trevor nodded. He'd figured out that several of the women were widows. He could certainly allow them the comfort of not having a strange man set loose in their homes. Though, they'd need to be a little more accustomed to it if they were going to rent out rooms. That, however, was not his problem.

"Also, Harriet will tell you that her son can do most of the work, but he won't. Andie will make sure she allows time for that in her schedule, for when he sprains his spleen or some such thing."

Huh.

Trevor hadn't worked on small jobs like renovating a few bedrooms and a bath for years. And he'd never been the architect in charge of projects like that. He was used to working with professionals.

Personal vagaries were going to be a factor on these jobs. Andie's local knowledge would be an asset. Perhaps he shouldn't be upset that they were apparently going to meet with the homeowners as a pair. It would give him more opportunity to watch how she worked and evaluate how trustworthy she was.

Andie stood. "Thanks for arranging this, Abigail. Do you have a date when you hope things will be completed?"

"Most of the timeline will depend on when the mill is ready. I don't want to add pressure on the two of you, because I know there will be factors outside of your control that can delay the work. I'll do what I can to smooth your path, but I won't make any major plans until we are closer to that being done."

Andie's forehead creased, her brows almost meeting over her straight nose. Trevor reminded himself that her nose was none of his business.

"Things went so well on Valentine's Day. There's nothing else going on?"

Abigail smiled. "As if Mariah would be content to let things ride. We aren't making any plans that include the mill or require the B and Bs to be functioning, but we have at least one major event planned for this summer, and there will be some smaller things, as well."

"That's good," Andie said. "People need that to look forward to, to give them hope."

Abigail's smile disappeared. "Exactly. I don't want to delay any more than I have to. Not to pressure you, but…"

Trevor knew Abigail had a lot of clout here, and this project of hers was going to keep the town and Kozak Construction busy. Was this maybe a nudge to take shortcuts to speed up the process?

He didn't want to think so. He admired Abigail Carter, but he'd been burned before, and he couldn't let it just ride.

"Do you mind, Andie, if I talk to Trevor for a bit?"

Trevor went very still. This was the first time someone appeared to want to separate the two of them for a discussion. He wondered what Abigail wanted to talk about and how Andie would respond.

"Not at all, but we rode over together."

Abigail shrugged. "This isn't a secret, so I'm not trying to keep anything from you. It just involves a potential project that could use Trevor's expertise after the mill is done, but it might not happen. If it does, you'll probably be gone from Carter's Crossing by the time a contractor is needed, so I don't want to keep you from your work. I know you're busy."

Wait. Andie was leaving town? When? Why?

Andie didn't appear to have a problem with being left out.

"It's fine, Abigail. I can stay here and answer emails. Or would you like me to go to the kitchen? I won't offer to wait in the truck, not today."

Trevor hadn't been watching the weather, but a glance out the window showed him that the wind had picked up and snow was blowing in the gathering dusk.

"As long as you can keep this quiet, Andie.

If things go well with Cupid's Crossing, I'm considering converting this place into an inn."

Trevor was mildly surprised, but Andie's eyebrows were now climbing to her hairline.

"An inn? But you—your family…"

Trevor didn't know Abigail's family, and he wasn't sure he could handle more names today.

Abigail looked out the window. "My grandson Nelson's the only family I have in town, and he won't be moving in here. I expect he'll do something about that house on his farm. This place is too big for just me, and I don't know that any of the others are coming back."

Andie was nodding, so Nelson and the others were familiar to her.

"But where would you live?"

Suddenly, Abigail didn't look sad. There was a look of mischief on that elegant face.

"I might not stay in Carter's—or rather, Cupid's—Crossing. I suspect Mariah will remain, and she can take care of things."

Andie was blinking, her mouth slightly open. Apparently, the idea of Abigail leaving town was a surprise. Trevor suspected finding out about Santa had been less of a shock.

It didn't surprise him. Abigail was beautiful, intelligent and incredibly competent, and he was more surprised to know that she'd lived in this small town her entire life. She had connections outside this place. She hadn't invited him to come and work here randomly. Someone in the city had given her Howard's name.

"Do you want me to look around and maybe come up with preliminary drawings?"

Abigail shook her head. "Not quite yet. But I'd like to show you around and get an idea of whether a conversion would be a big job, or a huge job."

Trevor smiled, pleased at the prospect of taking a closer look at the house. It was beautiful, both outside and from what he'd seen inside. He was pretty sure George hadn't done the work on this one.

"I'd love to see more of your home. It's beautiful. And I could probably give you a quick-and-dirty estimate of time and money."

Abigail turned to Andie. "Do you want to join us?"

Andie shook her head. "No, I should answer some of these messages. I'll just sit here and come to terms with the idea of Carter's Crossing without Abigail Carter."

Abigail's mouth twisted. "We're changing the name to Cupid's Crossing. And nothing is determined yet."

That might be true, Trevor thought, but Abigail looked like she'd set her mind on something, and he suspected she was not a person who failed often. If he lived here, he'd be changing his address to Cupid's Crossing.

CHAPTER EIGHT

ANDIE HAD HER phone in her hands but hadn't opened her email yet.

Abigail leaving?

That would be news. And a big change for the town. She couldn't imagine Carter's Crossing without Abigail Carter. Nelson Carter was here, true, but he was the town vet and showed no interest in taking up a leadership role.

Andie could see his fiancée, Mariah, stepping up. Those two had gotten engaged on Valentine's Day. Andie wondered if Abigail had had a hand in that. She shook her head. Nothing was set yet, and she had a couple of messages from her brother to deal with.

Trevor and Abigail took a while. She heard their voices echoing down the stairs as they examined the upper floors, and when they passed though the room she was in, she heard Abigail recounting the history of the building. Meantime, she agreed with her brother about sending the crew home since the wind and snow were now threatening the roads.

When they finally came back, Andie stood up, eager to get going. Her mother would be anxious, and she hated to make her worry. Most of the time, her mom's concerns were excessive, but when the weather was like this, she had good reason to be worried.

"I hope you don't mind, Abigail, but we should head out now. The roads are getting bad."

"You've got your truck?" Abigail asked.

Andie nodded.

"That's good. Would you like me to call your mother and tell her you're on your way? Maybe keep her talking for a while?"

Andie took a long breath. "That would be wonderful, Abigail. She'll fuss with the roads like this, and I need to return Trevor to his car back at the mill."

Abigail crossed to the window and pulled back a curtain.

"Maybe you should just drop him off at his place and take him to the mill tomorrow. The temperature has dropped."

Andie stood beside Abigail and looked out at the snow. Abigail was right. This snowfall had taken a twist toward snowstorm. She turned to Trevor. She didn't think he'd be very keen on that idea, but after taking a look out the window himself, he nodded his agreement.

"As I've been told, I don't have snow tires, so it might be wiser."

Andie shot him a glance. She would bet that if Abigail weren't here, he'd have argued rather than accept assistance.

"You're on Second Street, aren't you, Trevor? That's not far out of Andie's way."

Those eyes turned to her. "Do you mind, Andie?"

It was the first time he'd said her name. Why did she know that?

"No, I don't mind. We don't want to lose our architect."

She wasn't being sarcastic, not really, but she saw the slight narrowing of his eyes and the pinching of his mouth before he quickly wiped away the expression.

They bundled up in their outerwear. Abigail watched them as they headed out to the driveway and promised to call Andie's mom as soon as the truck was moving. Andie climbed in, turned on the heat and reversed so that Trevor could access the passenger door.

He slipped on his way up and gripped the door tightly. "Abigail was right. It's getting very slippery."

Andie was grateful for Bertha's snow tires and firm grip on the road.

Trevor didn't double-check her driving, which

was a relief. She concentrated on the road, turning onto Second Street and inching down the slick pavement until she arrived at the house he indicated. She was familiar with it. Kozak Construction had worked on it back when her father was alive.

She pulled to a careful halt in front of the house. She'd wondered where he was staying but had avoided taking any steps to find out. She didn't ask herself why.

"Flick the lights on once you're inside, and I'll head home."

His mouth opened, and she knew he was going to tell her not to bother, but then, he closed his mouth and swallowed.

"Thank you for the lift. Send me a text when you head out in the morning, and I'll be waiting on the sidewalk for you."

Andie nodded. She liked the idea that he wasn't going to arrive before her.

Trevor gathered his things and was careful exiting the truck, mindful of the slipperiness of ice under the coating of fresh snow.

He was very careful walking to his front door. The ice appeared to bother him. Maybe he didn't go out a lot in New York City when things were icy. Perhaps they didn't have a lot of ice like this in the city. If she stayed home when things got slippery, she'd stay home a lot.

Trevor made it to the door and used his key to open it. She put Bertha in Drive and kept her foot on the brakes, waiting for him to flick on the light that would release her.

She waited. It was dark enough now that she'd see a light, even in a back room. She frowned. It was very dark. She bent to peer through the windshield.

The streetlight beside her wasn't on. She could see one lit up farther down. The wind-driven snow whipped through its glow, but the one in front of Trevor's house was dark. So were the houses beside his.

He reappeared in the doorway. Andie put the truck in Park and hopped down, her boots and grip on the door keeping her upright. She headed up the sidewalk, remembering how he'd been cautious and wanting to save him another trip on the ice.

"What's wrong?"

He was frowning, phone in hand.

"The lights aren't working, and the heat is off. I'm calling the landlord."

Andie looked at the neighboring houses that were also dark.

"I don't think she can help. Looks like the power's out in a few of the houses around here."

He turned around, looking past her at… mostly nothing, since everything was dark. He looked at a loss for the first time since she'd met him.

Andie sighed.

"Go get what you need for the night. You can come home with me."

TREVOR WASN'T SURE exactly why he'd agreed. Well, part of it was because his place was dark and cold, and he didn't have a car here, but he hadn't thought through all that when he'd agreed and gone back to pack a bag. He'd been curious. What was Andie's place like? What was her family like?

This was his chance to understand her better and see how much trust he could place with her.

Andie didn't say much as they drove to her place. She was focused on the drive, and though her big truck gripped the road, he didn't want to distract her.

He remembered she'd said she lived out of town, back when they'd met at the pub and he hadn't known who she was. He'd heard her calls that day and while on-site and when she talked to her brother, so he knew she lived at home with her family.

He did wonder why but had never been able to ask. He might find out now.

Just outside the town limits, they pulled into

the driveway of a bigger house than he'd expected. There was a large garage and work shed, a big sign, and some oversize equipment in the shadows of the yard. This was obviously headquarters for Kozak Construction.

Andie pulled her truck into the garage. She handled her vehicle competently. From what he'd observed so far, she was surprisingly capable at everything he'd seen her do.

Maybe he had more chauvinism in him than he'd realized. It was a disconcerting thought, and he set it aside for later consideration as he slid out of the truck with his duffle bag.

An older woman was peering out the door, watching as Andie led the way, striding over the snow-covered path to the house, leaving footsteps for him to follow.

"Andie! Was it slippery? Joey got back a while ago."

"Mom, it was fine." Andie's tone was patient. "I was in a meeting over at Abigail Carter's, and that ran a little longer than I'd expected. She had all the women over there, so you know how that goes. Then I drove Mr. Emerson home. Since his place doesn't have power, I brought him to spend the night. Trevor Emerson, this is my mom, Marion Kozak."

He hadn't seen much family resemblance between Joey and Andie, but there was a strong resemblance between Joey and his mother. Presumably, Andie took after her father.

He held out a hand to Andie's mother, who'd stepped outside as they approached. "It's a pleasure to meet you, Mrs. Kozak. I hope I'm not an imposition."

A smile broke through her worried expression. "No, not at all. There used to be seven of us in the house, and with only the three of us now, it feels empty. We have lots of room, and with this weather—"

She broke off to cast another worried look at the snow blowing through the yard.

"Let's go in, Mom. It's cold out. We're all home and fine. What am I smelling?"

There was an appetizing aroma in the air. Trevor felt his stomach attempting to grumble, and he pressed a hand to his midsection.

Mrs. Kozak moved ahead of them into the kitchen. Andie pulled off her hat and gloves and threw them into a basket by the door. She opened a closet door and pulled out a hanger.

"I can hang up your coat."

Trevor unbuttoned his and shrugged the coat off.

"Thank you." He passed the coat over and carefully bent to undo his boots.

The entrance was roomy, leaving space for several people to don or remove their outerwear. He carefully stepped out of his boots and set them on a plastic mat already holding several pairs. Andie hung up her own jacket, removed her boots and led the way past a shabby living room with worn couches around a TV.

"Mom, I'm going to show Trevor to the spare room."

"Okay, Andie. I'll start serving soon." Her mother's voice echoed back.

Andie led the way down a hallway. She opened a door and flicked on the ceiling light.

The room wasn't as crowded as the rest of the house. It appeared to be a mostly unused guest room with a queen-size bed, a dresser and end tables.

Andie read the surprise on his face.

"Growing up, my sister and I shared this room. As you can see, it's a guest room now for when my siblings come back. Joey has the boys' room, and I have the other bedroom to myself.

"Why don't you drop your bag, and we'll get to the table. Mom is a great cook, but she likes to get dinner done before her game shows come on."

Trevor dropped his duffle and followed her back to the kitchen.

Joey was already seated at one end of the table, and Mrs. Kozak at the other. Andie headed to what was obviously her usual chair, and Trevor sat at the remaining place setting.

"This looks delicious, Mrs. Kozak."

He wasn't just saying that. The meal was homemade and emitting an aroma that was about to make his stomach embarrass him, with quantities beyond what four of them could possibly consume.

He felt welcomed but not overpowered.

Mrs. Kozak passed him a bowl to start.

"It's my *bigos*. The kids need a good meal after working all day."

The "kids" certainly wouldn't be hungry after this.

"You're new to Carter's Crossing, Mr. Emerson?"

Trevor almost whimpered at the aroma wafting from his plate. His own cooking was healthy and basic. This was something else. "Yes. I'm here to work on the mill. I'm the architect."

Mrs. Kozak's eyes widened. "Oh, really? Andie, love, perhaps Mr. Emerson could talk to you, give you some advice."

Surprised, he looked at Andie. Her cheeks were flushed.

"Mom, let me take care of it. Mr. Emerson is busy, and so am I."

"Oh, come on now, Andie. All we ever hear

is how much you sacrifice instead of going to study, so go ahead and talk to him." Joey jerked his head at Trevor. "Then you can escape Carter's Crossing and leave Mom and I here."

Andie's eyes widened, and her mouth turned down. "I'm not escaping. Can we just let this go? Trevor didn't ask to find himself in the middle of our family drama. Were there any problems on the site after I left, Joey?"

Trevor didn't want to be in the middle of family drama, but he was extremely curious about the issue he was supposed to offer advice on. And what sacrifices Andie had made. He was also very interested in whether there'd been a problem on-site. He was allowed to be curious about that.

Joey promised there'd been no problems. "Do you need a play-by-play of everything we did, or can you just accept that?"

Andie bit her lip just as their mother broke in. "Joey, I'm sure you did everything just fine, but Andie's a worrier."

"Wonder where she gets that?" Joey grumbled under his breath.

"Let's pass the food. So, Mr. Emerson, where is it you're staying?"

Trevor answered, and Mrs. Kozak commented on the place and what she knew of the people on the street, none of whom he knew.

He kept a polite smile on his face and indulged in the best meal he'd enjoyed in weeks.

Mrs. Kozak asked where he was from and what it was like to grow up in a city. From her responses, she obviously didn't believe that a childhood in the city could in any way compare to growing up in this small town. She didn't probe into his family, and he was relieved. She mentioned where her other children were living. Andie had three siblings who'd moved to other places. One was in Albany, one had gone to Boston and the farthest one appeared to be in Chicago.

They were all younger than Andie. Trevor wondered why everyone had left, but Andie had stayed. He wondered what had happened to Mr. Kozak, who was never mentioned. And he wondered why she had chosen to stay in this town and be a contractor, when her siblings had all gone to college.

But he didn't ask. Not when these were the issues that had sparked the drama at the beginning of the meal. Not when Andie had looked upset. For some reason, he didn't want to upset her. Not more than he already had.

He offered to clear up, but Mrs. Kozak refused. She shooed him away while she carried the serving dishes into the kitchen, and despite an urge to follow that delicious food, he let her go. Joey went to the living room and turned on the television. Trevor asked for the restroom and escaped from there to his room. He didn't want to intrude, but he'd forgotten his phone charger, and he needed Wi-Fi if he was going to do anything more than stare at the walls.

He could see the access point, but he needed a password, obviously. He hooked his laptop up to his phone data, but after fifteen minutes, it was almost dead.

He brought his laptop out to the living room where Joey and his mother were watching television. Andie worked on her own laptop at the dining room table.

"Um, can I use your Wi-Fi?"

Andie gave him a polite smile. "Sure." She scratched a random-looking code on a scrap of paper and passed it over to him.

He should return to his room, but he was tired of lonely nights with the internet, and he was curious.

He sat down across from Andie and typed in the password. Since the other two were immersed in a loud game show, he leaned over the table, seeming to catch Andie by surprise.

"What advice did you want me to give you?"

Her cheeks flushed again. She frowned and shot a glance over at her relatives.

"I have no plans to trouble you, don't worry."

Her reluctance made him push. There was something about her that made him prickly and juvenile. "I'm here, and you're not troubling me now."

As her mouth firmed in an upcoming denial, he added, "Or I could ask your mother."

Now she was frowning harder, forehead creasing. She glanced to the side and then back.

"Fine. Just remember that you insisted, I didn't ask." She waited for his nod. "I had planned to study architecture."

He blinked.

She had her head down and was facing her screen again, carefully avoiding his glance.

Oh, he wasn't letting that go. "So, why didn't you?"

This wasn't irrelevant; he knew it.

Andie sighed, as if hard done by, and stood.

Trevor stood, unsure of where they were going, hoping it wasn't someplace difficult.

"Mom, I'm going to the office with Trevor."

Her mother nodded, gaze never leaving the TV screen.

Andie headed toward the door they'd used to enter the house, but instead of pulling on her outdoor gear, she turned down a short hallway and opened the door there.

She flicked on the overhead light, and he saw they were now in the offices of Kozak

Construction. Not only was it recognizably a business office but it had Kozak Construction painted on the walls. And photographs.

There were black-and-white photos of a man he didn't recognize but who bore more than a passing resemblance to Andie. Color photos of presumably the same man with a younger version of himself. A couple of Andie on job sites. A lot of pictures of projects presumably completed by Kozak Construction. None of them were basement renovations.

Andie sat behind what must be her desk and waved for Trevor to sit across from her.

"We grew up working for Kozak Construction, all of us kids." She pointed to the photos. "My grandfather and my dad. I loved the buildings, so I applied to Pratt when I was a high school senior. I got in. I was pretty excited, and my dad was so proud.

"I was working with my dad on a job one New Year's Eve fourteen years ago, and after we closed up, my dad and I stopped at the Goat and Barley to have a celebratory drink. I couldn't have alcohol, so I had a soda, and we talked about my going to school and what the new year would be like. I was gonna be the first kid in the family to go to college. He said that someday he'd make a building I designed."

She paused, straightened some papers on the desk. "I headed out to a party with friends."

Trevor's muscles tensed in a futile effort to help. He remembered the soda she had stared into at the Goat and Barley on New Year's Eve. An anniversary, she'd told him. Something bad was coming.

"Mom called me at the party. Dad had a heart attack as he was driving home, went off the road, and that was it. He was gone."

Trevor opened his mouth to offer sympathy, but she held up her hand. He could see her throat working.

Now he understood the drink at the bar. He wondered if she'd just happened to be there this past year or if she went every year.

"Anyway, the company was how this family survived financially. Dad's foreman, Sid, tried to keep the business running, but he wasn't that kind of guy. He needed someone to direct him. I had worked the most with Dad, so Sid and I did our best to stay on top of things till I was done with high school.

"Then I took over. I couldn't leave to go to school, or Mom would have had to sell the company, and then how would she support us all? I learned the business. Each of my siblings went to college. Joey graduated in December. I was going to apply, to go somewhere this fall, but Abigail told me about her plans for the mill renovation. This is a big job for us, and Joey isn't ready yet."

Her head shot up, and her expression stilled. It was like she'd just remembered who she was talking to and regretted sharing with him.

He regretted it, too.

He didn't want to know that she was someone who'd put others first. That she cared for her family and sacrificed for them. That when you were in her inner circle, she would be there for you.

He didn't want to feel the urge to reach out to comfort her. To be in that circle. Because this story didn't give him any more confidence in her abilities. It made him remember how Geoff Compton had taken over from his father and how that had changed his life.

She'd learned by necessity on the job. Did she have any training? Did she know what she was doing? Did the crew do the work, leaving her as a figurehead? Did she keep people on her crew because they were old friends?

Would she be willing to take shortcuts like Geoff, to try to keep things afloat in that crisis? Probably not. She'd been the head of the company for a long time. But he'd trusted Geoff, too. He just couldn't shake his suspicions.

"Don't worry. I'm not going to ask you for

anything. I won't impose. If my mother says anything, just let it slide."

He nodded and rose to his feet. "I should probably..." His voice trailed off, and he had no idea how to end the sentence.

He wanted to get away to someplace he could think. He had no advice to give her on a career. She was starting late. If she hadn't been in school for the past fourteen years, would she be able to handle it? Would her brother be able to take over?

That wouldn't be Trevor's problem, since he'd be gone by then. *But* she was planning to leave. How invested would she be in this job?

He hated that he was this paranoid, but the need to protect himself came from a place deep, deep inside.

Even when people meant the best, they could still hurt you. Badly.

CHAPTER NINE

ANDIE SHOOK HER head at how fast Trevor left.

Why had she blurted all that out?

Part of it had been because she knew her family was going to spill the news of her academic dreams anyway. The guy was so spooked, any new information was evaluated as if it were going to blow up in his face. It was better that she told him than have her mother ask him to talk to her and put him in an embarrassing position. But if she was honest, part of it was because she wanted to show him they had something in common, a bond.

She wanted the guy from the bar back.

Andie leaned back in her chair and sighed. Somewhere in that stuffy package Trevor presented was the guy who'd helped her get through New Year's Eve. He'd made her laugh, made her feel seen and appreciated. She had no idea where that guy had gone, or why.

Andie didn't date a lot. Part of it was the lack of potential partners in Carter's Crossing.

Since her construction company was one of the few employers in town, some of the single guys worked for her, and dating any of them was out.

She'd tried that once, and the repercussions had dogged her for most of a year. It was too hard to earn respect in this field to jeopardize it for a few dates. Honestly, none of her current staff tempted her.

Some guys also didn't like the way she looked. She had calloused hands, unpainted nails and muscles. She wore dirty jeans and work boots most of the time, often wearing orange for safety, and she knew orange was not a flattering color for her.

She spent long hours keeping the company going, and she lived at home. It didn't all add up to a totally appealing package. But for that one afternoon, Trevor had made her feel attractive and witty. He'd talked to her about things she loved.

She needed to acknowledge that whoever he had been that afternoon, he didn't feel the same way about her now that he knew more about her. And yes, that was a depressing thought. It would be better for her to shove that afternoon away and forget about it, because there wasn't going to be a repeat.

Maybe she should have planned to go away to school this fall. She wasn't sure staying was worth it.

She didn't sleep well but woke up at her usual time the next morning. Her mother was up making coffee and breakfast.

Living at home when you passed your thirtieth birthday might sound depressing, but there were perks beyond the fact that her business was here within walking distance. Her mother making a big breakfast before a long morning of hard work was one of them.

"Morning, Mom." Andie got her coffee cup, filled it and added sugar and milk. At least her job meant she didn't have to count calories.

"Morning, Andie. Will your friend want breakfast?"

Andie's lips twisted. "Friend" was a stretch. She wasn't sure he'd even admit to being her coworker.

"Don't know, Mom. I didn't ask him last night."

By the time Andie had come back from the office, Trevor had been hidden in the spare room, their conversation over.

Her mother began to twist her fingers. "Would you ask him? I don't want to make something that he doesn't want or that he doesn't eat, but it doesn't seem right not to offer and—"

Andie held up her free hand. "It's okay, Mom, I'll ask him. I'll take him a cup of coffee and ask if he's hungry."

She set her cup down and took a clean one from the cabinet, filled it with coffee, milk and the tiniest bit of sugar she'd seen him add to his coffee in the trailer. As if taking a full spoonful was somehow an admission of weakness.

She hadn't heard any movements behind his door when she'd passed, so maybe he needed a caffeine jolt to get started. She tapped lightly on the door but got no response.

She checked the bathroom. Joey was in there, grumbling as he fussed with his hair. She'd been hearing him do that for years.

She returned to Trevor's door and knocked a little harder. Still no answer.

Had he left somehow? Called someone for a lift and snuck away? Was he that determined to get to the site before her? She wouldn't put it past him.

She twisted the handle of the door quietly and slowly pushed it open.

The early light coming through the curtains showed her enough to make out shapes. There was a person-shaped lump in the bed, a duffle on the floor beside it and a prosthetic leg...

She gasped, and the figure on the bed shot up, revealing a male head and torso.

"What?" he asked in a sleepy voice.

"Sorry!" she squeaked, her cheeks hot. "Um, we're heading out in about twenty minutes, if you can be ready then. And my mom asked if you want breakfast, and I, um, coffee." She held out the cup in her hand as if it would vouch for her.

He ran a hand through his hair. It was tousled in a way she was sure he never allowed anyone to see. He reached to the side table. "Phone died. I'll just..."

Andie realized she was staring at him, the messy hair, the bare chest, the...leg on the floor.

She finally managed to close her mouth and left him, closing the door firmly behind her. She stood for a moment, not ready to go back to her mother.

It was a good thing she would never be in a position to see a newly awakened Trevor again, because he looked too much like the man from the bar, and it was way too appealing. She was dealing with the architect now, not him. Without glasses, his eyes looked vulnerable, and without that prickly air, he looked younger and approachable. And annoyingly appealing.

Gah!

And he had a prosthetic?

She wanted to ask him what had happened. Did if affect him day-to-day? Did he need help sometimes? That was undoubtedly why he didn't tell people about it.

It was none of her business what had happened or how it affected his life. It didn't mean any adjustments to the work they were doing, and she needed to proceed now as if she hadn't seen anything.

She was embarrassed. She shouldn't have opened the door. If she'd thought he was gone, she should have asked Joey to check the room.

She straightened and headed back to the kitchen, still carrying the coffee. She told her mom their guest had just gotten up, so he probably wouldn't have enough time to eat. Andie did her best to eat most of her own breakfast, with Joey showing up not long after.

She heard the sound of a door opening down the hallway and then another closing. She expected their guest was making use of the bathroom now that Joey was done. By the time Trevor showed up with his bag, she and Joey were finished with their food, and her mother had prepared a takeaway container for Trevor.

Andie was tempted to offer to help carry something but restrained herself.

She wasn't surprised when Trevor ended up

getting a lift to the site with Joey. Having him spend the night at the house had just made things more uncomfortable between them.

COFFEE. HE DEFINITELY needed coffee.

Trevor never slept in. He had his phone alarm, and he was used to getting up when he needed to. Even last night, when he'd realized his phone was almost out of battery and that he'd forgotten his charger, he'd been sure he'd wake up.

This was the worst morning for him to sleep in.

It had been a strange, strange night. After leaving Andie, he'd gone to his room and done his best to immerse himself in work, but instead, he'd found his thoughts circling around the Kozaks.

Andie had lost her dream so young. It had been brave to take over the company and support her family when her dad died. He'd wanted to go back in time and offer her help. Support. Had she gotten that from someone? Was she lonely?

He understood lonely. He'd been lonely growing up. Even during his relationship with Violet, he'd felt like he was on the fringes, not the center.

That had reminded him that if anything went

wrong, he was the one on the outside here in Cupid's Crossing. Being isolated had been why he'd been blamed last time.

Again, he wondered if Andie was counting down till it was time to leave, and if that meant she really cared about this job. Could he have confidence in Joey as the head of the company? Her crew appeared to respect her, but he wasn't sure they felt the same about her brother.

His only concern was how it touched the job. He had no other reason to dwell on it, but he hadn't gotten to sleep for a long time with more thoughts of Andie than of the mill in his head. Despite being in a strange bed, he'd slept in until Andie had woken him up.

And now, she knew about his leg. She'd seen it.

He was braced for questions. For a change in how she looked at him and how she treated him. He didn't want that. He'd leaped at the opportunity to drive to the mill with Joey.

The storm had passed overnight, and now, with the rising temps, the snow was melting, leaving the roads bare and wet. Joey was quiet on the drive, listening to the radio and drinking from his travel mug. Trevor had been given a mug, as well, by Mrs. Kozak. The coffee inside was exactly the way he liked it.

Either Mrs. Kozak was clairvoyant, or one

of her children knew how he liked his coffee. Since he drank it in the trailer and since he thought Andie had been carrying a mug when she opened his door, he knew which Kozak he'd bet on.

His thoughts circled back to Andie and how they were going to get along after last night. It wasn't as if they'd had an easy relationship before.

Andie had arrived on-site just before them. She was unlocking the office trailer as Joey parked his car beside her truck. Trevor thanked him for the lift. Joey nodded and headed into the mill. Trevor dropped his overnight bag in his car and then braced himself before opening the door to the trailer.

Andie was on the phone, so he was able to make his way to his desk and pull out his laptop, finally getting his phone on a charger before he had to face her.

Someone had called in sick, and Andie was dealing with it as Trevor passed her again on his way to walk through the mill.

He checked over everything each morning and again in the evening before he left. So far, everything was going well, and he'd like to think it was because Kozak did a good job rather than because he was checking, but he couldn't take the risk.

He lingered in the mill, spending time staring around the open space where work hadn't yet begun. He crossed to one of the windows and pushed up to watch the stream burbling past. The days had warmed enough that the ice was mostly gone. The weather yesterday was probably the last bite of winter.

He was avoiding Andie. He needed to stop that.

He made his way back to the trailer. Andie was frowning at her laptop. She looked up as the door opened.

"I have a question for you."

Trevor's stomach clenched, and he was glad he hadn't yet eaten any of the food Mrs. Kozak had sent with him. He continued to his desk, wanting the security of some space between them before she asked questions. Questions he hated answering. Questions he was tired of. Questions about his leg.

She looked up and met his gaze. He saw a flicker in her eyes and knew it was coming. He didn't have to answer. Could he be rude enough to say that to her?

"Our supplier in Albany has a problem sourcing the fire-suppression hoods you requested. They're offering us a couple of substitute options."

It took a minute for his brain to catch up. That wasn't what he'd been expecting.

"Ah… Can you send me information on the substitutes?"

Suddenly, everything was fine. It was a typical workday with no talk of family dramas or artificial limbs. He was relieved. But for some bizarre reason, he was also disappointed.

Why didn't she ask about his leg?

Andie didn't bring it up, not that morning or in the weeks that passed. Winter turned into the ugly part of spring, and she'd still never mentioned it. He spent too much time trying to decipher if she'd seen his prosthetic and decided to ignore it or if she hadn't noticed.

If she had seen it, had she understood that he didn't want to talk about it? Could he trust that? It was a lot like trusting her.

And that was scary.

Still, he stepped back from reviewing every invoice that came into the trailer. He'd been taking copies at first, double-checking prices, quantities, looking for any possible scam he could think of. He could no longer justify doing that. He hoped he wasn't being a fool.

THE SNOW WAS GONE, leaving dirt and debris behind. There were indicators that green things were about to sprout and make things better.

For now, there were crocuses and scilla promising what was to come. The mill was proceeding on budget and on schedule. Trevor knew his stuff, and that definitely helped.

Andie hadn't asked Trevor about his leg, and he hadn't offered any information. They spoke about work and never touched on personal matters, which was fine. Really. She didn't expect anything else. But she found the slow march of spring to be frustrating. She was restless, as if she were waiting for something and it was so slow in coming, she wasn't sure if it was going to arrive in time.

A call from Denise was perfect timing.

They had been waiting on an inspection for two days now, and the inspector was finally scheduled for tomorrow. Since everything was on track here at the mill, Joey had taken the crew to a couple of the homes that needed to be renovated for the B and B business. Trevor had gone to watch them, as well, leaving Andie with some quiet time to process payroll and pay some invoices.

"Denise! How are things going?"

Denise told her husband to run away for a bit, and Andie heard her settle down for a talk.

"Things are going…well. Actually, there's a lot going on. You got a minute?"

Andie sat back and propped her boots on a handy waste bin.

"You couldn't have timed it better. I was about to pay vendors, so I'm happy to put that off for a bit."

Denise laughed. "Anything better than accounting, right? Okay, first, thanks for not telling anyone I'm pregnant."

"I promised." Andie didn't normally see much of Denise's family now that Denise was gone.

Andi knew her own mother would like to know about the pregnancy, but telling her that Denise's parents were about to become grandparents would only make her mom talk about the grandchildren she was missing. Or how Andie should find a nice boy.

Andie hadn't found any nice boys here in Carter's—no, Cupid's—Crossing. Well, maybe one, but that wasn't going to go anywhere. She'd decided to wait till she was finally away and following her own dream before considering a relationship. She didn't need any more ties to keep her here.

"Well, we have some more news on the pregnancy front, and I've told my mom."

That meant it would no longer be a secret.

"Are you going to tell me, or should I ask your mom about this news?"

"We're having twins!"

Whoa.

"Do I offer congratulations or condolences?" Andie was only partly joking.

Denise had a moment of silence. Oh, maybe that wasn't a great joke for an expecting mom.

"It's kinda both. I mean, twins are going to be a challenge, obviously. But Mom and Dad have decided to move down here. Like, I told her yesterday, and today, she told me they're going to list the house."

Andie's feet dropped to the floor. "What? That's crazy."

"Totally. So you can offer both congratulations on the babies and condolences on their move."

Andie knew Denise's mom was difficult.

"Is it going to be that bad?"

Denise sighed. "I hope not. I mean, having help with the babies will be great. But you know Mom."

Denise's mother was a person who seemed to enjoy not being happy. She always found the glass half-empty. And she complained about it.

"I'm dealing with that. And now Dave is mad because he thinks Mom just wants an excuse to avoid his wedding."

Andie didn't know the story firsthand, because she didn't hang out with Jaycee and

Dave, but Denise had told her that their mom had made Jaycee feel unwelcome. As a result, her brother Dave had put his foot down with her not long before the Valentine's Day party to celebrate his engagement to Jaycee.

The skating party at the mill. It had been an incredible event, but there wouldn't be any more events like that till the mill was done. Currently, they were hoping for an October finish, if they could keep on deadline.

"Maybe it will be nicer for Jaycee if your mom isn't there."

"Well, whether it would be or not, we won't know. That's the other news I have for you. Dave and Jaycee are getting married on the Fourth of July, and we're coming up for it. It'll be the last chance I have to travel before the babies arrive."

Andie sat upright.

"You're coming back? This summer? That's great!"

"I know. I need to go a little crazy once more before I have to become a responsible mom."

Finally, Denise was sounding like the happy woman Andie was familiar with.

Andie snorted. "I have so many stories to tell your kids about you, O responsible mom."

Denise giggled. "I know. It seems impossible that I'm going to be a mom, let alone to two unfortunate kids."

"Hey, you're going to be a fantastic mother. Those kids are lucky. I'll make sure I can take some time off while you're here. We'll have fun like you're still single."

Denise groaned. "I'm going to be as big as a whale. There are two babies being incubated in here. And I can't drink, and there's food I can't eat... I'm not sure how much fun I'll be."

"Hey, Dee. You are plenty fun. I'd love to see you on the rope swing at Weyman's Creek."

Denise snorted and then laughed. "Oh, we will have to go there. But I won't try the swing. I'll likely break it."

"I promise to take pictures if you do."

For the rest of the call, Andie was happy to reminisce and make plans. In just under three months, her best friend would be here. It would be great.

After they hung up with promises to talk again soon, Andie turned back to her invoices. That call had been just what she needed. Talking with her best friend, getting good news and having something to look forward to.

She needed something to look forward to, something that wasn't work. She still had months before the mill was done and she could plan for something beyond Kozak Construction for herself.

As she went through the paperwork, she wondered what was going on with Dave and Jaycee's wedding. It wasn't happening at the mill, obviously. Over the summer, they'd be taking out part of the wall to open up to the stream, and there'd be no place for a wedding. Not like the party they'd had here in February.

Andie had to banish those thoughts and concentrate on her paperwork. She was down to the last invoice, but there was a packing slip missing from a month ago. She remembered working on it yesterday. There'd been a discrepancy in the amounts shipped, and she'd planned to send all the details back to get the invoice corrected.

She went through her papers again. No packing slip.

It had to be here. Had some breeze from the door opening blown it somewhere? But she always put a paperweight on her stuff because of that. Still, she got up and began to look farther from her desk.

She looked under the desk. In the garbage, which fortunately hadn't been emptied. Under the table with the coffee maker.

She even checked through the paper they recycled to use for printing internal documents.

And when she did, she found a copy of another packing slip. It was covered with notes in Trevor's careful handwriting. She found herself reading them before she thought about whether she should. Suddenly, she was gloriously angry.

CHAPTER TEN

THE CREWS HAD done well at the two Victorians they were converting to B and Bs.

Abigail Carter wanted Cupid's Crossing to be a first-choice destination for people looking for a romantic getaway, not a cut-rate, nothing-else-is-available one. So while it would have been easy to add a couple of bathrooms to the homes and call it done, they were making sure the walls were soundproof, the electrical systems were upgraded to handle a larger load, and the walls and windows well insulated. They'd added air conditioning, extra outlets and made sure there was lots of water pressure.

He hadn't worked on small projects like this for a while, but he enjoyed it. Partly because he was working for himself and partly because he kind of enjoyed the seniors of Cupid's Crossing.

They plied him with tea and cookies and wanted to know if he was single because they knew someone. He politely turned down the dating offers, but their easy acceptance of him was flattering.

It was possible they were trying to soften him up to cut corners or do something to harm his reputation, but that was difficult to believe. They were too open and honest, or maybe he just didn't want to suspect nice old ladies.

They were all too happy to tell him about every renovation or change in wallpaper that had happened in the home's lifetime. Some of those changes had been unfortunate, but the homes mostly spoke of the elegance and crafts-manship of a previous time. He enjoyed them. These people were practically adopting him.

He truly hated being suspicious and guarded all the time, but he couldn't risk something happening at the mill, so he maintained a distance with the construction crew. That meant he was cut off from nonbusiness, human contact.

Except for Mavis's overly friendly Great Dane, who wanted to get to know him and lick all the places that had been covered up when he changed her tire, it had been a lovely afternoon. He was going to head back to the mill, check that nothing had changed and then maybe risk going to the diner on his own tonight. To get away from his own cooking and to see some faces that weren't digital.

He pulled into the parking lot at the mill and noted Andie's truck was still there. She'd often left by this time. She had the office at the family home, so she didn't need to be on-site, especially when they hadn't done any work to the place today.

Maybe she'd lost track of time. Maybe she had a question for him. Maybe he should ask if she wanted to join him at the diner.

Not like a date, but they could talk about buildings. Or work. Yeah, not a date, but it would be a change. Maybe he should try to warm up the relationship. So far, there'd been no signs of anything suspect going on. Maybe she was totally legit and so was Abigail Carter.

Maybe he could risk being friendly with his contractor again and not have everything blow up on him.

Or maybe those cookies Mavis gave him were spiked.

In any case, he was in a good mood until he opened the door of the trailer and met Andie's gaze.

Her furious, laser-like gaze.

He took a quick look over his shoulder to make sure she was looking at him. Since he'd been gone most of the day, it seemed unreasonable that she'd be this angry with him. He hadn't been around to do anything.

"I didn't expect you to still be here."

Her lips moved upward, but with enough tension that he didn't consider that it was a real smile.

"Did you come back to double-check the vendor order? Maybe go and count everything we received, see if we were keeping some back, trying to cheat? Or wait." She pulled out the copy he'd made of the packing slip that had been short shipped and the notes he'd made. "Perhaps you want to check if we're conspiring with the vendor, either to cheat Abigail or to substitute inferior product?"

He didn't have an answer to her accusations, because she had his words, written on the paper, asking those very questions.

The delivery was from a month ago. He'd stepped back since, after finding everything going well. Hadn't he thrown that paperwork out? Obviously not. How had he been so careless?

"Were you snooping through my papers?" Pivot and deflect was all that occurred to him.

"It was in the recycling. Maybe I should have checked that more carefully. How long have you been doing this?"

His cheeks warmed. He apparently wasn't as good at espionage as he'd hoped. He didn't think telling Andie he'd stopped checking things a few weeks ago was going to help.

"You've been doing it since the beginning, haven't you? I thought I was confused, because sometimes the papers would be out of order. I assumed things had fallen off the desk, and someone put them back wrong. Maybe Joey had been looking for things. But it's been you.

"What are you trying to do here? Are you trying to destroy my reputation, or are you looking for some way to cheat things yourself?"

Trevor's temper spiked. He wasn't going to be called the bad guy again, not when he was the one trying to make sure things went right.

"What's the matter, Ms. Kozak? Hiding something? Afraid of a little scrutiny?"

Andie stood, matching anger on her face. "I've spent years building my reputation. You have no idea what I've gone through, heading this company as a woman. And you are not going to destroy our company by bad-mouthing me to my vendors and clients. I've had it."

She grabbed her bag, threw on her jacket and pushed past him, heading to her truck. Trevor watched her go, his fury ebbing.

She'd left his notes on her desk. Everything else was locked up.

Maybe she'd done that because she had

nothing to hide and was angry that he'd been through her files. He had access to digital copies on a shared folder, but they could be changed, reworked. After all, everything came to Andie first.

Her anger could be because she had planned something, and now he'd thwarted her. He remembered the expression on her face. She'd been angry but also…hurt?

No, she wasn't upset because he'd stopped her in an evil plan. She was upset because this showed his lack of trust in her.

He'd thought he was mostly over it. That he could just take a few precautions, watch over things, and he'd be fine. But he wasn't. His first response to her anger was to wonder what she'd been hiding.

That had hurt Andie.

He had to fix this, if he could.

ANDIE PULLED INTO Abigail's driveway, fueled by righteous anger.

She'd cried many a night when she'd started, out of fear and grief and frustration. She didn't cry now. She took care of things.

If this guy, fancy architect Trevor Emerson, was going to call around, asking questions to double-check on everything she did, it was going to sow doubt in people's minds. No smoke without fire. This was a small community, and they relied on trust. She'd earned that trust the hard way, with men second-guessing her every step of the way. She couldn't let him do that to her, or to her family business.

She was hurt, too. She'd thought she'd shown Trevor that she was good. Trustworthy. She'd thought they were past his initial doubts.

She was wrong.

She couldn't work like this. She wouldn't. And she was going to tell Abigail that.

She knocked on the door and stepped back. Looking down, she saw her boots were dirty, but before she could worry about it, the door opened, and Abigail was there, a question on her face.

"Andie. Is something wrong?"

"Can we talk?"

Abigail gave her an assessing look and then stepped back. Andie hesitated.

"I'll just take off my boots out here."

"Don't bother. Having some mud to clean up will be the highlight of Rebeccah's day tomorrow. Come on in and tell me what the problem is."

Abigail held a hand out for Andie's jacket, and after passing it over, Andie unlaced her boots, flinching as the mud flaked on the floor.

Abigail led the way to a front room and waved Andie into a seat.

"Can I get you anything?"

Andie shook her head. Her anger was cooling, but her determination was not.

Abigail sat. "What's the problem?"

"Trevor Emerson."

Abigail cocked her head. "How so? Mavis was very happy with him today."

Andie frowned. Trying to get into their clients' good graces? What did he have planned? His suspicious nature was wearing off on her.

"Today, I found out he's been going through my paperwork, trying to find ways we might be cheating either our vendors or you. He double-checks everything we do, apparently convinced we're all in on some kind of scam. If he starts calling people to ask them to verify the information I'm providing him, it's going to hurt Kozak Construction. I can't have that. I can't work with him."

Andie sat back. She hadn't planned to give an ultimatum, but there it was. She couldn't risk her company's future, not for any single job.

Any personal hurt was beside the point.

Abigail stared at the coffee table, her lips pursed.

"I see. I guess it makes sense."

Andie shot to her feet. Did Abigail suspect her? "Do you think—? Could you possibly suspect—?"

"Andie."

Andie wasn't sure what it was about Abigail, but she stopped her outburst and drew in a breath. She sat back down in her seat.

"Andie, I know you. I don't suspect anything, or I wouldn't work with you. I'm not a fool."

Andie swallowed.

"Would you let me talk to Trevor before we get to the stage of ultimatums? He is gifted at his job, but I appreciate that you are, as well, and that you need to protect your family and your company."

Andie nodded. "I'm not sure what you can do, but I know not to underestimate you. Thanks for listening, I don't want to be difficult, but this is a major problem."

Andie rose, calmly this time, and Abigail followed.

"I'm very glad you came to talk to me." A smile touched her lips. "I do understand the difficulties of a woman leading a company in a masculine industry."

Andie nodded.

"Tell your mother hello from me. I hope she's doing well."

Andie shoved her feet into her boots, not bothering to tie them up.

"She is. Thanks for asking. I'll wait to hear from you."

Abigail smiled. "Dealing with people is the most difficult part of the job, isn't it?"

Andie paused, wondering if Abigail was implying that Andie was failing with this particular skill. Trevor's lack of trust was infecting her. That was something she couldn't put up with.

Abigail rested a hand on her arm. "I forget sometimes that meddling can stir things up."

Andie didn't think she'd done any meddling, so Abigail must be talking about her own actions. She didn't know what meddling Abigail had done, but the drama had exhausted Andie. She wanted to go home, have a quiet dinner, call Denise to complain and then maybe find out what Abigail had been able to do.

TREVOR ANSWERED THE call from Abigail. It was an hour after Andie had left, so he was confident he knew why his client had requested they meet. She asked him to join her for dinner.

She hung up after his acceptance, so he didn't know what to expect. If she was going to fire him, he wouldn't stay for the meal. He'd head back to his place to pack up.

He locked the trailer up carefully, making sure all his own belongings were in his bag. There wasn't much. He didn't want to have to return for anything. The thought of Andie smugly watching him pack up his stuff was more than he was prepared for.

It was ironic that he was in trouble for his lack of trust when he'd finally begun to show some.

The roads were clear, making it a smooth drive to Abigail's house. He paused for a moment to admire the lines of the building before he mounted the steps to the front door.

Abigail answered, dressed as elegantly as always. She invited him in and led him into her parlor, where a tray of cheese and olives was set out. She offered him a drink, and he decided the condemned was allowed that much.

Once they were seated, he waited, letting her start the conversation.

"Trevor, I looked into your story before I asked you to come to Cupid's Crossing. The friend that recommended you told me I had the opportunity to get a gifted architect who would normally not consider working here, because you were in the process of reestablishing your reputation."

Trevor nodded.

"We didn't go into details when we first met,

but I wouldn't have offered you this job if I didn't know you weren't at fault for the accident in New York. I understand the owner and contractor blamed you for their own misdeeds and being cleared so long after the fact meant that there was a mark on your reputation, and I took full advantage of it."

He nodded again. She'd summed it up well. She pinned him with her gaze.

"It must have been difficult when people judged you based on lies."

Difficult was one way to put it.

"And it must be very frustrating when people judge you now based on the misdeeds of someone else."

Trevor nodded. He was trying to figure out where Abigail was going with this conversation. Andie must have complained to her, and because this was a small, tightly knit town, he'd expected he'd be let go.

How was Abigail going to terminate his contract?

She paused long enough to ensure he was paying attention.

"I did not expect, Trevor, that you would do the same thing to someone else."

His jaw dropped. He wanted to argue, but he had to catch his breath. It took him a minute to understand her point.

"Pardon?"

"I appreciate that you're cautious and skeptical. But you've been here for more than two months now. I expect you've carefully monitored everything that's going on with the work at the mill. Have you found any issues of concern?"

He narrowed his eyes. "No."

"So are you judging Andie based on the actions of your last contractor?"

And there it was, the hit coming under his guard with the skill of a master.

He struggled to regroup. "I needed to ensure that the job is being done properly."

"True." Abigail smiled at him, but there was little warmth in it. "There's due diligence, and then there's…paranoia. As you probably guessed, Andie spoke to me. She feels that your, shall we say, concerns have moved beyond the normal due diligence?"

His cheeks warmed.

It was like Abigail had seen him looking through the papers, watching over shoulders, going online back at his rental to double- and triple-check everything that was going on. He'd even kept his own time sheets of the crew that first month.

Yeah, that was well beyond due diligence.

He'd been at offices being audited, and he'd surpassed that level of inspection.

He rubbed his forehead. "I lost a lot in that accident."

Abigail nodded. "All the reports I read indicated it was a serious event. And you were injured quite seriously."

He had been. Without thinking, he rubbed his leg. The one that wasn't really his. Her words sank in. She was wasted in this small town.

"You make a good point, Abigail. I was too trusting, too naive on that job, and I paid. I've…" He took a breath. "I've overreacted here. I know that. I did stop some of the checking. What Andie found was from the first month. Still, I might…no, I have…gone too far."

She held back a smile. "A smidge."

He felt the corner of his own mouth tilt up. "Maybe more than a smidge. So am I fired?" She'd made her point first, but if it was just to support her decision to fire him, he wanted to know.

She raised her eyebrows. "Oh, I hope not. I haven't gone through this much trouble for no payoff. Do you think you could speak to Andie? I would, but I feel the two of you need to find some common ground here, and I don't want to be your intermediary the whole time you're working together."

That was fair. But it wasn't going to be an easy talk. Andie was angry and hurt, and she had every right to be.

He was going to have to explain things to her. He would rather do almost anything else. But the alternative was to leave like a child who couldn't handle cleaning up his own messes.

That was not the man he wanted to be.

"If she doesn't take a hammer to me, I'll try to explain."

Abigail smiled at him approvingly. "If it turns out you do need my help, I'll do what I can, but I have confidence the two of you can work things out. Are you ready to eat now that we have this cleared up?"

"I would be happy to."

CHAPTER ELEVEN

THREE HOURS LATER, Trevor sat at home, replete after excellent food and wine. He'd also enjoyed the conversation. Abigail was well-read and intelligent. She'd led him to a discussion of buildings in New York, a topic he could speak on for hours, and she'd seemed to enjoy it.

He was home now, and it was time to deal with his problem. His contractor might not be coming to work tomorrow if he didn't reach out.

It was his fault. And he hated that he'd hurt her.

He debated calling but wasn't sure she'd pick up the phone. He needed to get her attention and convince her to listen to him before she had a chance to delete his message or hang up. He carefully selected the subject of his email, hoping it would be sufficient.

I owe you an apology and an explanation.

With any luck, the apology part would make

her consider listening, and the explanation would make her curious enough to meet him.

Would you meet me at the diner for lunch so I can provide both?

He could work from home for the morning and let her have the trailer to herself. It was a struggle, but he'd let her meet with the inspector without him. It was a token of trust.

He had to step back, at least a bit. He would still do his due diligence, and it might be more than anyone else's normal due diligence, but he had to step back from the paranoia. It was a line he'd crossed.

He hoped it wasn't too late.

ANDIE WAVED THE inspector off, trusting that his promise of a positive report coming to her email once he was back at the office would hold. Tomorrow, the crew could get back to construction on the mill. They were almost wrapped at Mavis's house now.

She went back to the trailer and sat at her desk. The place felt…odd without Trevor at the other end. It should be a good *odd*, and she should get used to it, since she wasn't spending time with him ever again. But the email was there, flagging her attention.

She'd wavered over that email from Trevor for longer than she'd admit to. She'd been tempted to call Denise to parse it out, like they used to with messages from boys, but this wasn't a social question, this was her business. She should be able to handle a business decision without depending on her best friend.

That she'd even considered doing that meant there was more than a business hurt happening, and that was a problem. She didn't need Denise to recognize that.

Abigail had spoken to Trevor, as she'd said she would. He must want to save his job, which meant he had to apologize to her. She was grateful that Abigail was backing her up, but that didn't mean she was going to accept a half-hearted apology from Trevor.

If his apology included anything along the lines of "I'm sorry *if* you took my behavior the wrong way," she was out. She was not working with a jerk, and she was not risking her company's reputation.

She couldn't imagine an explanation that would change her mind, but she couldn't go back to Abigail and say she wouldn't listen to Trevor. She'd listen to what he had to say, assuming he got through the apology without messing up, and then she'd calmly and collectedly tell him they couldn't work together.

Her crew would be able to keep on with the plans at the mill until Abigail found a solution. Another architect. They knew what they were doing at the mill and could handle it till Abigail found someone else.

She sighed and slammed her computer shut before heading out to Bertha. She had taken longer than she should to get ready this morning. She pretended that she'd wanted to look good for the inspector, but she was glad Joey was working on the houses this morning and hadn't seen her wearing nice jeans and some lipstick.

She told herself she was just preparing herself for battle. She didn't want to admit that the battle wasn't with the inspector.

Her stomach was churning as she pulled open the door of the diner. Trevor was sitting in the same booth as before. Probably not a good sign. But she held her head high and crossed to the table, sliding in opposite him.

She scanned his face, looking for anger, resentment or false cheer. Instead, he looked resigned, and tired. She didn't need to soften just because of that.

Jean came over with her coffeepot. Andie flipped her mug and placed her order. Trevor already had his coffee in front of him. Jean walked away, and Andie waited. He'd asked for the meeting. She wasn't speaking first.

He met her gaze. "I'm sorry."

She still waited.

Trevor moved his cutlery over an inch and then back again. "I should not have done what I did. I do have a reason I was so…paranoid. It's not an excuse, though. I crossed a line."

Andie put creamer and sugar in her cup and stirred. Then she picked up her cup and took a sip. Trevor cast a glance up at her.

She put down the cup and lifted an eyebrow. "The explanation?"

His eyes dropped. He moved the cutlery again. He took off his glasses and polished the lens with a napkin. He looked younger, more vulnerable.

"Two years ago, I was in charge of my first major, solo project. I'd set up my own firm. It was in New York, and I had big dreams."

Andie knew it wasn't going to be a happy story. No one behaved like Trevor because something good had happened. The journey from his own business in New York to doing bed-and-breakfasts in Carter's Crossing was one with a downward trajectory.

She resisted an urge to put her hand on his. He was apologizing and explaining his bad behavior, and it wasn't her job to make him feel better.

"I believed the contractor and owner were good people. The contractor's father had recently resigned, and he'd taken over. Their reputation was excellent. I thought we had a relationship. Friendly. Close.

"I double-checked things at the beginning. It was going well, and I trusted them. So while I didn't shirk on anything, I didn't look any deeper than I needed to."

Andie's hands clenched, and she dropped them onto her lap. She could see where this was going.

"There was an accident on-site. I was there. I was hurt."

Her eyes dropped of their own volition to the tabletop, the section above where his legs were. When she looked back at him, he nodded.

"Yes, I was in hospital for a while. I lost part of my leg. And once I was able to pay attention to things going on outside the hospital, I found out that the owner and contractor had blamed the accident on me.

"There was an investigation, of course, and I was exonerated. But by the time that happened and I was able to work again, people remembered the initial claims, not the truth."

Trevor stopped there. He put his glasses back

on, Jean arrived with their meals and, after checking on their coffee, left again.

Trevor was breathing carefully, staring at his food. He lifted his sandwich to his mouth. Andie grabbed a French fry, waiting for what else he had to say.

That appeared to be it. What was she supposed to do with that?

"You were screwed over by a crooked contractor and owner. So now you plan to micromanage the job at the mill to make sure Abigail and I don't do the same thing."

He set his sandwich down and swallowed. "I need to take precautions, yes. I went too far, but I hope you understand why I'm not willing to accept things at face value."

It wasn't a pretty story that he'd shared. But if you'd been in a relationship where your partner cheated, you were not allowed to put a tracking device on your next date. As tempting as the thought might be.

Andie grabbed another French fry. "You didn't ask for more access to what we were doing because you thought we might just hide things better."

Trevor nodded. "What you saw, that paper with those notes, was from the first few weeks we worked together. I haven't been going through things like that lately, but it was something I shouldn't have done behind your back."

Andie considered. Yes, she understood why he was so worried. But he had to consider other people, as well. He wasn't the only one who'd had a difficult past.

"When my father died, and I had to take over Kozak Construction because there was no one else, I was eighteen and female. I had, and still have, men insisting they have to double- and triple-check everything I do, simply because of my gender. It's insulting, sexist, and it bogs down my schedule."

Trevor had paused in his eating, watching her. "I'm sorry if you thought I was questioning you because of your gender. Or age or experience."

Andie raised her brows. "Instead of just questioning me because you thought I was crooked."

The corner of his mouth lifted up. "But I didn't think you couldn't successfully fool me just because you're a young woman."

Andie couldn't resist smiling in return. "So I should thank you for questioning my ethics the same as you would an older man's?"

His shoulders sagged. "I don't think thanks are in order."

Andie took a bite of her burger while she

considered the situation. They couldn't continue working the way they had, but she was at least willing to consider working with him. And that was something she hadn't thought possible before their conversation.

Because, after all, if you'd dated a cheater, you might not put a tracking device on your next partner, but you'd be much more careful of what he was doing. You might be tempted to look at a text message popping up on his screen.

"Can we find a way to work together that won't drive me crazy and will give you more confidence that nothing improper is going on? Something that doesn't involve you being my shadow all the time or going through my paperwork?"

Trevor finished his sandwich and used a napkin to wipe his mouth. "They fudged the invoices on that job."

"I can ask vendors to copy you on all emails. You'll end up with a lot of stuff to go through, but if that makes you happier, I'll do it. I just ask that you don't malign me and my company's reputation while you try to reassure yourself."

"How so?"

"If you ask them to independently verify every piece of paper you get, it will imply that you think I'm doing something wrong. I have earned my good reputation with most of the suppliers in this area, but if a rumor starts, it'll be almost impossible to fight."

Trevor started shifting his empty coffee mug around. Andie wondered if that was his tell. As well as playing with his glasses and the cutlery.

She liked that this situation made him nervous. She was out of her depth and didn't want to be the only one.

"You could be using a separate email account or chain to get different invoices."

Andie raised her brows. "I hadn't even thought of that possibility."

His smile was mocking. "There's a lot you consider after you've lost what I have."

Andie understood, but she also couldn't spend all her time reassuring him or risk her reputation by having him independently verify everything she did. The man had more ideas about how to cheat on the job than she'd ever considered. Maybe she had been too trusting with him.

"What about an audit?"

"When the project is done?"

Andie shrugged. "I'm not that familiar with all the possibilities, but perhaps someone could randomly verify transactions. Abigail would probably know how to set it up. But then you don't trust her, either. Or is it only me?"

Trevor shrugged.

"Why don't I ask Abigail if there's a way we can do that and then, perhaps, agree on an auditor? Because you might take advantage of us."

Trevor sat back. He blinked at her and then nodded. "I get it. Trust goes both ways."

He moved his coffee cup again.

"Let's start with sharing emails. Since I don't have a lot of projects going on here, I'll spend time at the mill site and let you know if I have questions. If I feel unsure of how things are going, we can explore a midterm audit."

Andie nodded. "I can live with that."

Trevor smiled, an honest smile, and Andie couldn't hold back her own smile in response.

She'd been sure nothing he could say would reconcile her to working with him. And now here they were with a way to move forward.

In theory.

He might not be able to keep to this. She understood that he'd been betrayed, and the results had been catastrophic for him.

But her first commitment was to her family and her company, the people who depended on her to support their families. They trusted her, so she needed to watch who she trusted, as well.

Trevor might have a smile she found hard to resist, but that didn't mean he was going to follow this plan. They'd have to wait and see.

TREVOR FELT LIGHTER after their conversation.

He hadn't enjoyed repeating the story of that last job, but everything was out there on the internet if someone was going to look. Andie didn't sound like she'd heard the story before, but as much as he might wish it, it wasn't that easy to get over his suspicions.

Still, if he was going to see the emails with the suppliers, he should be able to track the materials, which was where things had gone wrong on that last job.

Maybe, if he could trust the information, he could relax and get to know the people he was working with. Maybe he'd even hang out with people. It had been getting very lonely in his rental with no one to talk to.

He had family back in the city. Maybe even a few friends. But he'd been so bitter after the accident, after he'd let Violet out of their engagement, that he'd lost touch with most of their friends. He'd been reluctant to reach out. He and Violet had been together for three years, so his friends were their friends. He'd lost his confidence along with his trust.

With the warmer weather, they were about to start the major renovations on the mill. Now came the big test on the project. They were opening the back wall to bring in that view through new doors, windows, skylights. They were doing all this while maintaining the structural integrity of the building and its complex history.

They needed to finish up the commercial kitchen and get fixtures in the newly designed bathrooms. And everything needed to be right, before they added the final finishes that would cover up the skeleton of the building.

He couldn't relax. He wouldn't till the job was done and all inspections had been passed...and maybe not until they'd had years of use behind it. He couldn't undo what that accident had done to change him, but he could *try* not to be paranoid.

He could keep a close eye on things and ask questions before he rushed to conclusions. Like the packing slip Andie had found his notes on. After he'd written that down, he'd worked out that every item had been reconciled. There had been nothing wrong. So far, everything Andie had done should have earned her his trust.

He was first on-site the next morning, and

he had Andie's mug of coffee ready for her when she arrived, full and filled with enough milk and sugar to make him cringe. She smiled and thanked him, and that was surprisingly rewarding.

The crew showed up, ready to get started on this next phase. This time, as he followed Andie through the building, her shoulders weren't hunched up in discomfort. He'd thought it was how she did her walk-through. Now he realized he'd caused that.

When one of the crew had a question, she turned to let him answer. She was smiling instead of pinching her mouth up in frustration. Now that he wasn't pushing, he was being invited and she was treating him as one of them, not an outsider.

It was almost enough to make him relax. He hadn't felt part of a group like this since before the accident. Back when he'd had a full life. His new company had been busy and he'd had an unlimited future. Violet was making wedding plans, and they had their friends to hang out with. He'd never realized how tenuous his life had been.

It still was.

He reminded himself to be wary, but a couple of weeks later, when he was invited to the Goat and Barley for trivia night by the Kozak crew, he agreed to go. It didn't mean he was giving up his due diligence. Mostly, he was tired of his own company every night.

He knew where the Goat—as locals called it—was, but he hadn't been there since New Year's Eve. He'd planned to check it out, to try to find the woman with the soda once he was settled into the town.

Instead, he'd found her at the mill.

He could almost imagine it was a different place, with spring warming the air and the winter snow gone. He recognized some of the vehicles in the parking lot, including Andie's truck. He opened the pub door and blinked to adjust to the dimmer lighting.

He looked to the bar first, pausing as he saw the place he'd sat with Andie at New Year's, but he didn't recognize any faces. He looked around the room and spotted the people he knew. Andie, Joey and a couple of other guys from her crew were at a table at the other side of the restaurant from the bar. They'd saved him a seat, and he felt warmed. Wanted.

Something he wasn't used to any longer.

The others already had their beverages, so Joey got the attention of one of the waitstaff and ordered a beer for Trevor.

Andie leaned over and asked, "Is this your blind-date beer?"

She was smiling and relaxed, and he recognized the woman from the bar more than he had in any of their encounters since.

He bit back a snort of laughter. "No, that relationship wasn't meant to be. But I'm hoping for good things from this one."

Joey had the papers for the quiz in his hand. "So, Trev, what do you know?"

Trevor hadn't heard that diminutive nickname for a long time. He swallowed his first taste of beer. "Um, buildings?"

Joey rolled his eyes. "Andie's already good at that. What else?"

Trevor searched his memory banks. "Sports? At least, up till fifteen years ago."

His family was sports crazy. He'd joined in as a kid, hoping to feel more like an essential part of the family. He'd always been different and done his best to try to fit in with them. Fifteen years ago, he'd realized it wasn't going to happen, and he'd stopped forcing it.

"We've got hockey and baseball covered. Know basketball or soccer?"

"Some."

Joey turned to another teammate, and Trevor took another sip of his drink. He wondered, for the first time, just how serious these people were about their quizzes and if he was going to look stupid.

Andie nudged him. "Don't worry." Apparently, he didn't have a poker face. "These aren't super difficult," she said. "Sports questions that aren't related to hockey tend to be more about what team won whatever was the final trophy."

He smiled at her. "That much I can handle."

"So why did you give up on sports fifteen years ago? That wasn't because..." Her glance dropped to his legs.

He stiffened.

"I'm sorry. Foot in mouth."

She wrapped her hand over her mouth. Her cheeks were bright red. She dropped her hands and closed her eyes. "I had no idea I could be that offensive, totally by accident, I mean, without meaning to. I'll just shut up and not speak anymore. I'm so sorry."

He stifled his amusement at her embarrassment. "No, not because of the accident and prosthetic leg. That was only a couple of years ago. My family was crazy about sports, and I...wasn't."

He saw her watching him and hoped nothing much was showing on his face.

She grimaced. "Family... Yeah, that can be complicated."

He was relieved that she let it go, but also disappointed. He didn't want to talk about it normally. But he'd like to get her perspective.

Did she ever feel like she was on the outside with her family?

Was that why he felt a connection with her?

TEAM KOZAK DIDN'T WIN. But they weren't the worst team, either. And Trevor wasn't the weakest link on the team.

There weren't any questions on architecture, but there were some history questions he'd helped with. It turned out having studied buildings in previous eras helped him with some history knowledge. He'd known a question about when New York last won a basketball title. His dad brought that up every postseason.

After the points were tallied and the winning teams won vouchers, the Kozak team stayed at the table, sharing some surprisingly good onion rings, drinking responsibly—Andie was the designated driver—and talked. For a while, he was peppered with questions about working on big job sites in NYC. Before he'd been out on his own, he'd worked on some jobs using the biggest cranes, and everyone was interested. Trevor wasn't comfortable being the center of attention, though, and he was relieved when the conversation veered to stories of the jobs Kozak Construction had done.

Trevor listened and did his best not to piece out details to check for mistakes or accidents.

He needed to rein in his suspicions. But the only accidents they mentioned were small ones, mistakes that tended to be embarrassing rather than dangerous.

When they stood up to leave, not too late since they rose early in the morning, Trevor was disappointed. Not the disappointment of having wasted an evening or not having his expectations met—he hadn't had expectations—but disappointment that the evening was ending. It had been the best evening he'd spent in Cupid's Crossing since that first night when he'd met Andie. When he was asked if he would join again, he was happy to agree.

He wasn't sure who was more surprised by that. Joey, who'd extended the offer, or Trevor himself.

Trevor even volunteered to drop one of the crew at his home to save Andie some time on her trip back. The smile she gave him was worth the extra mile.

He hadn't wanted to share what had happened on that last project with anyone, but now that he'd told Andie and promised to stop his secret investigation into her work, a load of tension had vanished.

He might even enjoy the remainder of his time in Cupid's Crossing.

CHAPTER TWELVE

ANDIE CONSIDERED THAT night at the Goat to be a turning point. It marked a change in the workplace dynamic that had been troubling her more than she'd realized.

She didn't wake up the next morning stressed about getting to the job site. She hadn't been worried about work that way since the early days when she first took over. She didn't feel judged and micromanaged every minute of the day.

In the following weeks, she tested Trevor to see if he was keeping to his word. She left some paperwork around with notes on it that could trigger questions or further snooping on his part. She felt like James Bond trying to entrap him, but apparently, he was no longer checking her stuff.

The work was still demanding and often physically challenging, but more than just things with Trevor improved. The change of season helped. With the increasing warmth, as spring aimed for summer, the whole crew could gather outside the mill for lunch.

Before that first trivia night, Trevor always ate lunch in the trailer. Now, as they gathered by the stream, sitting on rocks or makeshift seats made of construction materials, Trevor joined them, but always on the edge. Not totally one of the group. Andie didn't know if he preferred the distance or was reluctant to intrude without an invitation. She decided it was time to find out.

She grabbed her thermos and her sandwiches and moved to sit near him. "I hear you helped the team last night."

Andie had missed trivia night last night. There'd been a meeting of the local business owners at Abigail's. The new B and B owners had been there representing new businesses in town, and that had dragged the meeting on a lot longer than usual. They were just so keen and wanted to discuss everything in detail.

Trevor smiled in response to her comment, and when he did, he was…attractive. Very attractive. Warm ribbons curled inside her, and she gave herself a mental swat.

"Apparently, there aren't a lot of classical music fans at your pub on trivia night."

Andie wasn't surprised Trevor knew classical music or that he was the only one of the team that did. He was different from most of the guys in town. More like Nelson, Abigail's grandson, than her brothers and their friends.

She was more like those guys. Not that she was upset by that. Not at all.

"Glad my absence wasn't missed." Andie didn't know classical music, either.

Trevor glanced away. "I didn't say that."

Andie was embarrassingly aware of her heart thudding and the chill running down her arms.

He'd missed her? But—

"How was your meeting?"

She shook off the strange feeling to answer him. "It was…long. I should send Joey next time so he knows what it's like."

She should, she decided. Next month, he could attend the meeting for business owners in Cupid's Crossing business while she went to trivia night.

Trevor looked over at Joey, who was joking with some of the other young guys on the crew. Guys who were his friends. They played hockey in the winter, and baseball had just started up again for the summer.

"I have a difficult time picturing Joey sitting at Abigail's, talking business."

Andie did, too. She wrapped up the remains of her lunch. "It's not a fun part of the job, but he's got to be able to handle it when he's in charge."

Trevor looked back at her. "When's that?"

Andie shrugged. "That partly depends on how the mill project goes. We're doing well now and are on time, but if it drags into the new year… It's probably better if I don't plan on going anywhere until next fall."

"That's more than a year away."

Andie smiled at him. "Nice to see you didn't waste your time at college."

He didn't smile back. "You don't mind waiting another year?"

She shrugged and looked away. Her fingers tightened on the lunch wrappings. "I made my decision when my dad died. I'm not second-guessing it now."

She'd done that enough over the years. Smiling at college graduations for her siblings without having one of her own. Waving them off as they left Carter's Crossing while she stayed. She couldn't change the past, and she wouldn't begrudge her siblings achieving what they wanted.

"Was it difficult? Making that decision?"

Andie glanced over at him. He narrowed his eyes like he did when he was frowning at his computer.

Apparently, she had noticed that.

She normally glossed over how difficult that time had been after her dad died, but for some reason, she didn't now. Not when Trevor appeared...invested in what she'd done.

She cleared her throat. "Yeah, it was difficult. It wasn't like there was one moment when I just decided I had to do this. It was more...a series of small decisions that built up until it was either my family or me.

"I couldn't do that to Dad, his memory and all the work he'd done to make Kozak Construction what it was. I couldn't let it all fall apart. That first tuition deadline I had... I told my mom I'd wait another year to get things settled."

The relief on her mother's face had been overwhelming. It had soothed her when she'd felt so unsure of what she was doing.

Trevor put his lunch containers back into his bag. "A year?"

She nodded. "At first, it was just a decision to wait another year. And then just one more. Then Arlie was supposed to go to college, and two of us studying at the same time was too expensive. I was getting good at running the place, so it made sense to wait."

"And you're still waiting."

Andie couldn't read his expression, but the words weighed on her.

She was still waiting. And maybe going now was a little scary. But that wasn't something to dwell on, not now, and not with this man. She'd shared enough. She stood up, dusting off the back of her pants.

"Hey, guys, let's get back at it."

Everyone slowly got to their feet, picking up scraps and papers and complaining good-naturedly. Trevor stood, too, still watching her.

She flashed a stilted smile. "No rest for the wicked."

She went back into the mill, all too aware of Trevor standing in place. He must think she was silly. Small. Lacking in ambition.

She'd had big dreams and lots of ambition, but she'd had to channel it into her family, the family business and being strong for everyone.

She wasn't sure if she'd lost her dreams and used up all that ambition. She'd spent a long time shoving all that down until it was her turn. It was hard to get excited about school now.

Maybe she'd missed her chance.

TREVOR FOUND LIFE more pleasant after he and Andie declared a...détente? He wasn't sure how to word it, but they were cooperating. And maybe just a bit more.

He was welcome on trivia nights. He wasn't the best player on the team, but he wasn't the worst. And he was greeted warmly even though he didn't have a lot in common with the rest of the team. He wasn't from Cupid's Crossing, but he'd been asked if he played baseball. No one minded that he was quiet or asked him if something was wrong because he didn't talk a lot. Thursday nights had become the highlight of his week.

He'd been working on some ideas for the next round of B and Bs and had questions about what materials were available locally. He took advantage of the warmer relations with Andie to ask if she'd grab a drink with him while he picked her brains.

That was a Tuesday, and Tuesdays at the Goat was darts night. Darts was something Trevor was good at. He convinced Andie to pair up with him, and they won.

Afterward, Andie introduced him to the two men they'd played against. Their names were Dave and Nelson. Nelson was Abigail Carter's grandson and Mariah's fiancé. They sat at a table together and talked, and it was a fun evening. Trevor was invited back next week for darts, and it seemed he now had, if not friends, people to spend time with outside of work.

Now that he wasn't doing an audit on the job every day, he had more free time. He didn't want to spend that time isolated in his rental, alone and lonely. He felt that he was getting to know the real people in town.

He hadn't planned on trying to fit in, not when he was going to be here for only a year. But the job was going well, and he was growing tired of the isolation he'd imposed on himself since the accident.

Since he and Andie hadn't talked about the B and Bs on darts night, they stayed the next night in the trailer, bouncing ideas back and forth. When it got a little late, Andie's mother messaged about dinner, and Trevor ended up invited and spending the rest of the evening there.

It wasn't awkward, like the last time, and he didn't take refuge in the spare room. That would have been weird, since he wasn't staying over. Instead, Andie showed him around the construction yard. It wasn't exactly the way he would set things up, but nothing looked problematic. He imagined this was the way Andie's father had arranged things, and she wouldn't want to change what he'd done.

By the end of May, the work on the mill was progressing without a hiccup. Trevor was checking things but staying on the side of due diligence. He had a life in Cupid's Crossing, complete with friends and regular plans.

Mariah stopped by to see them on-site one

day. She'd texted Andie and Trevor to let them know she was coming. Once she'd arrived, Andie offered to show her around the mill, and after carefully donning a hard hat, Mariah got the tour. Trevor let Andie take the lead, interested in hearing Mariah's opinion.

"I'm so glad you're opening up that wall to the stream. It's going to make this venue stunning. It's not going to get too hot in summer with all that glass?"

Andie let Trevor explain how he'd dealt with that concern. Finally, Mariah asked if there was a place they could sit and talk.

Andie offered the trailer. Mariah had been appreciative of the work they'd done, but Trevor was leery about why she was here. He suspected Mariah hadn't come here to get a tour.

Trevor braced for last-minute design requests or demands to shorten the timeline. Mariah wouldn't have any say on the budget, so at least that wasn't going to be the topic of discussion, but any alterations would have financial repercussions.

He'd come across clients who wanted to switch things up once it was no longer possible to make changes. Abigail was the owner, but Mariah wasn't just engaged to Abigail's grandson, she was also in charge of the romance business the town was setting up. She had clout with Abigail and with this project. She was definitely in a position to have a say in how things went.

Andie offered coffee, which Mariah accepted. Once they'd gone through that social obligation, they settled behind their desks with Mariah on a chair in front of them.

Mariah took a sip of coffee and then set the cup down by her feet. "I have a reason for this visit, as you've probably guessed. I wouldn't stop by and interrupt your work out of simple curiosity." She grinned. "But I *was* curious. I got a walk-through last fall, and what you're doing is impressive.

"The real reason I'm here isn't about the mill, at least not directly. Well, it is, but I should explain.

"I want Cupid's Crossing to be a place people think of for romantic events. We made a start on that in February, and we've got the website up now so that people can actually find this place. Thanks to you two and your work, we have a few of the D and Bo now open and getting reservations. That's all great."

Trevor had been in meetings like this before. There was a *but* coming. Mariah looked at Andie and then at Trevor.

Here it was.

"But we need the mill before we can really get under way."

He knew it. Trevor opened his mouth to explain the timeline, but Mariah put up her hand.

"I know that's going to take time. I warned the committee from the beginning about that. This is a big project, and big projects can't be rushed, not if they're done right.

"It's now May. February is long gone. We've got Dave and Jaycee's wedding happening in six weeks in the park, so that will be more buzz for the town, but I want to keep online interest going. That means we need content on our website, and one wedding isn't sufficient."

Trevor suspected what Mariah wanted. He knew that the mill had been used for an engagement party on Valentine's Day preconstruction. They couldn't host any kind of event till the job was done. There was too much going on now that the mill was a construction site rather than an empty building. It wasn't safe for a crowd. They could block off the areas currently being worked on, but in his experience, signs and fencing didn't keep the curious away, and at a party?

He couldn't allow something like that. He leaned forward, ready to present his objections once Mariah paused.

"This is my idea. I'd like to have ongoing videos about the transformation of the mill."

Mariah stopped then, giving them time to come to terms with the idea. Trevor had been about to launch into a list of reasons why they couldn't have people at the mill, and it took him a moment to switch gears.

Trevor's eyes met Andie's. She had her brows pulled together, looking as unsure as he was about what Mariah wanted.

"What exactly are you asking for, Mariah?"

Mariah glanced at both of them and then held up her hands. "I should have thought of this from the beginning, but I was a little distracted before the events in February."

Which included her own engagement.

"I thought the two of you might have taken photos or video as the job went along."

Trevor saw Andie nodding just as he did.

Mariah smiled. "I thought it was something you would do. Are you planning to continue doing it?"

They both agreed.

"Good. I don't have a video crew, and I'm not sure if I could put one together here."

Trevor saw Andie's expression. Yeah, they didn't think she'd be stopped by that.

"Once a month, we could put together a video showing how the renovation is progressing. I'll add my plans for events, and hopefully, it can keep us in the public eye till we can really get our romance initiative under way."

Trevor thought that between Abigail and Mariah, there was no way they wouldn't succeed. It pleased him that his building would be used and admired in future.

But…

The photos and videos that he'd taken were for his own purposes. They focused a lot on structural things that would have no appeal to the general public. Did he really want to share them?

"I'm afraid, Mariah, that what I have isn't something to post on your website. There's not been any editing, and most people would find a lot of it boring. I don't have any skills at making video."

He turned to Andie, wondering if she had some previously undetected talent in that direction.

Andie shook her head. "Same here, Mariah. It's boring stuff for the general public."

Mariah was unfazed. "If you provide me with rough footage, I can take it from there."

Of course she could.

"Oh, right," Andie said. "You've done wedding videos, right?"

Mariah shook her head. "Oh, not me personally. Definitely not something I'm good at. I don't do everything. I just arrange it."

Trevor was curious, but he didn't know the town and most of the residents, so he stayed quiet. Andie, however, asked his question.

"Will you send the photos away to someone?"

Mariah smiled. "We actually have someone here in Cupid's Crossing who makes videos of his repairs all the time for his YouTube channel. I thought this would be right up his alley. Can you send whatever you have to me and to Benny Gifford? Here are our email addresses, and we'll make sure you get copies of the finished files to use for yourself. If you can add an explanation of what's happening in the videos or photos, that will help."

Mariah finished her coffee and then left. Andie looked at Trevor after she was gone. Had they actually agreed to that?

"That was...unexpected."

He nodded. "I was sure she was going to pressure us to move up the timeline. Or ask us to allow them to use the parts of the mill we aren't actively working on."

Andie frowned. "First, Abigail would be the one to do that, if anyone did. And Abigail is smart enough to know better than to pressure us."

Trevor didn't respond, but Andie kept her gaze on him, so he finally nodded.

"And Mariah is also smart enough not to ask us for something impossible."

Trevor didn't like being suspicious all the time, but he'd paid too much for his previous complacency. Time to change the subject.

"Have you been taking videos or just photos?"

He'd seen Andie using her phone around the site. She'd never shared with him what she was doing.

And neither had he.

"A few videos. A walk-through at the beginning and some showing the major and interesting things we've done. You?"

Trevor had a digital camera. He brought it with him every day.

"I did a walk-through when I first checked out the place with Abigail last fall, and I've taken a lot of photos and videos as we go. Maybe we should compare before we swamp this guy Benny with everything? And we can make sure we don't send anything we don't want in the public domain."

Trevor knew he'd documented almost everything they'd done. Last time, that had helped exonerate him. Late, but still, he'd been cleared of any wrongdoing or neglect. He reminded himself that sharing the material didn't mean he'd lose it.

Andie cocked her head, and the corner of her mouth kicked up. "You have a lot, don't you?"

He nodded.

"Okay, probably a good idea, then. When do you want to do this?"

He had to think about it. With darts night and Thursday trivia, he suddenly had a social calendar. "Tomorrow night? After we close up here?"

Andie looked at her phone. "Should work."

"My place?"

Her eyes widened.

"I have a nice rental. And we won't be interrupted."

Wait, did that sound skeevy?

Andie nodded. "I remember. The old Sussex house."

"Is this a small-town thing, or have you been checking up on me?" There was a flicker of something at the thought that she had been checking up on him. Was it concern or pleasure? Could he complain, though, after what he'd done?

She grinned. "The small-town thing is basically everyone checking up on you. But I tried to drop you off the night of the storm, remember?"

Right. How had he forgotten that? Stupid paranoia.

"I can cook. And there's a decent TV we can Bluetooth the computers to."

"Sure."

After giving him one more long look, Andie said she needed to talk to her crew. Trevor nodded and opened his photo file. Probably a good idea to do some pre-weeding. He did have a *lot*.

ANDIE WAS NERVOUS as she knocked on Trevor's door. She knew the house, but this was more intimate than she and Trevor had been since that chat in the bar.

It was a little concerning that she desperately wanted to regain that kind of closeness. He couldn't be using this to check up on her, could he? To see if there was anything in the photos that he should pounce on and critique?

Perhaps paranoia was catching.

Trevor opened the door dressed in a T-shirt and khakis. He had a tea towel over his shoulder and looked better than he should. Why that tea towel made her catch her breath, she wasn't sure.

Andie wore a sundress with a lightweight cardigan thrown over. She'd wanted to look different than she did on-site, where safety and function were the biggest factors. She'd shaken her head at herself while she'd gotten ready, but here she was.

Trevor blinked at her for a moment, then stood back and welcomed her in with a wave of his arm.

Had she overdone it?

As Trevor shut the door behind her, Andie held out a bag with a bottle of wine.

"I don't know if you like wine or red wine, but—" She shrugged.

Trevor accepted it, took a peek and smiled at her. "Thank you."

They stood for a moment awkwardly, then both began to speak at once.

"I've got my—"

"If you want to come into—"

They both stopped.

Andie lifted the hand that was holding her computer bag.

"Right." Trevor said. "If you want to drop that in the living room and come through to the kitchen."

"Sure. Go ahead, I know the way."

Trevor's forehead creased, but then he turned and left. Andie appreciated that he didn't jump on her about that. It was almost like he trusted her. She pushed through the doorway into the living room, curious as to what the room looked like now.

The last time she'd been in here, the room had been bare, newly renovated by her dad. She'd helped.

The paint now was a little dull, but the furnishings were nice. Trevor was either neat or had cleaned up before she arrived. She set her bag down on the coffee table and looked around.

Her dad had done good work. She ran a hand over the door frame, one of the things she'd done herself, and then headed back to the kitchen.

Trevor was working at the stove. Andie forced herself to look away from him, something that shouldn't have been so difficult. She looked around the kitchen to see there had been some changes in here.

"They painted."

Trevor turned to her. "Who?"

Andie shrugged. "I don't know exactly. Fifteen years ago, our company did some renovations here. The rest of the house hasn't changed much, but these cupboards weren't green."

Trevor looked around as if he hadn't noticed the color. "Kozak Construction worked on this?"

Andie nodded. "We updated the kitchen, added a bath, opened up the dining room and living room into one space."

Would this freak him out?

Trevor looked around the room and then back at her. "I guess you know this place as well as I do."

Andie paused. "It's been fifteen years—more could have changed. I didn't mean to make you feel uncomfortable."

He shook his head. "The small-town thing still surprises me."

Right. He was used to the city. This must seem…gauche to him.

"I guess I'm used to it."

Trevor blinked and then smiled again, like it didn't bother him.

"I hope you like pasta carbonara. I'm only a so-so cook."

She would have bet money he was understating his abilities.

"Mom never lets me in the kitchen, so you're better than me."

Trevor grabbed potholders and drained some of the water into a bowl. The rest he tossed into the colander, spaghetti tumbling with it.

"If you'd take the salad to the table, this will be ready in a few minutes."

Five minutes later, they were sitting across the table from each other, a plate of warm pasta in front of each of them.

"Thank you." Andie found herself fiddling with her fork. "This is really nice."

Trevor shrugged. "I hope you think so after you eat."

The food was good, exactly as she'd expected. He relaxed after she reassured him it was. There was a silence, and she searched for something to say.

"Do you cook a lot?"

"I've been on my own for a while. It was a survival thing. I have a limited repertoire of easy meals, but I've gotten pretty good at them."

"I've never been on my own," Andie confessed.

"No?" She didn't hear judgment in his voice, and by now, she knew exactly how he sounded when he didn't approve of something. It was enough to encourage her to keep talking.

"You know that when my dad died, I took over the company. With four younger siblings, I was busy doing a lot of the things he used to do, things my mom hadn't done and didn't want to handle. It made sense to live at home with the office right there. I could focus on work and not worry about the domestic stuff."

"So no time spent learning to cook."

That would have to change.

"After the mill is done, maybe I'll have my

chance. I'll have my own place. I'll ask you for some of your recipes. Mom tends to make complicated dishes without precise measurements."

Trevor swirled the spaghetti with his fork. "Not to pry, but why didn't you ever find your own place here?"

Andie set her fork down. It was an obvious question, but she'd never found an obvious answer.

"At first, we all leaned on each other after dad died. My mom kind of fell apart and worried about us kids all the time, so living together worked. I think if one of us had moved out, she wouldn't have been able to function.

"Then it was a money thing, since there was a lot of tuition to cover. I had so much to learn, and living at home meant I could focus totally on the company."

She risked a glance at Trevor, worried that she might see pity or contempt on his face, but he showed only interest.

"Mom still worries. After my oldest brother moved out, I had my own room, so that was an improvement. And it seemed like if I moved into my own place here in Carter's, I was telling everyone that I was staying here. That I was giving up on my own dreams. And I wasn't ready to do that."

He was watching her intently. "Do you have regrets about giving up your plans?"

Andie shook her head, fingers pushing her plate around.

"Well, for what it's worth, I think it was an admirable thing you did."

Andie's chest warmed, surprised by the compliment.

"And I hope you get to achieve what you want."

Embarrassed, she searched for a change of topic. "Did you always want to be an architect?"

A smile tugged at the corner of his mouth. "From my first Lego set, I wanted to build things. It grew from there."

He moved the base of his wineglass in a precise clockwise circle. "What about you?"

She put her hands in her lap to hide the nervous fidgeting. The two of them fiddling with their place settings showed just how ill at ease they were. "After working on so many buildings while I was growing up, I wanted to be the one designing them. I guess I always wanted to be the boss."

They exchanged a glance, sharing something together. And it made Andie feel…restless. She grasped for another question. "Your family supported you?"

Trevor's face closed up, and Andie remembered how he'd done the same back in the bar when she'd mentioned brothers.

She remembered a lot about Trevor. More than she should for someone leaving at the end of the project.

He still had walls, ones that didn't allow anyone across. She didn't know if she'd ever see the real man.

CHAPTER THIRTEEN

TREVOR TOOK A bite of his meal, and Andie tried to think of a way to retract the question.

"My parents have always supported me."

He spoke carefully and deliberately. Had they been overprotective, the way her mother had become? Had they been cold and remote?

Somehow, the latter seemed more possible.

"I'm sorry, I didn't mean to pry. If you're uncomfortable talking about your family, that's fine."

Trevor set down his fork on his plate. "I'm adopted."

Andie didn't know what to say to that. She'd had no idea. She wondered how old he was when that happened. Maybe there had been some tragedy, and he was reserved and quiet as a result.

Trevor stared at his plate. "It was the usual story—teenagers not ready to be parents. I've known about it for as long as I can remember. I was adopted by a lovely couple who couldn't have their own child. And then, right after the papers were signed, she discovered she was pregnant."

"They gave you back?"

Andie couldn't imagine that.

Trevor shook his head. "No, they kept me. I have a brother. He's ten months younger than me."

It all sounded...nice? But Trevor was holding himself stiffly, still staring down at the table, so there was something happening here.

"Do you get along with your brother?"

His mouth kicked up, but it didn't look like a smile. "Yes, we all 'get along.'"

Andie narrowed her eyes. "Then, what's the problem?"

He finally looked up at her, drew a breath and then focused his gaze out the window.

"My parents kept me, kept their promise. They wanted to treat us the same. Every Christmas, birthday, graduation, everything was equal and fair. I'm pretty sure they kept a spreadsheet to make sure that they treated me exactly as well as they did the son that shares their DNA."

That sounded very rigid. And it didn't explain what was setting him on edge. Or did it?

"But?" Andie asked.

His gaze swung to her again. "But some

things don't fit on a spreadsheet. The things you can't force, or measure, or distribute fairly."

Andie put her fork down, appetite gone. "Feelings?"

Trevor shrugged. "It took me a while to figure it out, because I was just a kid. I knew something was...different. Somehow, I always felt like I'd done something wrong. They couldn't help how they felt. And they bonded more tightly with my brother." He was playing with the wineglass again.

"The three of them are extroverts, happy in big crowds of people. My dad sells cars, and my brother will take over for him. They are all like each other, and I'm the oddball, so obviously we aren't as close, but—"

He was trusting her with a secret. But she couldn't let him accept thinking it was right that they never fully brought him in to their circle.

"No." Andie said. Her voice was a little loud.

He stopped in the middle of whatever excuses he was making up.

"No. It's not obvious. You're not supposed to love someone like that—in levels. Blood kin here and adopted relatives one step down. I've known people who were adopted. They had parents who loved them just as much as ours loved us. Sometimes I thought more. My friend

Liv was adopted, but when she got sick, her parents were devastated."

"But if they'd had their own kids—"

"Trevor, you're saying that once a child is orphaned, they'll never be loved the same as children who are with their biological parents. And that's just…wrong. So wrong.

"Do you know Ryker Slade? The guy who's designing the town website? He grew up here with six siblings, and his dad…was terrible. He didn't love those kids. He couldn't, not the way he treated them. And they were his DNA. He wasn't a fraction of the parent that Liv's were. The biological bond didn't do anything for those kids."

Trevor focused on her face, watching her closely. She couldn't imagine growing up thinking you were always second-best. What that would do to a child, and how that would shape the person they grew up into… If you couldn't trust the people who raised you, how could you trust anyone?

She absolutely knew that it had shaped Trevor. And what had happened in that acci-dent had built on that lack of trust.

"Family is not limited by blood connections. Your value, your lovableness is not based on having blood relatives raising you. And to sug-gest otherwise is horrible for kids who are adopted. I'm sorry that happened to you. They did you a disservice. People can love you, even if you don't feel like your parents do."

There was silence then. Andie wondered if she'd crossed some line, and if the friendship she'd thought had been growing between them was damaged.

Trevor cleared his throat. "Thank you."

Andie blinked, her eyes watering.

"No one has ever said that. I somehow felt that I shouldn't have expected more. That it was my mistake."

Andie twisted her hands, gripping them tightly together in her lap. "No. It's never the kid's fault."

Trevor cleared his throat and picked up his fork again.

She unclenched her fingers and tried to lighten the tensions. "Unless we're talking about Joey."

Trevor looked up and flashed her a smile. She smiled back.

"It's always Joey's fault."

TREVOR WASN'T SURE which surprised him more—that he'd told all this to Andie, or that she'd defended him. Passionately and in a way that made him believe that there really wasn't something wrong with him.

Intellectually, he knew that. But as a kid, always coming up short of his brother when it came to his parents' affections, it had taken root in a way that went deeper than intellect. Andie's passionate defense reached down to those levels. He'd felt warmed inside, like he'd been given a hug.

Trevor refused Andie's offer of help with the dishes, insisting the dishwasher would handle most of them, and he'd be happy to deal with the remainder. They had work to do, and he suggested they start on that.

He appreciated what she'd said, but now he had to put that behind him. They were working together, and he needed to maintain that level of relationship. He could trust that, more than something emotional.

They sat on the couch in the living room. Trevor had gone through the photos and videos he'd taken and thinned out the number considerably. There was still a lot to share. Andie had just as many.

Most of his shots were better, since he'd used his camera rather than his phone, but Andie had some things he'd never seen. She'd taken pictures while her crew was working. She'd also taken some with him in them, photos he'd been unaware of. That was...

He wasn't sure how to define how that made

him feel. Surprised. Wary. And maybe... pleased?

Trevor shook his head. "No one wants those."

Andie disagreed. "You insisted we send some of the ones I'm in. Fair is fair."

He had taken additional shots of Andie, ones he hadn't included in this file of photos to share. She was the contractor, so of course, she was there when he took his photos. She was in a lot of them.

Of course.

Had she taken more of him, as well? He banished those thoughts before he could dwell on them.

"I doubt the man who edits these will want pictures of me, so it doesn't matter."

"Why not?"

Trevor paused. Why would he?

"I'm not someone local."

"The videos on the website for Cupid's Crossing aren't meant for the local people. This is supposed to bring in strangers, people who wouldn't come here otherwise."

True, but...

"After the accident...I was blamed for what went wrong. People remember that more than that I was cleared of any responsibility later."

Andie snorted. "Are you so important that everyone remembers you and what happened? I mean, here in Carter's—Cupid's Crossing, everyone would know and remember the story, but they'd also know you were cleared. We keep track of what happens here. I thought in a big city that would be different, that people would have forgotten or ignored it."

"Maybe, but other architects and contractors…"

"Would they examine a tourist website? Are there that many people who remember your accident? I don't mean to be cruel, but are you that well-known?"

He opened his mouth, but he didn't know what to say. Truthfully, he wasn't.

He'd been living a small life since he got out of the hospital. Part of that had been dealing with his broken engagement and adapting to life with a prosthetic. But part of it had been fear of what he might see in someone's eyes, seeing they believed he'd risked lives for money.

But did anyone remember him? Anyone who didn't know him, or the building and the people involved with that job?

"You must think I'm very conceited."

Andie shook her head. "No, I didn't think that the first time I met you at the Goat, and not even working on the site when we were…

Well, I never thought you were conceited when we were having some issues."

He risked a glance at her. "Should I ask what you did think of me then?"

"On-site? Probably not."

She paused and bit her lip. Did she fear he'd take that to heart? Hold it against her? He needed to reassure her.

"I won't ask. I won't even ask how I compare to Joey."

A smile crossed her face, and he felt his own in return.

Then her phone buzzed. Her smile vanished, and her brow creased.

She sighed. "That's my mom, worried about me making it home. I should get back. I need to be on-site early."

He remembered that first meeting at the pub. Her mom had called then, too. She would call frequently before Andie left for home at the end of their workdays.

"She worries about you?"

Andie's lips tightened. "She worries about everything. Excessively. But I went to the sites with Dad the day he died. He died on the way home, and ever since…it's like… I don't even know. I think she's somehow connected me to Dad and that day, or something? Sometimes it feels like I'm still a fifteen-year-old kid in her eyes."

Andie stood. "I didn't mean to bore you with my problems."

"It's not a bore. And I asked."

He didn't find her or these details about her at all boring.

"Still, my mom worrying so much is not your problem, and there's nothing you can do."

She had a point. He didn't want to push. He didn't like to be pushed himself, so he respected her boundaries.

He stood and followed her to the door. "You're right. There's nothing I can do. But I do understand worrying, perhaps to the point of paranoia."

She smiled again, and it loosened something in his chest.

"I seem to inspire worry in everyone around me."

Trevor wanted to deny it. He didn't want to burden her. But he was worried about her. Just like her mom.

No, probably not just like her mom.

"I'm sorry, Andie. I'll try to do better."

ANDIE WAS STARTLED when Jaycee interrupted her on darts night.

Tuesday nights had been darts night at the Goat and Barley for a long time, but those nights tended to include more male patrons than female. Andie, working mostly with men, was comfortable being outnumbered, but she also knew none of the guys she played with or against were interested in her romantically.

There had been one memorable Tuesday last fall when Jaycee had come to play. She'd brought Mariah with her. That wasn't long after Mariah had come to Carter's Crossing to set up the romance initiative Abigail had come up with to bring the town business opportunities. Mariah, who'd grown up sailing the world with her family, was a darts champion. She said it was popular in many places around the globe, so she'd had plenty of opportunity to practice.

People still remembered that night. She'd beaten all comers, handily.

Mariah was with Jaycee tonight, but they turned down invitations to play. Instead, they wanted to talk to Andie.

Andie didn't know Jaycee that well. They had been in different grades in school, and Jaycee had no connection to anything related to Kozak Construction. Their only connection was that Jaycee was marrying Dave, Andie's best friend's brother.

The pub was a little loud, so they went outside to talk. They were into the month of June now, so the days were long, and there was still light enough for Andie to see the other women clearly. The weather was warm, even at dusk. It was a beautiful time of the year, and one where Andie was grateful to be working outdoors so often. She didn't feel that way in January.

"What's up?"

Jaycee looked at Mariah, and Mariah nodded.

Curiouser and curiouser.

Jaycee took a breath and blurted out, "Andie, will you be one of my bridesmaids?"

Andie blinked at Jaycee, not sure she'd heard her correctly.

"I'm sorry, this is so late, and it's rude, but Dave's mom…"

Andie knew very well what Deirdre was like. Andie put up a hand to stop Jaycee's apology.

"I understand, Jaycee. What's she done?"

"She's insisting Don, Dave's brother-in-law, has to be one of the groomsmen, and that means I'm short a bridesmaid. I know she's just causing trouble, but I'm trying to keep her happy so she doesn't skip the wedding and make Dave angry on our day. The guys are renting suits to wear, so they'll be fine, but for the women…"

"And you think I can help?" Andie wasn't sure how.

Mariah answered this one. "I've done some research. We have a bridesmaid dress, a sample dress that works with the other bridesmaid dresses, that should fit you. You're good friends with both the groom's sister and husband, so having you as a member of the wedding party isn't strange. I hope you aren't offended that we didn't ask you at first."

Andie rushed to assure them, "Don't worry, honestly. I'm not upset. I know exactly what Deirdre is like, and I've heard all about how stressed she's been making you and Dave. I'm happy to help anyway I can.

"Do you just need me to stand up there on the day, or are there other things I can do to help?"

Jaycee's relief was almost comical, except that Andie knew the woman Jaycee was dealing with.

"We can pay for the dress, if you'll just go and get it fitted. You don't have to do anything else, but you're welcome to come to the bachelorette party. And thank you, thank you so, so much."

The woman was seriously wound up. Andie could only imagine how Deirdre was behaving. Andie wrapped her arms around Jaycee, who collapsed against her in obvious relief.

"I can pay for my dress, unless it's so ugly I'll never wear it again?"

Jaycee gave a shaky laugh, and Mariah raised her brows.

"The dresses are not ugly. And I say that not as the bride but as someone who's seen some truly horrible dresses."

Andie gave Jaycee another squeeze and let her go. "Jaycee, you've got a lot on your plate dealing with your future mother-in-law. Don't worry about this. I'm glad for the chance to spend more time with Denise while she's here. I've missed her."

Jaycee sniffed. "Thanks, Andie. I swear, I can't wait for this wedding to be over."

"Hey, I lived through Denise's wedding. I know what it's like."

Mariah mouthed a thank-you to Andie, and then after more reassurances on Andie's part, Mariah dragged Jaycee away, and Andie returned to the pub. The crew was still sitting at the table, and other teams were busy at the dart board. Andie dropped into her seat.

"What was that about?" Joey asked.

"I'm going to be one of Jaycee's bridesmaids. Dave's mom insisted on including Don as well as Denise, so it unbalanced the number of male and female attendants."

Joey frowned. "Wait, isn't the wedding in just a couple of weeks?"

Andie nodded. "It's on the Fourth of July. The whole town is invited."

Trevor looked at them as if surprised by the information. Hadn't he been invited? Or was he just surprised that people would come without specific invites?

Joey grabbed a French fry and leaned back in his seat. He had that troublemaking look on his face, so Andie braced herself.

"So, sis, who's gonna be your plus-one?"

Andie blinked. "What plus-one?"

"For the wedding."

Andie shook her head. "I don't need a plus-one."

"Sure you do. Who else is in the wedding party? Nelson Carter and the wedding planner, right? Your buddy, Denise, and her husband. Jonas over there has a girlfriend, so you really should have someone."

Andie decided to humor him. "You can be my plus-one, then."

"Uh-uh." Joey finished his beer. "I've got a date. Jonas asked me to take his girlfriend's sister."

Andie paused for a moment to work through who else was in the wedding party, wanting to prove there was no need for a date to an event the whole town was invited to.

Rachel. Rachel was Jaycee's best friend, so she was definitely part of the wedding. She wasn't seeing anyone, was she?

"You should take Trevor," Joey said, smirking.

Andie felt her face heating up. Sure, she and Trevor weren't in opposition the way they had been in the beginning, but they weren't dating. She kicked out her foot, catching Joey's shin.

"What was that for?"

"For being an idiot. Don't put Trevor on the spot like that. I don't need a plus-one, and if I did, I could find someone for myself."

"Who?" Joey asked, moving his legs before she could kick him again.

She glared at him. "Someone."

"It's okay," Trevor interrupted the squabble.

"What's okay?"

"I'll be your plus-one. I mean, I don't mind if you don't, and if you need someone…"

Joey grinned. "See, sis? I took care of things for you."

Andie was sure her face must be bright enough to light up the bar.

"Joey, don't even."

"No need to thank me, sis. I'm off now. You two can work out the details."

He stood, giving her one more evil grin before heading out of the pub.

There was an awkward silence. Andie couldn't bear to look at Trevor.

"It's okay," Trevor repeated.

Andie shook her head. "Ignore Joey. He's just trying to cause trouble."

"I mean, not if you don't want to."

Andie lifted her head. Trevor was pulling at his napkin. His cheeks were flushed.

"I don't want you to feel obligated."

He swallowed. "I don't know many people in town. No women, other than you and Mariah and Abigail. If you need someone to go with, it might be nice not to go alone."

Andie put aside her own mortification and considered Trevor. She never saw him around town, except for these nights at the Goat with Kozak Construction people. Considering that Trevor wasn't an extrovert, he might not have gotten to know a lot of people.

"Are you staying here for the holiday?" The Fourth was a long weekend. She'd expected Trevor to head back to New York City.

He nodded.

"You're not staying because of the job, are you?"

She thought he'd overcome most of his suspicions. If he wouldn't leave for a couple of days, days when they wouldn't even be working on the mill...

Trevor shook his head.

"You don't have plans with your family?"

"They have plans, yes, but I'd rather not be part of them."

Andie remembered that first time she'd met Trevor in the bar on New Year's Eve. He hadn't wanted to be with his family then, either. And the night they'd gone through the photos of the mill together, he'd told her that he felt that he wasn't loved the same as his brother.

Her family was so tight, so connected that sometimes she didn't realize people could have a different experience with their relatives.

Maybe he really would like to go with someone to the wedding, if he was planning on going. This man who wasn't comfortable with the family who'd raised him.

"You want to go to the wedding?"

"If the whole town is invited, there's not going to be much else to do, is there?"

That was true. Even the annual fireworks display was interwoven with the wedding celebration.

"So we'd go as...friends?" She wasn't sure if that was the proper term, but this was certainly not the invitation of a man who wanted to date her. And she was not disappointed about that. No, no, no.

He considered her question and then nodded, carefully.

Well, this was not how Andie had expected the evening to go.

"You're sure you don't mind?"

He gave her a small smile. "Do you?"

No, she didn't. She'd have to make sure her mother didn't make a fuss over this, especially with Joey's big mouth, but she'd been a little lonely since Denise moved away. And with Denise's brother getting married that day, she wouldn't be able to spend a lot of time with Andie.

"Okay, then. You're my plus-one for the wedding."

She found herself hoping desperately that Mariah was right and that the dress wasn't a horror.

CHAPTER FOURTEEN

TREVOR PACKED UP his laptop and notebook. The trailer was quiet. Normally, he enjoyed this quiet part of the day after the crew left. He and Andie would wrap up paperwork. They'd talk. They were becoming friends.

He couldn't forget to be watchful, but he thought they had a connection.

Today, Andie had gone out with Mariah. Trevor was on his own. No darts, no trivia.

He stepped out of the trailer and locked it up. He did his usual walk-through of the site. Everything looked good.

The idea of going home to his lonely house was not appealing. After making sure the mill was closed up, he wandered to the back.

The little valley that the mill was placed in looked very different in late June than it had last fall when he'd first come here or during the winter when they'd started work.

The leaves were out, showing shades of green patterned like a quilt over the hillside.

The creek, burbling through stones as it passed the mill, no longer looked forbiddingly cold.

In fact, with the temperature increasing as summer took hold, the creek was tempting.

Trevor looked around, but he was alone. Totally alone. He put his bag down on a stone and sat to peel off his socks and shoes. He then rolled up his pants.

The prosthetic leg stood out as jarring as it always did. He couldn't look at it without remembering Violet.

She'd been at his bedside for those first terrible days in the hospital. But as the weeks went by, her visits grew shorter. She was fidgety when she came by. It took him a little while to realize she couldn't look at his legs.

Leg. He had only one complete leg.

She was uncomfortable with him and with his injuries, but she couldn't admit to herself that this made a difference to her. To their relationship.

He'd been the one to suggest they end their engagement. The relief on her face had been blatant, even though she'd protested. Weakly. She'd promised they'd still be friends. But her visits grew further and further apart. It was a relief when she stopped coming by altogether.

Trevor stood and made his way carefully down to the stream. He put his right foot in the water and felt the shocking coolness of the water. Then he moved his left foot in for balance. The temperature wasn't an issue for that foot.

He didn't wear shorts, not anymore. He'd stopped swimming. After Violet, he hadn't wanted to show his prosthetic leg to anyone.

Andie had seen it that morning at her house when he'd slept in. She hadn't treated him any differently since. But then, they didn't have that kind of relationship. They weren't dating.

Would it bother Andie?

He stepped out of the stream and sat down, letting his feet, flesh and plastic, dry before putting his socks and shoes back on.

Maybe, someday, he'd find someone who wasn't bothered by his leg. Someone who hadn't known him before, and who wouldn't compare him to who he'd been. That made him think of Andie, and he was more optimistic.

MARIAH DIDN'T WASTE any time getting Andie to the bridal salon to try on the dress she'd found for her last-minute bridesmaid. Mariah ensured the process was as streamlined as possible. The dress and a seamstress were at the ready when they walked in the door.

Andie was all too aware of her jeans, boots

and grimy nails, since she'd come straight from the mill.

The dress was waiting in the change room for her. It was a vivid shade of blue, cocktail length, with broad straps and a heart-shaped neckline. Andie loved it on sight.

Mariah helped her into it with practiced ease. It was wide at the waist, which Andie found all too common when she tried to get dresses to fit her chest and shoulders. That didn't faze Mariah.

Andie stood on a raised platform in the salon while the seamstress and Mariah got to work. The waist was pinned, and the hem shortened. Andie watched herself in the mirror and stood straighter as she saw herself in the reflection.

Her hair was pulled back and messy, and she didn't have a bit of makeup on, but she looked good. The dress, once fitted, accentuated her curves in all the right ways. She hadn't realized how small her waist looked when properly set off.

Mariah walked around Andie, still on the platform. "Perfect. You can have that ready in a week?"

The seamstress nodded. "This is a straightforward job. I'll call you when it's ready."

Andie stood for a moment, until she realized they were waiting for her to move.

"Oh, right. I'll change."

She was reluctant to take the dress off. It made her look...different. She liked that, but she stepped down and into the change room. She removed the pinned dress carefully and passed it to Mariah before changing back into her work clothes. The dress would be useless on a job site, but she was going to enjoy wearing it to the wedding. And she was definitely going to find another time to show it off.

Mariah was waiting for her when she stepped out of the change room.

"It's a beautiful dress, Mariah. I'll find a way to wear it again."

Mariah smiled. "I'm glad you feel that way. There wasn't another option. One thing about this rushed wedding is that Jaycee hasn't been able to fixate on her perfect wedding plan, so she's gone with what we can do in the time frame. More stress in one way, less in another."

"I'd never have thought Jaycee was the bridezilla type."

Mariah sighed. "If she was marrying anyone else, she probably wouldn't be, but Dave's mother—"

Andie nodded. She had no problems understanding what Jaycee was going through. "I know. Denise and I were best friends all through school, and she much preferred being at my place than at hers."

"You really understand why Jaycee needed a last-minute bridesmaid?"

"Totally. But I should maybe have warned you that Deirdre is not one of my fans. Not after I took over the construction company. She's big on traditional gender roles."

Mariah grinned. "Rachel mentioned that. Deirdre can't really complain when her daughter's best friend is in the wedding party, but she might want to."

Andie laughed. "I can't believe Rachel said anything that uncharitable."

"Rachel is changing."

Andie thought of the quiet woman, a pastor's daughter and always the first to help when trouble struck.

"It's probably time. People have taken advantage of her. So, are we good now?"

Mariah raised a finger. "One question. Shoes."

Andie grimaced. "I can check what I've got, but I'll probably need to buy something."

"The other bridesmaids are wearing flat sandals. Want to go get some now?"

Mariah wasn't leaving anything to chance. Andie was happy not to have to make another trip to find sandals, so she was willing to deal with everything now.

"Lead the way."

They found sandals without much difficulty. Andie appreciated that they wouldn't be too hot for an outdoor, afternoon wedding in July. It wouldn't be too difficult to walk on the grass in them, since the wedding was taking place in the park in the middle of town.

When Mariah suggested they grab something to eat before heading back to Cupid's Crossing, Andie was happy to agree to that, as well. She hadn't thought she and Mariah would have much in common, but she was enjoying the time they spent together.

Andie had felt alone after Denise moved away. She hadn't found another girlfriend and had resigned herself to being lonely till she left town for school.

She was going to spend some time with Denise at the wedding, and also Jaycee and Rachel and Mariah. Maybe she didn't need to feel lonely. Maybe she didn't need to put off her life. She just needed to make an effort.

"I'M REALLY PUTTING a downer on your bachelorette, Jaycee, aren't I?" Denise sighed as she lowered herself into a chair.

Abigail Carter had offered the use of her home for Jaycee's party, though everyone knew who had engineered the event. Mariah lived in the house and was taking care of everything connected to the wedding.

The party had been designed with Denise's pregnancy in mind. There were no strippers, little alcohol and no going out. Instead, Mariah had arranged for a spa to come to them.

Jaycee was currently getting a massage while Rachel and Mariah were getting pedicures. Andie couldn't see the details of what was going on, since it was her turn for a facial and she had something over her eyes.

Didn't matter. This was bliss.

Jaycee's voice was languid and slurring. "Shut up, Denise. This is awesome."

"We needed to get this all done for tomorrow anyway." That was Mariah. "There isn't going to be a lot of time on the day, since the ceremony starts at two. And I really don't need a bunch of hungover attendants when we're having an outdoor, summer wedding."

Andie wanted to shudder at the thought of a hangover and the bright afternoon sun, but she'd already gotten in trouble for moving while she was being worked on.

"What about the guys? Are they going to be in trouble tomorrow?" Denise was invested, since this was her brother's wedding.

"If they are, the hangover will be the least of their problems."

Now that Andie had seen Mariah in action, she had no doubts about it. Since Joey wasn't in the wedding party, there was a good chance Nelson would be able to keep them in line.

Andie was content to lean back, eyes closed, while the conversation moved around her.

"Can I ask you guys something?" said Denise.

Andie knew Denise. They'd been friends all their lives. That was her troublemaking voice.

"Sure, ask whatever you want." Rachel had been mostly quiet, which surprised Andie. Not that Rachel was someone to take over a room, but she had circles under her eyes, and her smiles looked forced.

Andie had asked Mariah if anything was wrong with Rachel, and Mariah had explained Rachel and Ryker Slade had fallen out. That shocked Andie. She'd heard Ryker was back, but she'd never dreamed he and Rachel would ever spend time together. Ryker must've changed.

She'd never imagined Rachel with him. She hadn't had time to get the details, but she hoped she'd get a chance at some point. There had to be a story there.

"Someone tell me about Andie's architect, because she won't."

It was good for Andie that she had a mask drying on her face, or her heated cheeks would

248 A NEW YEAR'S EVE PROPOSAL

have been visible to all. And good for Denise that Andie had to keep still, or she'd have gone over and muzzled her friend.

That, or strangled her.

"He's not mine" she growled and was shushed by her attendant.

"Well, Andie's working with him. Closely. Every day."

Denise made that sound like something must be going on. Andie worked with a lot of men, closely and every day. Andie started to growl again, and suddenly a cloth was laid over her mouth.

"And he's going to the wedding with her."

"Ooh." Rachel was awfully interested in Andie's affairs for someone who had her own problems.

"He's good-looking, in a slightly nerdy way. Messy hair, glasses, lean, like he's a runner." Jaycee ticked off his attributes, and Andie wondered why she was checking him out so carefully when she was getting married tomorrow.

"Is he nice?" Denise wasn't giving up.

"Do we have to call people *nice*?" That was unexpected, coming from Rachel.

"He's quiet," Mariah said. "He and Andie put some video and photos together for the website, so that's how I've got to know him. He's very good at his job, doesn't talk a lot, doesn't seem to think he's God's gift, and he's kind of reserved."

As the mask was gently removed from Andie's face, she agreed with Mariah's assessment. Mariah didn't know his story, not like Andie did, but she'd described Trevor well.

Andie could have added *paranoid* and *suspicious*, but he hadn't been, not lately. And that made her feel better than it should.

"And he's from New York City, right? Is that one of the places you're going to apply to study, Andie?"

Andie was happy for the need to keep quiet while her face was done.

"Andie's leaving?" Rachel asked.

Denise grimaced. "I'm sorry, Andie. Was that a secret? You get your turn to go to school now that your siblings are all taken care of, right?"

With a final swipe, Andie's technician cleaned her face and left for the kitchen, so Andie had no excuse not to answer. She saw four faces, women she would call friends now, as well as a couple of the estheticians all watching for her to answer.

She sighed. "In theory, yes, but I've got to wait till the mill is done, and honestly, I'm not sure Joey is ready. I'm not sure he'll ever be ready."

Suddenly, she had a whole team of women ready to talk, suggest, condole and stand by her. It was wonderful.

Rachel had made plans to leave Cupid's Crossing before her uncle's recent accident. Andie was slow to put the pieces together. Ryker had been on his motorcycle when he'd been hit and seriously injured by Rachel's uncle. Rachel was her uncle's paralegal. Ryker was out of the hospital but still on crutches. With Rachel's uncle in rehab, Rachel had put her plans to leave on hold to try to help sort out the mess this left for his law practice.

Rachel was on Team Leave.

"You've done so much for your family. You deserve your own chance," Rachel told Andie.

"I know," Andie said. "But after putting everyone else through school, there's not much of a buffer left in the company's bank account. If Joey messes up, I'm worried about how Mom will survive."

"No one else has worried about that for the last fourteen years. It's time one of your siblings stepped up," Denise countered.

Denise had argued for this frequently. She was also on Team Leave, the unelected captain.

"Well, do I really want to start college now? If I want to be an architect, there's years of school, plus apprenticing… It's going to take a while."

"You should ask Trevor about that. He'd know."

Andie wanted to move the whole conversation away from Trevor. Her future plans and what would happen to Kozak Construction were a big problem, but she knew all the variables connected with that. She knew the problems, the possible solutions…but Trevor was an unknown.

She wasn't sure how she felt about him, she wasn't sure how he felt about her, and she had no idea what he was doing once the mill was done. None of that should have any impact on her planning process.

They had a truce, a tentative trust. She enjoyed spending time with him. She wanted to know what his plans were and what he thought of hers. Sometimes, she let herself imagine that their plans could overlap. She was more attracted to him than she wanted to admit, and it was going to hurt when he left.

She didn't need to get closer to him.

Everyone was looking at her. Everyone thought that asking Trevor was a perfect solution. It wasn't, but she didn't feel like it was appropriate to share all the gory details of Trevor's story with them.

How could she explain that he knew her plans but hadn't offered to help? She thought it was because he wanted to maintain boundaries, hoped that was why he hadn't said anything further.

She didn't want to push, didn't want to bring back that suspicious, cold person she'd first worked with. She'd do a lot to maintain the warmer relationship they had now, even if it meant missing out on something that would help her plan her future.

They were staring at her, so she'd have to give them some reason. Or with her luck, they'd ask him themselves and trigger his paranoia.

"He was injured on the last big project he worked on when the contractor messed up. They purposely cut corners, used cheaper materials, stuff like that. Trevor is...wary about whether Kozak might do something similar. I'm trying to maintain a professional boundary so he doesn't think I'm... I don't know, distracting him so he doesn't notice me doing the same kind of thing."

"You'd never do that." Denise was a loyal supporter.

"I know, but it's not like I can just tell him that and he'll stop worrying."

"That is a problem." Mariah was frowning.

"But if you're trying to just be professional, how come he's going to the wedding with you?"

Andie felt her cheeks warm again. "That's because of Joey. And it's not a date. It's more, um, he didn't want to go alone when he doesn't know very many people."

Denise got it. "How did Joey involve himself?"

"On darts night, after you asked me to be a bridesmaid, Jaycee, Joey told me Trevor should be my plus-one...in front of Trevor."

Everyone groaned.

"You were at darts night together?" Denise asked.

She knew that look on Denise's face. Troublemaker. Mind you, Andie had been just as bad back before she had to take over the family business.

"Yes, I was there with Trevor, Joey and a bunch of other guys from the crew. It was *not* a date."

And now the idea of a date was in her head. *Thanks, Denise.* Andie had to change the focus of the conversation.

"So, have you told Deirdre whether you're having boys or girls or one of each, Denise?"

Jaycee swung around to look at Denise. "You know? And you haven't told her?"

Denise shot Andie a glare, but Andie grinned back. What were friends for?

TREVOR STOOD AT the edge of the park.

It was a glorious summer day. The sky was bright and clear, but there was enough of a breeze to keep people cool without causing damage to the decorations.

There were a lot of decorations.

The colors were red, white and blue. Fitting for the Fourth of July. Yet somehow, through whatever magic Mariah employed, the patriotic color scheme still looked…romantic. Appropriate for a wedding.

He was sure he wasn't seeing all of what Mariah had done for this wedding. There were too many bodies in the way. The park was packed. He wouldn't be at all surprised to learn that everyone in Cupid's Crossing was here.

He searched vainly to find Andie among the crowd. Since she was in the wedding party, she had told him she'd be busy taking pictures and other wedding-related things before the ceremony. He wouldn't see her, at least as her plus-one, until after.

He'd see her during the ceremony, since she was part of it.

Maybe. There were a lot of people here.

"Trevor!"

He turned, happy to find someone he knew. It was Joey, wearing a button-up shirt over khakis. Trevor looked down at his dress pants and jacket. He must have overdressed.

Joey slapped his shoulder. He was flanked by some of the other guys who worked for Kozak Construction.

"Come on. You get a seat since you're connected to the wedding party."

Trevor wanted to protest, but Joey was crowding him, and it seemed easier to let himself be shepherded to wherever Joey was taking him than argue with him.

There were chairs in rows in front of the gazebo. A central aisle led to the steps. If the park had looked prepared for a wedding, the gazebo was even more so. This close, he could hear strains of music underscoring the murmur of voices.

It looked like something out of a wedding brochure. Trevor had seen a lot of those — with Violet.

About half the seats were occupied. He didn't know what the protocol was, but he would have been happy to stand or slip into a seat at the back. Joey, however, headed to a row in the middle. There were two women sitting there.

"Hey, Rose, Amelia, this is Trevor. He's with

Andie, so you guys are together—dates of the wedding party."

This wasn't supposed to be a date. Was it? Andie said they were going as friends. That was fine. He shouldn't want it to be a date.

The two women looked up and smiled politely.

"Go on, sit, Trevor. They're with Micah and Jordan, the guys who are standing up with Dave."

"Hello."

They echoed his greeting. He sat beside them, and with unexpected dismay, he watched Joey leave.

Rose and Amelia continued their conversation. He had no desire to interrupt or vie for their attention, so he sat back and watched the people around him. Some greeted him or waved. He smiled or waved in return. It was… nice. Nice to know people. Even if he wasn't officially with Andie for this event, he wouldn't have been alone.

The seats rapidly filled up, leaving room only in the front row. The mothers were led down the aisle, and then the groom and his groomsmen climbed the steps to the gazebo to wait.

The music changed. Everyone turned to face the rear, waiting for the bridal party. Trevor was a half-second behind. He looked in the same direction as everyone else, ready to see the first bridesmaid walk down the aisle. His mouth dropped open when he saw her.

CHAPTER FIFTEEN

IT TOOK TREVOR a moment to recognize Andie. She didn't look anything like the contractor he knew. Her hair was up, and she was wearing makeup. That was one change. The other was the dress.

He'd thought her pretty when he first saw her at the Goat and Barley. She was more than just pretty now. She looked beautiful. It did strange things to his insides.

She was smiling as she walked down the aisle, familiar with the people watching her and making their own greetings. Then her gaze caught on him, and for a fraction of a second, she froze.

He was already still, watching her with who-knew-what expression on his face. He hoped he wasn't drooling. He felt his cheeks flush.

Andie recovered and looked to another part of the crowd, and his eyes followed her helplessly as she finished her trip down the aisle. One of the groomsmen met her, and together they climbed the shallow steps to the gazebo.

He was scarcely aware of the rest of the bridesmaids passing him. He stood when everyone else did, and the bride walked slowly down the grass aisle, holding the arm of a man who must be her father.

The rest of the ceremony passed in a blur. He tried to focus on what was happening, but he kept stealing glances at Andie.

Andie in a blue dress that lit up her face. Andie exchanging grins with the groomsman she was partnered with. Trevor didn't like him.

The service was short, the groom soon kissed his bride and the party retreated down the aisle. People stood, and Trevor stood with them, unsure of what to do next.

Rose took pity on him and led him around the back of the gazebo where photos were being taken of the wedding party. Andie and her groomsman had been joined by another bridesmaid, one who was conspicuously pregnant.

Andie looked over and smiled when she caught sight of him. He couldn't resist responding. She said something to her companions, and the three of them walked toward him.

Rose and Amelia left him to find their dates. Trevor barely registered their departure.

His eyes were on Andie.

She stood in front of him, a small smile crossing her face.

"Trevor, this is my friend, Denise, sister to the groom, and her husband, Don."

He relaxed once he knew this man Andie had been partnered with was married to the pregnant woman. Andie shook her head slightly as Denise stepped forward. Denise ignored Andie to give Trevor a wide smile.

"It's so nice to meet you, Trevor. I've heard so much about you."

Trevor shot a glance at Andie. Her cheeks were pink.

"Denise!"

Denise widened her eyes. "We're all pretty excited to see how the mill looks after you two are done."

Don took Denise's elbow in his hand. "Weren't you telling me you had to find a bathroom?"

Denise hesitated, then shrugged. "Hazards of pregnancy. I hope I see you later. I have *lots* of questions."

Andie poked her.

"About architecture, of course."

Don dragged her away while Andie shook her head.

"I'm sorry. We've been best friends since

we were kids, and she's suffering from pregnancy hormones."

Trevor was curious. About what Denise would have said had she not left and what Andie had told her friend to inspire those comments.

"I should just ignore whatever she's been hearing about me?"

Andie flushed and bit her lip. "You do understand small towns are gossipy, right?"

Flushed Andie was doing strange things to him. His palms were sweating, and his pulse quickened. What had she said? Right, small towns.

"It's become apparent since I've been here. I haven't seen Denise around before."

"No, she and her husband moved to Florida about a year and a half ago."

"I see."

There was an awkward pause. He swallowed.

"Um, you look very nice." Internally, he groaned. Why couldn't he tell her she looked beautiful?

Andie met his gaze. "Thank you. Bridesmaid dresses can be a bit of a crapshoot, but I love this one. Denise's dresses were... Well, I love Denise, but I will never wear the dress from her wedding again."

That sounded familiar. Violet had discussed the subject extensively. Without thinking, he spoke. "I remember there being a lot of debate about that."

He froze. He hadn't planned to say that. Of course Andie didn't miss it. Her eyebrows lifted.

"You've been through a discussion about bridesmaid dresses?"

He shrugged. "I was engaged."

Her mouth dropped open. She obviously hadn't expected to hear that. He braced himself, waiting for her next question. He understood he wasn't his best self anymore, so why would she think someone had wanted to marry him? Violet *had* changed her mind, after all.

"Married?"

He shook his head. He heard her exhale.

"Something you prefer not to talk about?"

"Exactly."

Andie glanced around, and a frown pulled down her eyebrows. "Is being here today a problem? I'm sorry, I didn't know."

That wasn't the response he'd prepared for. He'd prepared for curiosity and questions, not concern. He put his hand on her arm, wanting to reassure her. The tingle in his fingers when he touched her skin was not what he was expecting, or honestly, wanting. He drew back.

"It's fine, Andie. I could have made an excuse. I'm not bothered by weddings. I just prefer not to talk about why my engagement ended."

She grimaced. "She didn't leave you at the altar, did she? Sorry. I wasn't supposed to ask."

It hadn't been *that* embarrassing. "No, we never got that far."

"Good. I mean, I'm glad that didn't happen to you. It happened to Nelson, and it would be a little freaky if it had happened to you, too."

He almost turned to look for Nelson. He couldn't imagine the man waiting at the altar for a bride who didn't show.

"Nelson? And Mariah?"

"No, this was a few years ago. Someone else, not from here. I don't know all the details, just that it happened, and Nelson came back to Carter's after."

Andie turned and led the way toward the tables where food was being set out. Trevor quickened his step to keep pace with her, careful on the uneven ground. He was annoyed by how curious he was about what had happened with Nelson. The town was wearing off on him.

She considered. "I don't think Mariah would do that, leave someone at the altar. If nothing else, she wouldn't jeopardize all the work she put into planning something like this."

He glanced around. "She has worked hard. Everything's beautiful."

"It's way beyond any other wedding we've had here. We just might be able to pull off this romance-center thing." Andie sounded like she'd had doubts.

Trevor had been focused on his job, on getting the mill done, but he hadn't connected it to the whole concept of the town's survival. He wasn't pleased with himself. He wasn't the only person who'd had problems. He had no business being so self-centered.

"I think people would be willing to travel to have an event like this."

"I hope so. The whole town has united behind this idea. They've worked hard to make this look good. I mean, I've never seen Mr. Lawrence in anything but sweatpants for years."

Trevor had no idea who Mr. Lawrence was, but he'd seen a few older men in sweatpants around town. Not today. Today, it did look like the town was doing its best to shine.

"I was afraid I'd overdressed."

Andie's gaze traveled over him, and his cheeks flushed again. He hadn't been looking for a compliment, but her gaze was warm and admiring. He wasn't used to that, but despite his embarrassment, he liked it.

"You look good, Trevor. You're not more dressed up than the wedding party, so I don't think you need to worry. If you're comparing yourself to Joey, on the other hand, you'll always be overdressed, which probably means you're doing it right."

She grinned at him, the two of them sharing an inside joke, and he returned the smile before he was aware of it. His cheeks were feeling the effects of this much smiling, and a warmth that had nothing to do with the summer sun spread through him.

Denise and Don joined them again, which was good. He didn't think grinning at Andie was going to help his situation.

"Trevor, I'm very sorry if I embarrassed you earlier." Denise shot a glance at her husband.

Don shook his head. "Adding that '*if* I embarrassed you' negates most of the apology."

"No, don't worry about it. I'm fine." Trevor didn't want more attention or to upset someone so conspicuously pregnant.

Don tried to glare at his wife, but their obvious affection reduced the effectiveness of his stare. "Sorry, Trevor, but when these two get together, there's no telling what might happen."

Andie poked his arm. "Don, don't you dare tell stories."

Trevor was very interested in the stories Andie wanted silenced, and he couldn't even tell himself it was to better understand his contractor. He wanted to know her as a person. An attractive, interesting woman.

The four of them moved in a group to get some of the food spread out under tents. Andie and Denise and Don knew everyone. Trevor recognized only a few of the people, but Andie gave him a low-voiced bio of each person before they met.

"That's Mr. G, retired high school computer teacher with his son, Benny. Benny may be in a wheelchair, but he can fix almost anything."

Trevor remembered Benny was the person they'd sent their photos and videos to. It was nice to finally put a face to the name.

"That couple—Gord and Gladys. She's fussing over him now because he broke his hip this winter, right before their fiftieth wedding anniversary."

Gord looked pretty grumpy.

"And that's Judy, who works at the vet clinic, and her husband, Harvey. Just don't mention zombies to them."

Trevor couldn't imagine any circumstance in which he would.

He recognized Mavis Grisham, who was accompanied by her Great Dane, Tiny, who was wearing a tuxedo T-shirt.

"Don't ask," Andie advised, so he didn't.

He recognized some people from meetings and some who were working on the mill. Everyone was friendly and obviously enjoying themselves. The food was good, and he was startled to find that he was enjoying himself, as well.

This was the first big social event he'd attended since his accident. No one asked him about it or how he was doing. He was just one of many people at a party. A weight rolled off his shoulders.

It seemed like no time had passed before Mariah announced it was time for the throwing of the bouquet and the garter.

Andie groaned.

"I'm just going to hide behind you. Don't move, and if anyone asks, you haven't seen me."

Trevor didn't think her chances of hiding behind him, even this late in the afternoon, were very good. "I'm not sure that's going to work."

"Don! Cover me."

Denise chuckled. "You should hide behind me. I'm as big as a house."

Don held up a warning hand. "Don't agree with that, Andie. It's a trap."

Trevor allowed himself another smile.

Andie's maneuvering was in vain, since Mariah came up behind them, beckoning for Andie.

"Mariah, this is such a silly thing to do. It's embarrassing and—"

Mariah took hold of Andie's arm. "Don't worry. Jaycee has something planned for the bouquet, and it doesn't involve you catching it. You won't want to miss what's coming. Nothing embarrassing for *you*."

Andie allowed herself to be dragged away, and Trevor followed with Don and Denise. They were all curious.

Jaycee, glowing in her white dress, took her time getting ready. She fidgeted with the bouquet and looked over her shoulder, then she turned to where a man was making his way on crutches to the center of the park where everyone was gathered.

"Is that Ryker Slade?" Denise asked. "I heard he was back."

"Are you asking me?" Don rubbed her back where she'd placed her own hand. "I didn't grow up here. Never seen the man before."

Trevor had heard the name. Something to

do with the website for the town? Right. Andie had mentioned him. Big family, terrible dad.

Jaycee threw the bouquet to the man they thought was Ryker who struggled to catch it, and Mariah pushed Rachel to walk over to him. He dropped one of his crutches and fell on one knee. Trevor didn't catch everything, but it was clearly a proposal, and Denise was squeeing with pleasure. The whole park burst into applause as the couple kissed.

Andie came back to them. She had a dreamy smile on her face. Trevor would never have imagined his prickly contractor could look like that. Something else that would mess with his concentration at work.

"That was so romantic."

Denise was almost vibrating in place. "Was that Ryker Slade?"

Andie nodded. "Yes. He came back. He's changed, and he and Rachel are a thing. I had no idea, but that's so sweet. Not what I thought I'd ever say about a Slade."

Trevor didn't say anything. That proposal hit a little too close to home. The memories weren't welcome. He excused himself, pretending he needed to find the portable toilets.

He hadn't thought much about Violet for weeks, months even, but the wedding and the proposal were all bringing it back. At the last wedding he'd been at, he'd proposed to Violet. He'd thought his future was settled then. Everything had been planned out. The accident had upset not just his career.

He needed some time and space to get rid of this unsettled feeling. He found a bench at the edge of the park, away from the crowds, and watched from a safe distance.

The sun was setting when he roused himself to find his date. It wasn't fair to leave her hanging. He needed to behave like an adult, not a hurt child. Andie deserved to know why he'd vanished. His muscles tightened at the thought of exposing himself like that, but he trusted her.

He really did.

CHAPTER SIXTEEN

ANDIE WAS AWARE of Trevor's absence, and she fended off questions from her friends. Denise had to leave. The long day was trying on her ankles, which she swore were swollen to the size of watermelons. As soon as the newly married couple were sent off on their honeymoon, Don took Denise back to her parents' place.

Andie stopped to talk to her mother, avoided Joey and wondered if Trevor had gone. Wouldn't he have said something? Had something here reminded him of his broken engagement and caused him to leave? She wished she'd had some way to carry her phone, but since the dress had no pockets, she'd left it locked up in the truck.

If Trevor was gone, she might just leave, as well. People were staying to see the traditional fireworks display, but Andie had seen many over the years, and she could give this one a miss.

She took one final glance around. Then she spotted Trevor returning from wherever he'd been. He was scanning the crowd, and when he saw her, he smiled.

It was the smile she'd seen that first night at the Goat. When they'd been two people sharing an interlude, not adversaries on a job together.

She couldn't resist a smile in return.

"You okay?" He'd been gone a while, and she didn't want to pry, but she was concerned about him.

He glanced away. "I think so. Would you like to take a walk?"

"Sure." She asked Mavis to let her mother know she would be home later and followed Trevor past the tents and chairs that had helped turn the park into a wedding venue for the day.

The town was quiet once they left the park, where the crowd still enjoyed the food and music. They walked in companionable silence. She felt no urge to break it, and Trevor didn't speak, not till they'd covered two blocks.

"I'm sorry I left like that."

"Not a problem." That was true. She'd missed him, but she knew everyone in this town. She was used to attending things solo and enjoying herself. "This event was so informal, I'm not sure many people knew you were with me."

He made a grunty noise in his throat, whether of agreement or something else, she wasn't sure.

"I'm not a party person. I tend to be quiet. And this…" He waved his hand, indicating the wedding event. "It brought back some memories."

Andie wanted to slap Joey. Trevor could have avoided this if it hadn't been for her brother's big mouth.

"You should have made an excuse. It would have been fine. I've gone solo to lots of things here in Carter's—I mean, Cupid's—Crossing, and I'm good on my own."

Trevor shook his head with a jerk. "No, honestly. I don't dread or hate weddings. But that proposal threw me. It brought things back, things I don't think I've dealt with. I guess that's obvious since it hit me like that today."

Andie had never been in a serious relationship. She hadn't wanted to be tied down to Carter's Crossing when she'd been counting down the days till she could leave.

No. She was leaving. Still. She thrust that sense of confusion down. This was Trevor's moment to process things, not hers. She didn't have anything to process. Enough!

She turned to him. "Everyone gets to deal with things the way they need to."

She noticed the corner of his mouth quirk up. "Probably better to choose a healthy way.

I've mostly been pretending it never happened. That hasn't been completely effective."

"I can understand the appeal." Sometimes, though, pretending wasn't an option.

"I wish the easy way worked. I proposed to Violet after her sister's wedding. I didn't really plan it, but we were at the reception, talking about the wedding, and she said what she would like for *her* wedding, and I agreed with what she'd suggested, and... We knew we were ready. It was what we wanted. It was the next logical step, so..."

Ryker's proposal had been much more romantic. Andie pushed that thought aside.

"We got a ring the next week and told her family. I asked her again then so that her sister wouldn't think we'd tried to take any attention away from her wedding."

Andie didn't like the way her hands were fisting. This was not her story. She had no stakes in it, so there was no reason to feel upset. Except something had gone wrong, and it had hurt Trevor.

Trevor didn't speak for a few minutes, and Andie had to clench her jaw shut to restrain herself from asking what had happened. She had no right. Anything Trevor offered was a gift. Trust came to him with difficulty.

"We were going to get married the next winter. Violet wanted a winter wedding, and that worked with my schedule. I was busy getting the firm going, so she did most of the planning. I hadn't worried about the day itself. I was focused on what would come after. The two of us, living together, making our own family.

"The accident at the site happened about six months before the wedding was scheduled. After the accident, I was out of it most of the time. I wasn't in good shape. Violet had to cancel everything related to the wedding, because we had no idea when I was going to be able to walk again. It was a disaster.

"She came by every day, just like a good fiancée should. But once I wasn't lost in a world of painkillers all the time, I could see that she wasn't comfortable."

He rubbed his leg, the one with his prosthetic device. Andie wondered if it bothered him, or if it was a reaction to talking about the accident.

"When it was time to get the prosthetic, she couldn't look at it or the leg that was only partly there. I asked her if there was a problem, but she said there wasn't."

Andie wished she could somehow stop the end she saw coming.

"She was lying. She couldn't deal with it, couldn't handle that I was...damaged, but she was also afraid what everyone would think of her if she broke our engagement after what I'd been through. I couldn't imagine seeing that… repugnance for the rest of my life. So I broke it off."

Andie's hands were fists again. She wanted to hurt that shallow woman who'd not been able to look past a surface injury. She wanted to hurt her for hurting Trevor.

She could read between the lines. He'd trusted the people he'd worked with, and they'd betrayed him. He'd trusted his fiancée, and she'd abandoned him, even if he'd been the one to end things. No wonder trust was such an issue for him. Even his family had allowed him to feel less wanted.

"I could see the relief on her face. She said if I felt that way, it would be best if she returned the ring. She stopped coming by soon after that."

Trevor paused. Andie didn't want him to regret telling her. She wanted him to know that he'd done nothing wrong.

"Please tell me she went for a facial that went badly and scarred her, and she finally asked your forgiveness for being so shallow."

Trevor stopped. Andie paused, as well, wishing she could see his face in the dark.

"Andie, she isn't a bad person. It wasn't all on

her. She tried. She really tried, but she couldn't help the way she felt."

He was so forgiving, just like with his parents. Andie drew a breath, trying to be fair.

"She couldn't help the way she felt, sure, but when you agree to marry someone, you should care for the whole person, not just the superficial parts."

Trevor didn't respond for a moment. "You think 'real' love would accept something like that, like this?"

He pulled up his pant leg, his prosthetic showing in the pale light of the streetlamps. His skepticism came through loud and clear.

Andie let her gaze rest on his leg, neither flinching nor gawking. It didn't freak her out the way he obviously expected. She tried to choose her words carefully. "As far as your leg… It doesn't bother me. I work in the construction industry. We try to be safe, but accidents happen. My grandfather lost a couple of fingers, and my grandmother didn't leave him. In the same accident, my uncle lost his arm. He ended up moving to Arizona and is still there with his wife.

"Things happen in life. Bad things as well as good. You can be hurt or lose your money… And even if you're lucky, if you make it through life without major tragedies like bankruptcy or cancer or an accident on a building site, time is going to happen. Would you have felt differently about her when her hair turned gray or she got wrinkles or had to walk with a cane?

"If you can't handle those things, that's not love. If you love someone, the surface is that, the top layer. But you love the whole person, all the layers. If the surface changes, or one of those inner layers does, the love is still there."

"What if all the layers change? How can you trust that the person will still love them?"

She wasn't sure exactly what he meant. "I… I don't know. To be honest, I've lost track of the metaphor."

She heard him chuckle. It was a quiet sound, but it pleased her. She'd brought him something good after he'd been dwelling on something bad.

"I think you're using the onion metaphor. Only not saying that everyone has so many layers, but that a person needs to love all the layers."

"That's a good thought. Maybe Violet and I never showed each other all those layers. Maybe I never trusted her enough to show her."

Andie thought he'd just shown her more than one, layers he didn't share with many people. Maybe not with anyone. Her chest felt like something was turning over, expanding at the thought that he was trusting her with this.

She wouldn't betray that trust. She wouldn't be another person on the list of people who'd made Trevor feel like he was less, insufficient.

Her mouth opened, ready to say something reassuring, when suddenly, a whistle sounded and light shot through the sky. The fireworks had started.

They stood there, close but not touching, while the bright lights shot through the sky, punctuated with booms, crackles and more whistles. Abigail always put on a good show for the Fourth.

The finale firework lit up the sky, imprinting images on their retinas. They blinked, and their eyes started to grow accustomed to the dark again. Andie drew in a breath, feeling peaceful. Content. Ready to stay here for a long time yet.

"It's getting late," Trevor said.

Andie swallowed. Apparently, she was the only one having a moment. Or maybe Trevor was retreating after sharing with her. She needed to let him take the lead here, on whatever he was comfortable with.

"Let me walk you back to your truck."

Andie didn't want Trevor to feel obligated. If he didn't want to be with her, she'd rather be alone.

"It's not necessary. This is a safe town."

She knew almost everyone, and everyone knew her. Trevor didn't argue, he just waited till she started to move. He didn't speak till they arrived at Bertha.

Andie wasn't sure how to end the evening. Slamming the door and roaring away wasn't a good option.

"Would you like a lift?"

"No, it's only a couple of blocks. Good night, Andie."

"Good night, Trevor."

And that was it. She climbed into Bertha, turned the key, and the engine started immediately. Trevor nodded and headed toward his own place.

As she pulled the truck into the street, she glanced back at the figure almost swallowed up by the dark. He'd opened up to her, and she wasn't going to force anything more. She didn't want him to regret having shared with her.

She also needed to remind herself that he was not her project, not her concern...possibly not even her friend. They'd spent time at the wedding together, but Joey had forced that. They were coworkers, nothing more.

He trusted her now and she wouldn't abuse that trust. The reminder didn't make her feel any better.

THE NEXT MORNING was busy for Kozak Construction. They'd helped set up the park for the wedding, and now everything needed to be torn down, cleaned up and either tossed or put into storage for another event. None of that required Trevor's assistance, and that was good. Really.

Andie picked up Denise later that afternoon. Denise had kicked Don out to spend time with the guys at the Goat. Nelson was there along with a few other people in town for the holiday and the wedding. Denise told him to go be manly while she had her girl time.

Andie drove Denise to what had been a make-out spot in their high school days. At Andie's home, her mother would hover, and at Denise's, her mother would be Deirdre. They wanted somewhere they could be alone and be themselves without worry or disapproval.

Andie pulled a couple of lawn chairs and a cooler out of the back of her truck. They sat in the shade, watching the creek flow by. In daylight, this place didn't attract a lot of attention.

"So Dave is married. My mom is torn between pride at the wedding and disappointment that Dave didn't marry Delaney."

Andie spit out her drink. "What? Dave and Delaney? Delaney Carter? Were they ever even together?"

"Nah, not since that week in high school. But my mom really got her hopes up. She would have been happy for me to go out with Nelson, but that was never going to happen. He and Dave spent too much time together. Nelson is like another brother."

Andie leaned her head back, staring up at the leaves above her. "I remember that now. You were never interested in Nelson?"

Denise shook her head. "What's up with you and Trevor?"

"Nothing." Unfortunately.

"Oh, come on. I heard the two of you disappeared together after we left."

The town was full of busybodies.

"How did you hear that if you were gone?"

"Andie, this is still Carter's Crossing, no matter what they change the name to."

"The joy of small towns. Everyone gossips."

Denise reached her soda can out to touch Andie's. "Not like where we live now. We could die in our bed, and no one would know for days."

"Here, someone would know exactly the last time your door opened and be knocking to see if you'd fallen in the tub."

"Not the worst thing. Well, depending on what you were doing when they knocked. But that still doesn't tell me anything about Trevor."

Andie might as well talk. This was her best friend. "I'm not sure about him myself. We might be friends now."

"Friends?" Denise's eyebrows were inching up to her hairline.

Andie nodded. "We talked last night. He's had some things happen to him. He doesn't trust people much. And I understand. But it makes working with him difficult."

"Hmm." Denise took a drink of soda and let the silence settle.

There was rustling from the leaves and gurgling as the stream ran over stones. Sounds of people were distant. Andie soaked it in and realized she'd miss quiet like this.

"What about school?"

"Dunno." The day was peaceful, and Andie was reluctant to bring up any drama.

"Andie, you need to think about what *you* want for a change. You've been good to your family. All your brothers and your sister have had their chances. You need to take yours now."

Denise was right. Andie knew that. But...

"I know. But my mom still worries all the time and Joey isn't ready to take over."

"Maybe he can't be ready when you're here and everyone knows you're the boss."

Andie had wrestled with that idea. "But what if he makes a mistake?"

"What if he does? You made mistakes, didn't you? That's how you learned."

True. But when she'd been learning, she'd been burdened by the responsibility of her family. She didn't take risks, and she never relaxed. When she'd taken over, she'd been years younger than Joey was now, but he was much less mature than she'd been.

"He seems so immature. And he doesn't push to take over."

"Again, it would be difficult for him to do that when you're around. Maybe he doesn't want to try only to be told he's doing everything wrong."

Andie looked over at her friend. "Have you been eavesdropping on us?"

Denise smiled. "No, I just know you. No one else in your family could have taken over when your dad died. I know that. But you deserve some happiness, too. I'd like to see you find someone, but there's no one here in town, not if we're taking your architect out of the picture, is there?"

"I know. I just… I mean, I wanted to be an architect back in high school, but I'm not sure if I want to start that now. It takes years, and I may be too old."

Denise reached out a lazy hand to swat her. "Don't you dare say you're too old, because

I'm just as old as you are, and I'm still only twenty-two."

Andie snorted. "I think I'm too old to start school now. At least, not something that requires postgraduate work and apprenticing. I don't think I could relax enough to be a student and do nothing else."

"Maybe you should give it a try before you write it off. Spend a year at college. See what it's like. You could even choose a school in Florida… And if you have too much time on your hands, come and babysit."

Andie laughed. "This is all a ploy to get free babysitting?"

Denise reached out a hand for Andie's. "No, it's a ploy to get my best friend the life she deserves. You deserve to do something you want. If you weren't here in Carter's Crossing—"

"Cupid's Crossing now."

Denise rolled her eyes. "Fine, if you weren't here in Cupid's Crossing, your mom couldn't obsess over where you are all the time. You wouldn't have the burden of your family suffocating you. Don't argue. I know you'd rather have your own place. And I will nag you till you get what you want."

"I know. And thanks. I just have to figure out what it is that I want."

"When is this big project with the mill done?"

Andie huffed a breath. "If all goes well, before the end of the year."

"Then, I want you to make some plans for then. If nothing else, take a vacation. When was the last time you left Cart—this place?"

For any amount of time? Years. "I have thought about taking a holiday."

"Does it involve beaches, sunshine and men without shirts to drool over? Don't mind me, I'm not going to have that for a long time once these babies arrive."

Andie smiled at her friend. "It might, if you're having boys. You don't have to bundle them up with shirts down in Florida, right? Though they might be the ones drooling, not me. I thought I'd come down and see you in the fall, maybe help with the new babies?"

Denise sat up. "Are you sure? I mean, I'd love to have you, and I'm panicking about how I'm going to handle two kids, but that doesn't sound like a great vacation."

Andie was serious. She turned in her chair to be sure Denise got what she was saying.

"I can't picture myself taking a solo vacation. If I visited you, I could spend some time thinking about what I want, and maybe if I help with the babies a bit, I can talk it over with you as well as help you out. And you're in Florida. Beaches and sun all the time, right?"

"Totally. They close the borders when clouds roll in."

"I could give Joey a chance to step up, and we can see how he does while I'm away. And you could make sure I don't fuss too much."

Denise cackled. "Oh, I'll keep you busy enough that you won't fuss. But after the mill is done, you need a real break."

"Maybe I can look at schools in Florida while I'm there. Get some ideas."

Denise held out her soda can again, and they clinked. "Good. It's time you did something for yourself, Andie."

It was. If she could just figure out what she really wanted. And she pushed a picture of Trevor out of her head.

CHAPTER SEVENTEEN

TREVOR WASN'T SURE what things were going to be like when they returned to work after the wedding. He had no idea what had gotten into him, sharing intimate details with Andie. For that matter, why had he even agreed to be her plus-one?

He needed to remember that she was his contractor. He didn't need to be her friend. In fact, being her friend made it more difficult to retain that distance required. Friendship assumed trust. He couldn't let down his guard. Except, he already had.

He was trying not to be too overzealous, like he'd promised Abigail, but he needed to be cautious. It wasn't just about Andie. There were other people involved. Any one of them could jeopardize the project, if they wished and weren't monitored.

He was assuming she was totally on the level because he liked her. He'd liked the contractor that screwed him over, as well. Though that contractor had never worn a dress like Andie's blue one.

He didn't sleep well that night, but he made sure to arrive early on Tuesday morning when work on the mill resumed. He was safely behind his desk with his laptop open when Andie came in. He didn't look up right away, afraid she might think...

Might think he'd enjoyed spending time with her. That they were more than coworkers. More than friends.

When he finally looked up, ready to say good morning, Andie was about to head out.

"Sorry, Trevor, I just got a message that Pastern's is delaying the next shipment, so I'll have to deal with them. You must have gotten the message, too."

He'd been so anxious about seeing Andie that he hadn't read his email. "Right. Yes. Let me know how it goes."

Andie left the trailer, and Trevor wanted to bang his head on the desk. It was all too obvious that the problem wasn't Andie.

BY THE END of the week, Trevor had managed to settle their working relationship. At least, he thought so. He'd almost skipped darts night, but Joey had insisted they needed his skill.

He'd planned to sit away from Andie and talk to the others as much as possible.

He hadn't needed to worry. Andie had been sidetracked by Mariah, who was there with Nelson. Since Jaycee and Dave were on their honeymoon, Mariah was there to take Dave's place.

Mariah was the strongest competition Trevor had faced thus far, and she defeated him. Nelson beamed as if he'd had some impact on the win. Mariah didn't want to keep playing after the first round. Instead, she and Andie started a conversation that kept them busy.

On Thursday, they all went to trivia night, and he was no longer worried that Andie might assume too much after their time at the wedding together. It was like it had never happened. She'd been busy, and they hadn't discussed anything that wasn't related to the mill. That was good, he reminded himself. He found himself a little too aware of where she was all the time, but he threw himself into work to squash that.

Despite the Pastern's delay, construction had gone well this week. They were about to open up the wall on the river side of the mill. It was a big event, and the crew had been let go early on Friday afternoon. Andie was finishing up some payroll stuff in the trailer while Trevor was going through the plan for the wall removal again when they heard a car pull into the lot.

The door was open, and fans were spinning to dissipate the heat.

Mariah climbed the steps and stuck her head in. "Can I talk to you two for a minute?"

Andie looked up with a smile. "Sure, Mariah. Want to take a seat?"

Trevor shut his laptop. He'd gone over this process more times than he needed to already. He should have left when the crew did, and he didn't try to decipher why he'd stayed.

"Thanks for all you've done with the photos and video on the mill renovation. It's been great. You saw the first couple of videos I sent you, right?"

Andie nodded. "We're opening up the back wall next week, so we'll be sure to get good coverage of that."

Mariah made a note on her phone. "That's all great, but it's not the main reason I'm here. I have a business thing to ask you, but it's not mill or town business."

Andie pulled out a notebook. Trevor wasn't sure if he was supposed to take notes, as well.

Mariah sighed. "Nelson lost one of his horses yesterday."

Andie looked sympathetic while Trevor wondered how he'd misplaced something that large.

Andie shot him a glance. "Nelson has a farm where he has rescue horses." She looked back at Mariah. "Which one?"

"Sparky."

Andie shook her head. "That was the first one he rescued, right? What happened?"

Mariah blinked rapidly. "Nelson has the medical terms, but mostly, Sparky was just old."

Ah, that kind of lost.

"He's in a bit of a funk about it, so I was wondering if you wouldn't mind going out to the farm."

Trevor froze. He'd never been close to a horse in his life. What was he supposed to do on a farm?

"Does he need company?" Andie looked surprised, as well.

"He needs a distraction. I'd like the two of you to look at the house and tell us if we have to tear the place down and start from scratch or if we should try to salvage it. I know what I think, but I won't try to influence you."

Andie's blinked. "You two plan to live out there?"

"Once we're married." Mariah nodded. "Which reminds me. Do you have an idea when the mill will be done? I know you can't promise, but if nothing unexpected happens, when might we reasonably expect it to be ready?"

Andie turned to him. "I thought maybe the end of October, beginning of November. What do you think, Trevor?"

He frowned. He reviewed the schedule every day and adjusted it for any variables he could possibly imagine impacting their work.

They'd soon be mostly working indoors, and then there was less chance of delays since weather wouldn't be a factor.

"Why don't we say mid-November, just to allow for contingencies?"

Andie nodded. She had undoubtedly been working on her own projected schedule.

"Are you planning your wedding already, Mariah?" Andie teased.

Mariah shook her head. "No, I'm not going to have a big wedding."

Andie raised her eyebrows, and Trevor thought he must show as much surprise on his face as Andie did. After what Mariah had accomplished with Dave and Jaycee's wedding, he'd thought she'd be planning something even more attention grabbing for herself.

"I've seen enough big weddings, and Nelson doesn't like them. We'll do something small when the time comes. I did have an idea for a Christmas wedding for someone else, so it sounds like I can explore that idea."

Andie slid a finger over her lips, and Trevor watched too closely.

"I won't say anything. After all, there are only so many couples in town."

Mariah held in a smile. "I can neither confirm nor deny, but I appreciate your discretion. I need to talk to the couple involved if I decide it'll work. So can you take a look at the house? Then I can bother Nelson about it, and he'll have less time to mope."

Trevor wasn't sure he approved of Mariah's plan, but he was curious to see the place now.

"Are you in, Trevor?" Andie asked.

He nodded. "When would you want to go?"

Andie looked at the papers on her desk. "I can finish this up later if you're free now."

He was just doing busywork. "Probably good to go in daylight. Are you available, Mariah?"

"Oh, I'm not going."

Andie shot Trevor a perplexed glance, and they both looked over at Mariah.

"Don't you want to tell us what you've got planned?"

"Nope. I'm not going to make plans till I know if we're restoring or starting over. I've got other ideas to distract Nelson with for now, then when I hear from you, I'll have that option in hand for when I need it."

Andie had risen to her feet, so Trevor stood. "Are you really planning to do something with the house, or is this just a diversion scheme?"

Mariah's eyes widened. "Oh, we're absolutely going to be moving on to the farm. Nelson won't want to leave the carriage house until Abigail has settled her plans, but if you weren't tied up with the mill right now, we'd already be working on the place."

Trevor was glad to know this wasn't just a distraction, and he was glad of a break. Something new would be good for him.

Mariah waved goodbye and left, having ticked something off on her list.

TREVOR RODE OUT with Andie since she knew where they were going.

"Nelson bought the old Abbott place when he returned to Carter's Crossing and keeps some rescue horses there. The place was falling down, but he got us to help put the barn in shape. He lives in the old carriage house next to Abigail's house right now, but I get why Mariah would like her own place, especially if Abigail makes the house an inn."

"Do you have any idea what condition the

house on the farm is in? What was it like when you worked on the barn?"

Andie scrunched up her nose. "It was pretty bad, if I remember correctly. My guess is that it isn't reclaimable, but we'll see what you think."

Andie slowed to turn onto a smaller county road. The countryside was pretty in the afternoon sun. It was hot enough that Andie was wearing shorts, but Trevor still wore long khakis. Both were wearing T-shirts. The road was shaded by green trees that almost met overhead in some places. Behind the trees were fields. Most had some kind of crop growing, but he'd spotted cattle in one field. Andie signaled and pulled into a driveway.

It had been a gravel drive at some point, but it was mostly dirt now. The weather had been dry, so the drive was rutted and slightly dusty. Ahead, he saw a barn in good condition and a few horses in the field.

On the other side of the driveway was a house. At least, he assumed it had been once upon a time. Andie came to a stop and turned off the truck. Neither said anything.

Trevor had no idea what made Mariah think anything could be renovated here. He turned to Andie and saw she was biting back a grin.

"Shall we get out and take a look so we have a full report for Mariah?"

Trevor stretched a hand toward the house. "There's no way to restore this. You had to know that."

Andie let the grin escape. "It's gotten a lot worse since we were working on the barn. But it's a beautiful day, and I was ready for a break. Maybe we can reclaim some of the timber or something, if they want to try that."

Trevor shrugged, unclipped his seat belt and opened the truck door.

Once out of the truck, he took a moment to look around and drew in a deep breath. The air was fresh and warm, and some kind of insect sounded in the background. A slight breeze moved the leaves of the trees, many of which were now growing close enough to the house to make work there a difficult prospect.

Andie led the way to the building. There had apparently been a verandah out front and two stories, both of which had now fallen into the basement.

Trevor walked carefully over the uneven ground. Around back, the house was even worse. A sapling was growing in the rearmost room, a branch jutting out over what had been a backyard.

"I think this is a demolition job for you, not a renovation for me," Trevor said.

Andie looked at the remains of the farmhouse. "But once we remove the debris, you can start with a blank slate, plan any kind of house here."

He moved in a circle, looking not at the house, but at the surroundings, imagining what he might design. It was only speculation, of course. Mariah and Nelson would have their own ideas as to what the house should look like.

Andie slid to a sitting position under a huge old oak growing in what would have been the home's front yard. Trevor walked around the house, getting an understanding of its size and what it must have looked like previously.

He came back to Andie, who patted the ground beside her. "Sit."

He did, still slightly awkward with his prosthesis.

"Have you designed a lot of houses?"

"I'm always designing houses. Not always for clients. But I need to know the budget and what the owners want before I can start a project."

"But if Nelson and Mariah asked you for suggestions, what would you say?"

He relaxed his head against the tree trunk, enjoying the place, the quiet and the company.

"There are constraints, of course. I doubt Nelson and Mariah want a massive place. If they do, they'll have to overcome some of the landscape. Materials would need to be suitable for this climate."

"Of course, but within reasonable parameters, what would you suggest?"

He let his imagination free. "A mudroom, for coming in from the barn. A big kitchen. An informal place. Bedrooms on the second floor, maybe an attic."

Andie paused, as if imagining what he'd suggested. "What would you do the exterior in?"

"Stone is too heavy for what I'm picturing here."

"Brick?"

He shook his head. "Wood siding. A muted shade that would fit with the trees. Maybe even white."

Silence fell. "Not very progressive or avant-garde."

"This isn't the place for it. There aren't any breathtaking views, and no one is coming here to be impressed. You said Mariah grew up on a boat, and now she wants to stay put. I think she'd want something that looks like home, like you'd see in a movie. Something to match what she'd dreamed of."

Andie nodded. "I think you're right."

"I don't know Nelson, so maybe I'm wrong..."

"I don't think the guy who rescues horses

here is looking for a showplace. Right now, what he wants is to make Mariah happy."

Trevor grew up in the city. This sense of space and quiet, of time passing slowly, and of peace was not something he was used to. His first instinct was usually to compare places to the city and note how the city was superior. Sitting here, that idea took too much effort. He enjoyed just…being.

After a comfortable silence, Andie looked over at him. "Have you ever imagined your dream home? The one you'd want for yourself?"

The corner of his mouth hitched up. "Of course. I'm sure you have, as well."

Andie gave a noncommittal shrug. Didn't matter. He knew he was right.

She shot a glance his way. "What's yours like?"

He stared up into the leafy bower overhead. "When I was a kid, I imagined castles and mansions where I'd have rooms for toys and books. I'm pretty sure I used to have rooms for candy, as well. When I got older, I always focused on the interior, because there's not a lot of space for exteriors in the city. Everything was sleek and smooth and modern, maximizing the space and feeling bigger than it was."

He heard Andie sigh. "I'm going to have to get used to the city, I expect."

He looked over at her. She was gazing up at the leaves, as well.

"Do you want to live in the city?"

She shrugged. "I always thought so. I imagined a place of my own. Not too big, but something I didn't have to share. Our house was always full of people, and during the day, clients and the crew were often there. Now it's hard to imagine giving up space and quiet." Andie paused, as if she'd surprised herself with what she'd just said.

"Not every city is like New York. You might find another place where you can live outside the city but still be close enough for school and work."

"I guess. If you weren't in New York and had space, what kind of place would you design for yourself?"

Trevor knew there were other things he could be doing, though not necessarily should be doing right now, but he was content sitting under a tree talking about dream homes. It didn't matter what had happened on that last job in New York or what Violet had felt.

His time here in Cupid's Crossing was limited, but if it wasn't...

"I'd first want a lot with a view. A river, a

ravine, something. And I'd want to open up part of the house to invite that in."

"Open space, inside and out."

"Mmm-hmm," Andie murmured. "That sounds like more of a showplace."

Trevor pursed his lips. "No, that's not what I want. Think unpainted wood, warm colors—a place that welcomes in people as well as the outdoors."

"Really?" There was no missing the skepticism in her voice. He held in a smile. She was right.

"Okay, I wouldn't want that many people. But I'd want a place that could be comfortably lived in." There was a pause. It was time to flip the script. "What about you?"

He watched her face as she puzzled it out. Her brow creased and then smoothed. There was a ghost of a smile, and she bit her lip.

"Peaceful. That's what I'd like. A creek, maybe, instead of a river. But the open spaces, if they aren't cold and empty, sound good. We're all squished in small rooms at our place."

Trevor felt a warm flutter in his chest. It was silly. They were talking about a home that would never exist. He wasn't building a place here, and Andie wasn't, either. But he liked that she embraced his vision.

Quiet and peaceful. That sounded like a

great base for a home. Not that there wouldn't be noise from people living in it, but it would be an oasis from the rest of the world. That was it. A safe place to recharge to face the world again.

Something inside clicked. That's what he wanted. When he got his life back together, he needed that kind of space. But not an oasis for one.

For so long after Violet, he hadn't opened his mind to the possibility of having someone again. Surely there was someone out there who would be interested in an introvert who could play darts and had a prosthetic leg.

The sun was warm on his face as the trees rustled overhead. This town, where he'd come because he didn't have other options, was providing him with a safe haven while he finished healing.

This year in a small town was helping more than his reputation.

CHAPTER EIGHTEEN

ANDIE HAD BEEN counting down till her vacation in Florida, date set now that Denise had given birth to twin girls. Work on the mill was going smoothly. With Trevor looking over everything, making her more careful, things were going almost scarily well.

There were occasional hiccups. Supplies that came late. Inspections that lagged. But she'd built a buffer into her time budget, and they were still on track. They might finish just before the end of October, but she and Trevor had agreed not to mention it to Mariah again in case she planned a Halloween event that might need to be delayed.

The biggest challenge had been opening up the back wall so that the large event space was lit up and offered a view over the stream and hillside. Again, they'd planned and checked things over and over, and it had gone off without a hitch. The big glass doors and new larger windows were installed with shutters for protection and to shut out the exterior as needed.

Andie thought that even Trevor was almost relaxed. They'd worked together on the trickiest part of the whole renovation and it had gone perfectly.

Perfectly enough that she was willing to leave Joey in charge while she went away. All the supplies were ordered, the plans of what needed to be done while she was away were laid out, simple and easy. It was a perfect opportunity for Joey to step up and show he could lead the company.

Maybe she should knock on wood, in case it was too perfect.

Now, just before Andie left on her vacation, Abigail and Mariah were standing in front of the new glass doors in the mill, obviously impressed. Andie showed them how the doors opened.

The exterior area in front of the doors, where they planned a patio, wasn't finished yet, but that was a fairly simple project, especially compared to the work involved in installing the doors.

"You've done an incredible job," Abigail said.

"This is even better than I'd pictured." Mariah had accepted the verdict on the farmhouse without a flinch. Andie wasn't sure exactly what she'd said to Nelson, but Trevor would be meeting with them while she was away to discuss designing a new place for the two of them.

"What is the crew doing while you're in Florida, Andie?"

Abigail might not micromanage the project, but she kept up on everything.

"There's the patio here and out back behind the kitchen. We also want to get the portico done before there's any chance of bad or cold weather, and the exterior cladding."

Abigail smiled. "Yes, the unpredictable autumn weather."

"Then we can wrap up the finishes inside and should be done about when we'd hoped."

Abigail nodded. "Give Denise my congratulations when you see her. And try to enjoy yourself, as well. You've worked hard and deserve a vacation."

It was true. She did deserve a break. But while she was looking forward to seeing Denise and spending some time in a bathing suit rather than a hard hat, she was also looking forward to coming back.

She didn't want to consider all the reasons why that might be. Why she was reluctant to go. But she couldn't banish the image of the man she'd been working with.

Abigail and Mariah left, which left just her and Trevor.

"Are you worried about leaving Joey in charge?" he asked.

He must have picked up on something.

"It's stupid, I know. He's overseen most of the work on the B and Bs and the demolition of the house at Nelson's farm. But I've always been close by."

The corner of Trevor's mouth quirked. "You know I'll still be here."

"True." It was an indication of how far they'd come that they could joke about this.

They'd become...friends since that day out at the farm. They worked together weekdays and played together at darts night and trivia night with the rest of the crew. They had fallen into a routine of working on photos and video of the mill renovation together, and on the weekends, Andic showed Trevor some of the area, especially any interesting buildings.

He watched her, eyes keen behind his glasses.

"I thought you'd be a little more excited about taking a vacation."

She was, really. "I am. I mean, Florida, my best friend, not wearing a hard hat..."

"Those are all good things."

She nodded. "It's just...when Denise was here, we talked about what I was going to do after the mill is done. Soon it'll be time for Joey to take over Kozak, and for me to finally do what I want to do. I'm supposed to make plans for college."

She should be more excited about it. Instead, it felt like one more chore.

"Are you having second thoughts?"

She parsed his response for meaning. Was he judging her? Doubting her?

"I don't know. It's been so long, it's like I've forgotten how to be excited about it."

Trevor stood in front of her. "Is this a temporary, distracted loss of excitement, or is the excitement completely gone?"

She blinked at him. "How could it be gone? It's my dream. Those first years, when it was so difficult to keep the company going, I imagined attending classes and learning how to design beautiful buildings. I had sketches I worked on when I had free time. That got me through."

Trevor was still watching her, eyes intent behind the glasses. "I don't know if your dream is gone, but maybe it's…changed?"

"Yours hasn't."

He nodded. "That's true, but not everyone wants to be the person they imagined themselves being back when they were eighteen."

Andie paused. Those words hit something inside. She'd grown a lot in the last decade, almost fifteen years. Had her dreams changed? Really? Or was she just giving up? She couldn't imagine being a quitter. She'd never backed down from a challenge.

"Do the dreams really change, or do those people just give up?"

Trevor shrugged. "Some may give up. Some may have to acknowledge their dreams aren't realistic. Some may achieve their dreams and find they aren't what they wanted. And some people change, and their dreams don't fit them anymore."

The last sentence had a trace of bitterness. Was he thinking of his dream of his own architecture firm? Or of the fiancée who couldn't accept how he'd changed?

"How do you know if you've changed or just given up?"

"Maybe that doesn't really matter. Maybe the important thing is that you find what the dream is for the person you are now."

The conversation was approaching deep waters, and Andie wasn't sure she was ready to swim. She forced a smile.

"So you're telling me I should reconsider getting that Oscar?"

"I'm sorry." Trevor stepped back. "This isn't my business."

Andie hadn't meant to offend him. She'd

wanted to change the subject because of her own fear, not because she didn't appreciate and value what he was saying. Those words of his would have an impact on what she would decide to do.

She reached out and grasped his wrist. "No, I'm sorry. I appreciate what you said. It's just a little scary to think about big changes like that. I've had a plan for most of my life, and suddenly, I may have the rest of my life in front of me with no idea what to do with it."

He didn't break her hold. "It can be scary. But maybe it can be a little freeing? You don't have those limits anymore. Imagine doing anything you want."

Andie wasn't sure how they'd wound up so close. She could see the flecks of color in his irises, a bit of stubble he'd missed while shaving and that his lips were slightly parted. He was staring at her, and his words, *anything you want*, were circling in her brain. Suddenly, she was kissing him.

And he was kissing her back.

Andie had no idea why they were doing this, but her hands were gripping his T-shirt. She was tightly pressed against him, his arms around her waist, pulling her closer. He turned his head, and the angle was better, and she went up on tiptoe because she'd never had a kiss that felt like this. Like her center was burning while her skin pebbled with a chill that had nothing to do with the temperature.

She didn't know how long they spent kissing, pausing only for breath before meeting lips again. But eventually, they pulled apart, chests heaving, eyes wide, and reality slipped back in.

Trevor stepped back, clearing his throat. His hair was mussed, his shirt showing creases from where she'd gripped it. And his lips— No, she couldn't look at his lips, swollen with their kisses, without wanting to launch herself at him again. Andie dropped her gaze.

"I'm sorry—" she started. What had come over her?

He was staring at her, his brow furrowed. "We can't... We can't do this. Not when we work together."

Heat rolled over her cheeks, spreading down her neck. "I know. I won't do it again. I'm sorry."

Trevor was in front of her somehow, hand on her chin, tilting her head up. "It was incredible, but we can't be involved, not when we're working the way we are."

Could he not let this go? She was mortified.

"I understand, Trevor. I don't know what happened, but I won't kiss you again."

Her eyes dropped, unable to meet his.

"As long as we know this will never be repeated…" His breath hitched, and suddenly his lips were on hers again, and she wrapped herself tightly against him, determined to enjoy it while she could.

Everything had to end sometime. Even incredible kisses. When they finally pulled away, Andie could feel her lips, swollen, and her legs, shaking as they supported her.

Dusk settled as they left the mill. They didn't break the silence, because there was nothing to say. Andie let Trevor lock the doors, and they each went to their own vehicle.

She didn't know how to speak to him, what to say. The good part was that she was leaving the day after tomorrow. Tomorrow wasn't a workday, so she didn't have to face him.

Hopefully, by the time she came back from Florida, she'd have a better idea of how she felt, and what she might want to do about it.

She remembered his words about dreams, that facing a new one could be freeing. Would Trevor be part of a new dream? The mill would be done in a couple more months.

What happened after that?

"I'M SORRY. CAN YOU repeat that?"

Trevor found himself using that phrase more

often than he ought. He couldn't concentrate like he normally did.

All because of Andie and those kisses.

At first, he'd thought it a good thing that she was in Florida. They needed time and space to get back to their working relationship. He refused to work with someone he was involved with. The risk of trouble was too great. It was just a terrible idea. And yet he couldn't forget the kisses.

It shouldn't have been a problem. It wasn't like he'd never kissed a woman before. He hadn't dated that many women—he was somewhat shy—but he had gone out with women, and he'd been engaged to Violet.

Undoubtedly, it was some combination of forbidden fruit and the friendship he and Andie had developed that made it so...

No, he wasn't thinking about it again.

His phone ringing gave him an excuse to pull his attention from his desperate attempt to follow what Joey was saying about something they were going to do with the portico.

That *something* was exactly what he should be focusing on, since it was part of his job, something that kissing Joey's sister was not.

"Trevor Emerson."

Joey waved and left the trailer, giving him some privacy.

"Trevor, it's Howard. How are things going out in the woods there?"

Trevor relaxed in his seat. A call from Howard was just what he needed. "Things are going well."

Incredibly well.

"Good to hear. Nothing like the last job?"

Trevor's thoughts wandered to Andie again, but he shook it off.

"No, this contractor is honest and doing good work."

"But you're keeping an eye on him, right?"

"It's a *her*, not a *him*, and I am."

Howard whistled. "Let me guess, fifty and able to bench-press you if she wanted."

There was silence as Trevor tried to find words to explain Andie. "Um, not fifty."

Howard cleared his throat. "So, she's pretty?"

Trevor was defensive. "Yes, but she knows her job."

"Just don't take anything for granted."

"Thank you, but I of all people understand the importance of keeping on top of what my contractor is doing."

Howard sighed. "I'm just worried about you."

Trevor rubbed his eyes under his glasses. "I know. I'm sorry. I hope with some time people can see me without that accident being the first thing they think of."

"You're right. And I actually called you about a job."

Trevor's mood lifted. He was hoping the finished mill would be good for his reputation, but it wasn't done yet. He hadn't had a good prospect in ages. There were some projects here in Cupid's Crossing, and he'd wondered if he should stay a little longer. Going back to New York City was a little daunting.

"My boss has a buddy who's moving to the East Coast and is looking to build a place—big and splashy. He wants to impress everyone. I talked you up, and they want your number."

The light feeling grew.

"I'm not done here for almost two months."

"Guy still has to close on this lot he wants to buy, but he's excited to start, and I've told him you're someone who can design his house and that you'll be a new discovery. Impress his friends that way."

"Then, give him my number."

This was absolutely what he needed, wanted.

"He's going to be in New York next week. Can you meet him there?"

Trevor quickly scanned his calendar.

The portico was going up next week. Joey should be able to handle that. It wasn't as tricky a thing as opening the wall had been.

Trevor had been watching Andie and Joey

closely, and everything had been fine. He could miss a few days.

"Sure. I'll be there."

TREVOR RELAXED IN his hotel room. The tension eased out of his shoulders as the day replayed in his head.

The interview with the lead Harold had gotten him had gone well. It wasn't a done deal, but the man, Oscar, had expressed admiration for some of the work he'd done and found the mill project to be quite interesting.

They'd discussed what the property Oscar and his partner were purchasing was like and what they wanted in their home.

They were talking to other architects, but they'd talked to him as if they were already working together, so there was a fair chance he'd get this job. It would be a good one. It would put him back in the middle of things.

He should be a lot happier about it, but New York City felt more busy, noisy and smelly than usual. He'd grown up here, lived here all his life, and now he didn't feel a part of it.

He'd grown accustomed to Cupid's Crossing. The quiet and the space had been new to him, but it had all been a relief. He was slow to make friends, but in Cupid's Crossing, people knew him. They didn't wait for him to reach out. They drew him in. It made him feel a part of the place.

He considered calling someone he knew, maybe even his family, to let them know he was here for the evening. Instead, he sat and watched the dark shadow the room. The person he wanted to talk to was Andie, but that was wrong.

He'd talked to Andie about her dreams and what she might want in the future, but he was at a crossroads, as well. He wanted to keep his own firm. To have the chance to design and implement his vision. He'd never thought about doing that outside New York.

He'd considered the job in Cupid's Crossing a detour. A temporary diversion that he would accept because it would bring him back to where he'd started, to where he belonged.

Now, when he had a chance to return, he wasn't sure he belonged here in the city anymore.

Was it the location? Was he more suited for a quiet place? Or were Andie and those kisses messing up his perceptions? How did he feel about her?

He wouldn't change his future for her, would he?

He shook his head. No, Andie was nice enough. She was one of the best contractors he'd worked with. She took care of her family, sacrificed herself for others, was kind, pretty, could kiss like—

His phone rang, disturbing his train of thought. He was grateful for that until he answered the call and heard what had happened while he was gone.

"Go spend some time at the beach, girl."

Denise had bags under her eyes, mysterious substances all over her shirt, and her hair was partly braided, partly in a ponytail and all a disaster.

"Nope. I've seen what some of those women look like in bikinis, and I can't compete. I'm better off here." Andie leaned over and carefully picked up Twin One from her friend's arms.

"You go have a shower and a nap until these two need you again."

Denise sighed and then shrugged. "I should argue, but I can't. Bless you."

The twins were cute, and when they were asleep, they were totally adorable, but they didn't sleep all the time and not often at the same time. Denise and Don had looked exhausted when Andie arrived a week ago, and despite her assistance, they still did.

Don stumbled in from the kitchen with Twin Two, also mercifully asleep in the baby carrier.

Andie kept her voice low. "Don, I just sent

Denise to shower and sleep. Why don't you leave Two with me, and you do the same?"

He shot a glance at Twin Two and gave a longing look at the hallway to the bedrooms.

"I shouldn't leave you."

"Come on. I know these are the two most precious humans on the face of the planet, but I can handle them while they're sleeping. I can even change diapers. You guys won't let me help at night, and you need to sleep or you're going to fall over."

The torn look in his eyes was almost funny. Then she saw him lose the battle with his manners.

"Thanks, Andie. But call if you need me."

Andie nodded, determined to let them sleep for as long as she could. She was glad she'd come, not because she was getting a beach vacation, but because her friend needed the help.

Denise's mom, Deirdre, had moved from Cupid's Crossing to Florida to be near her grandbabies. Despite that, she was too busy to help much, so the two parents were running themselves ragged.

Twin Two stirred in the carrier. Andie set Twin One down carefully and picked Two up. She rocked her slowly the way Denise and Don did.

"Hey there, cutie. You're not going to cry

now, are you? You wouldn't do that to your mom and dad. They need some sleep."

The bleary eyes turned her way. Over the past week, the twins had become accustomed to her voice, and they now accepted her.

Andie stood up and jiggled Two as she walked around the living room. After getting #One and #Two cloth pins and tags to identify each twin, they were now being called by the numbers. Once Denise and Don got sleep, Andie knew they'd be able to decide on names.

"So, Two, can you help me here? I was supposed to talk with your mom, but you've made her too tired. Since that's your fault, you owe me."

Twin Two made faces. Andie sniffed to see if the baby needed another diaper change, but when that was clear, she continued her chat.

"I have a bit of a problem, Two. I don't know what I'm going to do with myself. Now, you're not worried about your future yet, but the time will come. If you help me, I promise I'll help you."

The baby blinked.

"I'm taking that as a yes. So do I finally get those applications in to school to be an architect? Huh?"

She paused, but Two just stared back at her.

"Or should I consider something different?"

The baby blanket was flopping over the baby's face, so Andie used a finger to push it back. Two gripped Andie's finger in a tight hold.

"You think I need to look at other options, right? I think you're on to something. But what should I do? Go to school and see if there's something else I want to do?"

The baby blew bubbles.

"You're right again. That's wasting money. But what else? Should I just keep doing what I'm doing?"

The tiny arms thrashed.

"I'm sorry, Two, but you need to do better than that. I don't know if you're disagreeing or agreeing with me on that one."

The baby yawned.

"Oh, I'm boring you, am I? Nice."

The tiny eyes closed, and the baby drifted off to sleep again.

Andie kept walking.

What if she did keep doing what she'd been doing? Would that be a good life?

She couldn't keep on exactly as she was. If she was staying in Cupid's Crossing and taking on the responsibility of Kozak Construction permanently, she had to find her own place to live. Somewhere totally separate from where her mom and brother lived.

There were a lot of projects being discussed for the new and improved Cupid's Crossing. There would plenty of work for the company. But what about Joey? If she stayed, what would he do? Could they share being in control of Kozak Construction?

Would he want to?

She suspected he might like to be free of that. But this was supposed to be her turn to go. Her turn to chase her dream.

Walking around this house, chaotic as it was, made it obvious to Andie that her dream included this—a home, a spouse, children. She might have to sacrifice that to become an architect if she was starting at this late date.

Did she want to return to school, to start over, to go back to books and classes after having been in charge of her own business for so long?

When she'd stepped up to replace her father, she'd hated it. Hated not knowing the answers to questions, hated making mistakes, hated the responsibilities.

But that had changed. She knew most of the answers now, and she didn't make mistakes. Responsibility was a burden, but she also didn't have to listen to someone she didn't agree with and do what they told her to do. Being the person making the decisions was part of her now.

She wasn't happy with her life as it was, but that wasn't because of her job. She didn't dread going to work in the mornings, and she didn't escape home the first chance she had.

The part she didn't like was her personal life. She'd been reluctant to move out, since it signified that she was giving up on school. But if she did, if she had her own place, then Cupid's Crossing was a good place to live.

Trevor.

There was a different issue.

She wasn't sure what they were to each other now. Not after the kisses. She couldn't deny she had feelings for him.

Would he be part of her future? With a pang, she realized he wouldn't be. Whether she stayed in Cupid's Crossing or not, she didn't see a future for them. He would go back to New York City, and she couldn't picture herself there. She was used to space, and there wasn't a lot of that in a big city.

If people came to Cupid's Crossing, maybe she could find someone else. Someone who'd like a contractor with an overdeveloped sense of responsibility and a mother who worried too much.

She decided to let the idea percolate, and if she had a chance to talk to Denise before she left, they'd discuss it.

The idea felt good. Cupid's Crossing was going to come back to life, and being part of it held a lot of appeal.

She carefully set down Twin Two, relaxing when the baby stayed sleeping. Andie picked up her phone to check what was going on in the world while the babies slept. Right now, her goal was to give her friends their own time to rest. Nothing she saw was that interesting.

She was starting to doze when the ring of her phone woke her and Twin One. She answered, hoping for a quick call and a chance to settle One down so that Denise and Don could sleep a little longer.

When her mom told her Joey was in the hospital, she knew that wasn't going to happen.

CHAPTER NINETEEN

TREVOR STOOD IN front of the disaster that had been the portico on the mill.

It had collapsed, with Joey Kozak underneath it. Joey was in the hospital. The mill had been taped off while they figured out what had gone wrong.

It was all too familiar.

Accidents happened on work sites. Workers slipped, cut themselves, fell, knocked things over. Since construction sites were full of large materials and tools, those little accidents had consequences. That stuff happened.

A building, or part of it, collapsing? That was different. That meant something had gone wrong with the design or the materials or the process.

It was a small accident in a small town, but something had collapsed with a human underneath, and Trevor had to shove his hands in his jacket pockets to prevent them from shaking.

He couldn't believe it had happened again. He'd been so careful.

He'd been less vigilant lately because of Andie. He'd been thinking too much about her and not enough about the job. Obviously. The evidence was in front of him.

He couldn't give up his dream for her. No matter what she'd done, deliberately or not, the result was another of his projects had a structural problem, and there'd been another serious injury. Thank goodness it hadn't been worse.

There would still be an inquiry. Last time, he'd been in the hospital and hadn't been able to give his side, and he'd been blamed. He wasn't taking the blame this time.

His phone rang. He was sure it would be Andie, and he had no idea what to say to her. But when he checked the name, it was Harold.

He hoped Harold hadn't heard about this. If it got through to these potential new clients… His stomach dropped.

He almost missed the call, between his hesitation and the shaking in his hands, but he managed to say hello before it went to voicemail.

"Trevor, you okay?"

That jolted him. If Harold was asking how he was, then somehow the information was out there. With Trevor's name attached.

"I'm fine. Why are you asking?"

"My boss saw something about a wall collapsing on a construction site in a place called Cupid's Crossing. That's where you are, right?"

Trevor nodded and said yes.

"Is it your site? Who got hurt? My boss is asking, worried about that referral he gave you."

No. Trevor couldn't have this happening again.

"Harold, it's my site, yes. But it's not me. It's something the contractor did. I don't know what. I was in New York meeting those clients, but you can tell them it was a contractor issue."

"Are you serious? How can that happen to you again?"

For a moment, Trevor wondered if it was him. Had he done something?

No. He hadn't done anything in New York, and he hadn't here. He'd gone through those plans over and over again.

This wasn't his fault.

"The contractor is the only local outfit, and the owner insisted on them. The head of the company is out of town, and her brother is in charge. He must have been the one to mess up. He's also the one who was hurt."

"Will he be okay? Was anyone else hurt?"

Trevor's hand clenched the phone. "Word is he's going to make a full recovery, and no one else was involved."

"That's a relief. I'll talk to my boss. Reassure him. Small-town contractor, didn't know their stuff, and you won't work with them again. That should cover it."

Trevor opened his mouth. He was about to say that it wasn't Andie's fault and that he'd happily work with her again. But she wasn't going to stay to run the company, so it didn't matter. He was going back to New York City, and she wasn't.

Harold and his boss wouldn't have any impact on Andie and Kozak Construction here in Cupid's Crossing. He let it go. Right now, he needed to protect his own future.

This wouldn't do any real damage to Andie. And the chances were good that it was Joey's fault. Something obviously had gone wrong, but not on Trevor's watch.

The blame would fall on Joey, not Andie. Andie hadn't taken shortcuts, but she had left Joey in charge. When it was your company, the buck stopped with you. That's what she'd said.

He didn't want to do anything to hurt her. If he'd only stayed here instead of going to New York.

If word of this got back to his client, if they heard it might be his fault, he'd lose that job. He might not ever get another.

And Kozak Construction?

This town would take care of them. It was probably Joey's fault, and that would have some impact, but Andie would be okay. People here loved and trusted her. They didn't feel that way about him.

He filed the necessary reports and met the investigator. He did his best to start the investigation with Joey, what he'd been doing and how.

This time, no one was blaming Trevor first. Of course, that meant they were blaming Joey instead.

ANDIE WAS RELIEVED to find a flight home leaving only a few hours after she received the phone call. She didn't know the whole story, but her mother had told her there'd been an accident at the mill, and Joey was in surgery.

Fortunately, the flight was short. Once she landed, her mother assured her that Joey was in recovery. Andie met her at the hospital where she was still waiting for Joey to wake up.

He regained consciousness the next day, and Andie was finally able to get her mother to go home with her.

After some sleep, she managed to pull her focus from worried sister to contractor. That was when she got the details.

Reports needed to be filed within twenty-four hours of the accident. With Joey being hospitalized, that was Andie's job. Since she'd been in Florida, on her way home and then in the hospital waiting to find out if Joey would be alright, Trevor had filed the report.

Trevor had met with the OSHA investigator. At first, she'd felt only relief that her inaction while she was dealing with her family hadn't led to any delays in procedure, but as members of the crew stopped by or called for word on Joey, they also shared what had happened with Trevor and the investigator.

Trevor had immediately placed the blame on Kozak Construction. It was inevitable and understandable, but it still hurt her deeply.

There were a limited number of things that could have caused this, but Trevor had immediately steered the investigator to Kozak Construction.

She understood that he wanted to protect himself after last time. But still. The materials from the supplier could have been defective. That wouldn't have put the blame on either of them, but because of what had happened to him, he'd immediately blamed her company.

She remembered how suspicious and defensive he'd been when he first arrived. But she'd thought they'd learned to trust each other since then. They'd talked to each other, become friends. And then…those kisses. Those kisses hadn't meant that much, it seemed.

He'd told her they couldn't do that, be like that. She wondered how long it had taken before he'd decided she'd kissed him to get away with something. She hoped she was wrong, but she was too afraid that she was right.

She didn't see or talk to Trevor for the first couple of days. She had to deal with work-related things, and she was spending the rest of her time in the hospital. She was there when the investigators came to talk to Joey.

There was a man and woman with laptops and serious expressions. They struggled with how to handle Andie and Joey. Normally, they preferred to interview witnesses without the employer being present. But Andie was the sister of the person injured, and Joey had been the employer at the time he was hurt.

Andie got to stay, but she had to promise to be quiet.

Joey had been alone when the portico collapsed. He explained that he'd gone to look at how it was holding up. There'd been some strong winds. He'd heard a crack, and he didn't remember much after that.

The investigators had already done a lot of work. Undoubtedly, Trevor had helped them find the paperwork relating to the building of the portico.

It was supposed to be a simple job, but… Joey had messed up. It was all too heartbreakingly obvious. There'd been a shortage of what they needed. Joey had decided to get what he could from a vendor Andie had stopped dealing with. They had promised they had an equivalent product, and Joey had accepted their word. The "equivalent" product hadn't met specs, but waiting for more materials would mean the project would fall behind. Since they were starting to nudge at the top of their budget, he thought it would save there, as well.

Andie bit her lip, but it was hard. She was angry at Joey and disappointed. She didn't understand why he hadn't realized what an obviously bad idea it was.

Joey was pale, but he answered the questions unflinchingly. Andie was just grateful her mother wasn't present. Andie had relieved her of watch duty and sent her to catch up on some sleep.

The investigators finished by asking Andie questions. She had some documents to send through to them, but the conclusion was foregone at this point.

The investigators had just left when their

mother returned. Andie couldn't hold her tongue any longer.

"Joey, I'm sorry, but what made you think you could ignore the specs we had?"

"He's in no condition for you to grill him like this, Andie." Her mother put a hand on his shoulder, standing between her two children.

"Mom, if he could talk to the investigators, he can talk to me."

"He needs his rest. You're upsetting him."

Andie counted to ten. "He made a stupid decision, one that put him in the hospital, and one that messed up our biggest job and damaged our company's reputation."

"He's too young for this."

"I took over the company when I was younger than him. He's never going to grow up if you don't let him accept some responsibility for what he does."

"I almost lost him."

"And I want to make sure he understands so that he doesn't do anything like this again."

They were arguing in whispers.

"Of course he won't."

"Yes, well, I didn't think he'd be that idiotic to begin with, but here we are."

"It's not his fault."

"Mom, the investigators were just here. It is *totally* his fault."

Her mother burst into tears, and Andie walked out before she said anything more. She leaned against the wall just outside the room, struggling to control her temper.

"She's right, Mom," she heard Joey say.

Sniffles. "You just rest. Forget about that."

"Jeez. I'm telling you she's right. I thought, I dunno, thought I'd impress everyone by finding a shortcut. It's my fault it happened."

"Shush, now. You probably hit your head and didn't know it."

"I didn't hurt my head. Andie's right. I made a mistake. I don't think I'm cut out for this. When I get out... I'm going to leave."

"What? You can't leave." Her mother's voice was shocked.

"Why would I stay? Everyone is gonna know it was my fault. Smitty was saying he could get me a job in Syracuse. Maybe I'll go there."

"You can't leave me, Joey!"

"I'm not *leaving* you. I'm just finding a job somewhere else. There's nothing else to do in Cupid's Crossing."

"But what if something happens?"

"Something just did happen, Mom. And it's my fault. You need to get your own life, you know?"

"You're my life. You and your siblings."

"We're adults now. You have to let go."

Andie stepped back into the room. "You're upsetting Mom, Joey."

Her brother was sitting up in his bed, eyes flashing, cheeks flushed. Their mother was on the verge of more tears. For the first time since the investigators had shown up, he met Andie's gaze.

"I'm done tiptoeing around everything because we can't upset Mom. I want to live my life, and I can't do it here. I'm sorry, Andie, but I'm not you. I can't run the company, and I'm tired of trying. It's not what I want. It's never been what I wanted."

The words resonated. It was what she'd suspected.

"Mom, I think we should let Joey rest. You're right, we're upsetting him."

Andie managed to lead their mother away.

"It's just the accident, Andie. He'll be back to himself soon."

Andie would normally agree with her to protect her. But denying what was obvious hadn't helped with Joey, and she needed to prepare her mother. She wouldn't be surprised if Joey did what he'd said.

He needed to find himself, and he wasn't going to in Cupid's Crossing.

"Mom, you need to be ready in case he does leave."

"He can't! You're leaving, and I'll have no one."

Andie sat her down in a seat in the waiting room. "Whether we move out of town or not, you still have us. We're still your children. But Joey is right that you need to have your own life. I may not go away to school, but if I stay in Cupid's Crossing, I'm going to get my own place. I need my own life, too."

Her mother's mouth was open, eyes blinking back tears. "You'd move out? But how will I know if you're safe?"

Andie grabbed her mother's hand. "Mom, you need to see someone. A counselor or a therapist. You worry too much. After Dad died, you said you could handle things on your own, but you're not.

"I understand that you were worried about us after Dad, but it's been a long time. We're grown up now, and you should have your own things to worry about, your own life to live. Maybe you just need a bit of help so you can let Joey and me go."

Her mother was still crying when they got home. Andie desperately needed to talk to someone, but she didn't know anyone to call. Denise was overwhelmed with the twins. Her siblings were all far away, except for Joey in the hospital.

She couldn't talk to Trevor, because he was one of the problems. She had no idea what she was going to face in the morning when she got to work. She was so anxious about what would happen tomorrow that she couldn't settle down to do anything.

She got in her truck, drove out of the yard and found herself at the mill. She stopped just inside the driveway.

There was a pile of rubble in front of the mill—the remains of the portico. They'd have to clear that away. They'd be behind schedule and over budget.

Her mind started scheduling, budgeting, seeing how they'd get things done. They'd have to restock on materials, and they'd need to do it fast.

She needed to talk to Abigail. Abigail was a smart businesswoman, and Andie was sure she'd give Kozak a chance to make up for this. Abigail knew the company was important to the town, and Abigail knew Joey. Kozak would bear the additional costs, and Andie would commit to finishing the project as they'd planned.

Joey was not going to take over the company. Andie would need to remain here if the company was to stay alive, and she was okay with that.

More than okay. She wanted this.

She'd find her own place here in Cupid's Crossing instead of waiting to start her life when she left for school. She was used to being the boss, and she enjoyed her job. She'd embrace that now and start making the life she had the life she wanted. The essentials were all here—work she enjoyed, people she knew, space and community.

It wouldn't include Trevor, and that brought a stab of pain. But the incident with the investigation had proven that he wasn't a part of her community. He'd put himself first. He needed his reputation untainted so he could return to New York City and live his dream life.

Despite the kisses, they didn't have any bond, not like she'd hoped. No feelings, no connection, no relationship. No future.

How could she be disappointed? She'd built up castles out of sand. But somehow, it still gutted her.

She hoped Trevor didn't think she was going to make any presumptions based on their kisses. No, they were business associates, and that was all. She'd make sure to act in such a way that he knew that. It was bad enough that she had to apologize for her brother's behavior. She didn't need any "talk" where he explained to her that they were only coworkers.

She might be ready to make Kozak her career now, but these next few weeks were going to be bad.

TREVOR GOT TO the site while it was still dark, an hour before there was a chance anyone else would show up. He wanted to be inside, behind his desk, laptop shielding him, before he saw Andie.

He owed her an apology. He'd been too quick to jump to conclusions. He'd been right but also wrong.

It *was* Joey.

Trevor had carefully listed the specs for all the materials for the mill, including the portico. The supplier had been short on what they needed, and Joey had accepted an inferior product from another supplier.

Trevor looked at the paperwork and was horrified at the laxity. It was obvious to him that the substitution would never have worked. He was sure Andie would have known, as well.

It all came out when the results of the investigation were announced. This time, Trevor wasn't blamed. There'd be no blot on his record.

He should be relieved. He'd done nothing wrong, but there was a lot of guilt behind the relief. He had lashed out and blamed Kozak

Construction before any of this was known. He hadn't said anything that was wrong. He'd been justified and correct in assessing the problem. Harold told him his boss had passed on word to the prospective clients.

He shouldn't feel guilty. But he did. He'd left Cupid's Crossing to see a potential new client after he'd told Andie he'd be here with Joey. If he had stayed, this wouldn't have happened.

His job wasn't to babysit Joey, but he'd known Joey wasn't reliable the way Andie was. Then he'd blamed Joey first thing. That kept him awake at night and away from the people he'd come to know here in Cupid's Crossing.

He hadn't heard a word from Andie or any of the Kozaks. Work on the site was halted, so he didn't need to go to the mill. He didn't want to be with anyone. He was afraid to see blame coming from the people around town, people he'd come to know and like. Last time, even those who knew him well had turned away from him. What could he expect in this small town?

He wasn't one of their own.

The site had been cleared, so they could resume work. He had to face the crew he'd been working with. And Andie. Joey wasn't out of the hospital yet, so it would be Andie.

He hadn't tried to reach her, and she hadn't tried to reach him. That said it all.

He pretended to bury himself in work, but he was listening for the sound of her truck. When he finally heard the rumble of tires, he found his hands clenching, his palms sweaty.

Her truck door slammed shut. He knew that heavy thump. He heard footsteps heading to the front of the mill.

More vehicles pulled in, and greetings were exchanged. He couldn't hear the words, but he could imagine there were questions about Joey and how he was doing. Questions about the mill and the job. He heard her voice, and he imagined she was assigning responsibilities.

Was she avoiding him?

There were footsteps on the steps to the trailer. He woke his laptop and focused his gaze on his screen. The door opened. His posturing was in vain, because he couldn't resist looking up.

For a moment, he just looked at her, at the direct gaze he was used to, the hair mussed by the helmet, the familiar work garb. But there was no warmth in her gaze today, and he shivered.

Right. He'd done that.

He opened his mouth, but she was quicker than he was.

"I apologize for what Joey did. Kozak will bear the cost of redoing the work, and it will be done right. I've told the crew you'll want to oversee everything they do, and they understand. They're putting in some extra hours, so you may want to hang around to make sure they do it correctly."

Trevor knew how inviting someone in to micromanage the work she was doing would cost her. And surprisingly, he didn't feel the obsession to do so. Joey might have taken a shortcut, but he knew Andie wouldn't. He trusted her. He knew that now, too late.

He interrupted before she could continue. "I owe you an apology, as well. I'm sorry, I shouldn't have immediately blamed Kozak. I'm a little wary after the last time, but that was wrong of me."

Her expression didn't soften. "You *were* right. We failed to do our job. I'll make sure we don't make any additional mistakes."

"I know—"

Andie turned and left the trailer, heading outside. When he stood and looked out a window, she was working with her crew, making up for what her brother did.

He had the urge to go out and pitch in, as well. But he stopped himself.

He could picture too well the rejection, being

told he wasn't needed. Wasn't wanted. He wasn't part of this company or this town.

Somehow, even though he'd not been at fault this time, he was still on the outside. That appeared to be his destiny.

He left at noon. He couldn't stand being alone in the trailer, sure Andie wouldn't do the work she needed to do in there if he was around.

No one said anything to him.

The next day, Andie did stay in the trailer to work, but she didn't talk, and she gave monosyllabic replies to his attempts to speak to her. He overheard her tell someone on the crew that she wouldn't be at darts night because she was going to see her brother. He stayed in the trailer until everyone was gone, and he didn't go to darts night, either.

He was at home, washing the dishes from his lonely meal when he heard a knock on his door. For a moment, he felt his heart lift. Maybe it was Andie. Maybe they could talk and somehow work this out.

He opened the door eagerly.

His smile fell. It wasn't Andie. It was Abigail Carter. There was no warmth in her expression, so it obviously wasn't a social call. She was going to fire him, even though he'd done nothing wrong. The unfairness burned inside him, and his voice was tight as he invited her in.

"Would you like a drink?"

Abigail shook her head. "Let's get to the point of this visit."

Trevor indicated a seat and was somewhat surprised when Abigail sat down. She folded her hands in her lap and looked at him with a frown. He was reminded of how his high school English teacher had looked at him when he'd gotten the theme of Macbeth wrong.

"Why do you think I'm renovating the mill?"

Just like in school, he attempted to work out why she was asking such an obvious question. "For the romance initiative. You need an event venue."

"And what is the purpose of all this effort? In case you wondered, I do *not* need the money."

He hadn't thought she did.

"As a family legacy?"

She snorted, a sound he hadn't expected from her.

"I've changed the name of the town from Carter's Crossing to Cupid's Crossing. It's not for my family name.

"The legacy I want for this town is for it to be alive. Growing and vibrant. And that's what this romance initiative is all about."

She paused, as if to make sure he understood. He nodded.

"We're a small town. We know each other,

and we look out for each other. We may seem gossipy or nosy, but it comes from a place of caring. Well, most of it. Like everywhere else, we have people here who aren't good people. We know who they are, and we work around them, and if we can encourage them to change, we do it. And possibly overdo it."

There was another pause and another nod from Trevor.

"I know you had a problem on your last job. Your reputation was damaged, through no fault of your own. This project was a chance for you to reestablish yourself. I was happy to provide that opportunity, because you are an excellent architect and would never otherwise consider working here. I thought—no, I *hoped*—you would appreciate that this community is more like a family than a band of cutthroats.

"You were unjustly accused of something when you were unable to defend yourself. I presumed that would make you more understanding of others who might find themselves in trouble. I was wrong."

Trevor wanted to argue. To defend himself again. After all, Joey *had* been responsible, not Trevor.

But Trevor hadn't known that when he first reacted. He'd wanted to protect himself, and he hadn't considered the harm he'd do someone else. He understood that now. He just wanted to know how badly he'd messed things up.

"Are you firing me, or would you rather I resign?"

Abigail frowned at him. "I certainly don't want to fire you, and I didn't think you were a quitter."

Trevor wasn't sure what she wanted. She was a couple of steps ahead of him, and he was tired of being flat-footed.

"I'm happy to finish my obligations here." He spoke carefully. "Did you come here only to express your displeasure, since you don't wish to end my involvement with the mill?"

Abigail sighed, and her expression was sad. "It seemed to me that you were finding your footing in this community. I spoke to you about turning my home into an inn, and there are other growth opportunities here. I'd hoped you might consider staying for a while."

For a moment, Trevor thought the ground had tilted under his feet, and he checked that nothing had fallen. But it wasn't a physical jolt.

Stay in Cupid's Crossing? Why did that thought suddenly excite him more than this big home he had a chance of designing back in the city? But Abigail was talking about hope in the past tense.

"You've changed your mind." His voice was

flat. The tilting was gone. The ground was stable, and his future…was exactly as it had been.

"Honestly, I don't think Andie would work with you again after the mill job is done."

He held back from saying he'd been right, that Joey had screwed up. Because the problem now wasn't about blame.

He understood that. This was about community. About working together. Finding out what was the truth and what was the best thing to do rather than immediately saying it wasn't his fault, as if he were a child being accused of misbehaving.

"You're right about that." Andie had been doing her best to avoid him while they were still working on the mill together.

Abigail stood. "It's unfortunate. Lately, we've been reclaiming people in this town, letting them show that they've grown and matured. You are, of course, welcome to stay through the end of the year, even after the mill is done, but I'll understand if you wish to leave earlier."

Trevor stood, followed her to the door and closed it after her. He hadn't been fired, not officially, but he felt just as bad as if he had been.

CHAPTER TWENTY

ANDIE WAS DOING her best to avoid Trevor. The first day back at work, she stayed out with the crew, helping to remove the rubble of the former portico. She had to be in the trailer the next day to track down materials to redo the work, but she'd done her best to ignore the man at the other end of the on-site office.

The trailer had never felt so small.

On the third day, he surprised her by joining her and the crew as they unloaded some of the new materials she'd managed to track down and expedite delivery on.

"Excuse me."

His voice wasn't loud, but as the nearest workers to him turned, the next looked to see what was going on. There was eventually silence as they all watched him.

He cleared his throat. "I wanted to apologize to you. On my last job, there was an accident and an injury. I was blamed by the contractor, though my work was cleared later. Because of that, I was too quick to react to what happened here. Before that happened, this job had gone as smoothly as any project I've worked on, and that's down to Andie and your hard work.

"I had some concerns that this project might be too much of a challenge for you, and I was wrong. I appreciate how you've pulled together to make up for the lost time. I have every confidence we'll finish up the project, and it will be great. So, um, thanks and sorry."

Trevor turned and almost fled to the trailer. The crew looked at each other and at Andie.

She shrugged. "We have a job to finish up, so let's get it done."

It was nice what he'd done. She knew the crew felt betrayed, just like she did. But she refused to let herself soften. The apology was one thing. That didn't mean he'd trust her or her company again.

She needed to keep that wall between them up, because there would be no more kisses, no more cozy discussions. She didn't need to get any more attached to Trevor. She was already more attached than was wise.

The next day, Mariah arrived. For a moment, Andie shot a look at Trevor, but he looked as surprised as she felt. Then she remembered they weren't a team now, and she needed to ignore him.

"Andie, Trevor, do you have a minute?"

Andie nodded, and Trevor shoved his laptop aside. "What is it, Mariah?"

"This is probably the worst time to ask, but do you have any idea when the mill will be done?"

Andie stilled, hating that Mariah had broached the topic that sat between Trevor and her, a landmine they couldn't discuss.

"The crew has been working hard to redo the portico." Trevor filled the momentary silence. "The last projections I saw had the mill ready about the third or fourth week in November, but that does include a lot of variables."

Andie had kept posting paperwork to their shared drive. She'd shot photos and video and posted them there, as well. Things they would have discussed in person prior were now all handled digitally. Trevor had been keeping up.

Of course he had.

Mariah turned to look at Andie, and she nodded. She was determined that the job would be done, no matter what, by the end of November, if she had to work 24/7 herself. Trevor could be back to his real life before Christmas.

"I don't want to pressure you, and I have a plan B if something comes up, but it sounds like I could tentatively plan something for mid-December in the mill?"

"That should work. Knock on wood. Dare I ask what you're planning?"

"Remember I'd mentioned a possible wedding? A Christmas wedding? And no, it's still not mine."

Andie could imagine what a great job Mariah would do. The mill would look beautiful, and since this town was now Cupid's Crossing, what better event than a wedding to kick off the new event center?

"Should I ask who's getting married then?"

Mariah grinned at her. "I need to tell the happy couple first."

Andie laughed, for the first time since her return from Florida. "That's probably a good idea. It's someone local then?"

Mariah held a finger to her lips. "Thanks, guys. That's all I wanted to know. Like I said, I have a backup plan, but I'd like to have the first event here be something the town can all be part of, and something that will look really good on the website."

She turned with a wave and left.

Andie knew whose wedding Mariah was planning. There were only two engaged couples in town, and one of those was Mariah and Nelson.

She wondered if Rachel and Ryker knew what was coming their way.

ANDIE WAS SURPRISED when Abigail stopped by the house one evening. Andie welcomed her in, since her mother was flustered. The Carters didn't normally visit with the Kozaks.

"You're looking good, Marion," Abigail said.

Abigail was right. After the argument with Joey, her mother had finally started talking to a therapist. She hadn't been going that long, but Andie was getting fewer frantic requests for her location. Her mother had also joined a committee at church. It was the first time she'd been involved outside the family since her husband died. They were small steps, but they were having a big impact.

When Andie told her mother she was looking for a place of her own after Christmas, her mother had fled to her room. After, though, she'd come out and promised to help Andie furnish the new place.

Joey would be home from the hospital soon, and her mother would have him to care for, but Andie wasn't sure Joey would be staying long. At least her mom should be able to handle it better now.

"Marion, I was hoping to tempt you into helping out on the romance committee after everything is settled with Joey."

Considering that Joey had caused the accident, Andie thought Abigail was being more than generous.

Her mother's eyes were wide. "I'd be happy to help."

"I'm pleased to hear that. But for now, I'd like to talk to Andie."

Andie nodded and led the way to the construction office. She'd known at some point that she was going to need to talk to Abigail.

Andie had called her, but Abigail had promised to speak to her later. Later was now.

She didn't think Abigail would fire them from the mill project, but she might not wish to work with Kozak again, and that would make it difficult for the company. Abigail carried a lot of influence in this community.

"This has nothing to do with the accident. Or at least, nothing directly." Abigail opened the discussion after settling herself in a chair.

"We're absorbing all the additional—"

Abigail held up a hand, so Andie stopped.

"I know. I also understand what happened, and as long as Joey will be supervised until such time as he's able to take this kind of responsibility again, I have no qualms about working with Kozak Construction in the future. But perhaps I need to ask if Kozak Construction will still be operating here in Cupid's Crossing."

Andie gripped the arms of her chair. Abigail wasn't following the script she'd expected, but unsurprisingly, she was going directly to the heart of the matter.

"It wasn't much of a secret that you'd hoped to go to school after the mill is done."

Andie nodded but remained silent.

"You've certainly earned the opportunity to fly the nest and stretch your wings."

For the first time, Andie tried to put her feelings into words. "My wings have been pretty well stretched here, heading up this company."

A slight smile tugged at Abigail's mouth. "Was it enough of a stretch to change your plans?"

Andie pulled in a breath. "It was. Mom has been getting some help, and I'm going to move to my own place in the new year. I want to stay here and run the company. Permanently. If you haven't lost confidence in us, that is my plan."

Now the smile on Abigail's face was complete. "I'm very pleased to hear that. There's going to be a lot of work in the immediate future here, and I'm pleased to have Kozak Construction available."

That feeling fluttering in Andie's stomach was relief. Joey's irresponsibility hadn't harmed the company, and she could continue a job she'd grown to love. One that gave her satisfaction, not just by doing good work but by helping to keep the community thriving.

"I had a meeting with Mr. Emerson."

Suddenly, Andie wasn't feeling so light anymore. Her feelings about Trevor were many and confused.

He'd hurt her, hurt more than just her professional pride. She understood that he'd be defensive after what he'd been through. Lashing out without proof had been bad, but he had apologized to the crew for that.

This hurt was personal.

She'd thought he trusted her. That they'd become friends. She'd thought their kisses had promised there was potential for something more in the future when they weren't working together.

But he hadn't trusted her. He hadn't even talked to her before he'd placed all the blame on Kozak. And as the head of Kozak, on her. She'd put up a reserved wall of politeness and wariness between them. She wasn't opening herself up to any more hurt.

She suspected that when he left, it was going to hurt badly anyway. Still, she braced herself for whatever Abigail was going to say.

"I let him know that there's no chance of him continuing to work here on future projects if he can't work with our local construction company."

Future projects? What was Abigail talking about? "But he's going back to New York anyway, isn't he?"

Andie was counting the days until he left. She'd told herself she wasn't counting with regret.

Abigail shrugged. "We have projects coming up. I know he's been talking to Mariah and Nelson about the house on the farm. We've also talked to him about converting my house, and Gerry's project. Realistically, I don't think you'll want to work with him again, and Kozak Construction is more essential to Cupid's Crossing than Trevor Emerson. We'll find someone else. Hopefully, someone more congenial."

Andie bit her lip before she said anything about being quite happy with how congenial Trevor was. That had been before.

She rose to her feet when Abigail did and followed her back to the door.

Abigail left, inviting her mother to a planning meeting next week on her way out, and Andie closed the door behind her.

"What did she want?" her mother asked. Abigail had never come to their office before.

"To let me know there's going to be work

coming up for the company. She wanted to know if I was staying to keep things going."

Her mother's smile wavered at the corners. "I'm glad you are. Your father would be very proud."

She pulled her mother into a hug. "You're sure Joey won't mind?"

Her mother sighed. "I don't know. But he's not ready."

Andie was. She was ready to claim her life now. She wasn't waiting anymore. She was living it. Now she needed to take the necessary step to make it what she wanted.

Unfortunately, it was going to be a single life for a while.

THE MILL LOOKED GORGEOUS.

Snow had fallen the night before, dusting the ground, and everything was white and fresh, as if the weather had been specially ordered for this day.

Rachel and Ryker's wedding day.

Rachel had been the town's good girl, Ryker the bad boy. He'd come back after serving in the Air Force and had become a town asset.

Rachel had learned to stand up for herself with his help while learning to ride a motorcycle. It was a story Andie would never have believed. But after that proposal at the wedding in July, it was all too real.

There was greenery and lots of red, candles and mistletoe. Mariah had managed to hit winter and romance without detouring too much into Christmas.

The wedding service had been held at the church where Rachel's father was pastor, and the reception was at the Mill, as it was now officially called. And like Dave and Jaycee's wedding, it was a town-wide event.

Mariah had arranged transportation for guests from the town park, since the parking lot at the Mill wasn't large enough to hold every vehicle in town. Andie hadn't been at the service. She'd come straight to the Mill, parked at the rear and walked through the building again, just to enjoy the results of a successful job. This building represented a future for Cupid's Crossing. It was a visible symbol of its new life.

The kitchen was busy. There were professional caterers from Oak Hill as well as offerings from the town. It wasn't a sit-down meal, but the smells Andie encountered as she passed the doorway made her stomach growl, and she placed a hand on her tummy to calm it.

The bathrooms were spotless. In the main space, long tables near the back were waiting for food, while high tops were scattered through the rest of the room so that people could mingle while enjoying the food and beverages.

A large cloakroom near the doors already had some high school students waiting to handle the coat check. There was a grouping of photos of Rachel and Ryker in one corner and a place for presents to be set next to it.

The shutters were open on the glass doors they'd installed, and the hillside above looked like a Christmas card, with trees and outcrops dusted with snow.

Cupid's Crossing was open for business.

THREE HOURS LATER, the official part of the reception was winding down. Rachel and Ryker were leaving for a weeklong honeymoon and would return for the holidays. Andie ducked away from the bouquet toss, and later, she saw Mariah carrying the bride's bouquet.

The town saw Rachel and Ryker off and then settled in to celebrate until they were kicked out.

Abigail was present, with Mariah's grandfather keeping close to her. Mariah had been busy coordinating all the activity, but somehow she never looked flustered or upset. If this was an indication of how events would go in the future, the town would be a success.

Andie was reluctant to leave. Joey was home, and her mother was helping him while keeping up with her new venture on the town romance committee. Joey's friends were often there, and Andie was unsettled. She blamed it on the fact that she was moving out so soon.

There was nowhere else to go tonight. Families with small children had made their exits, but everyone else was here. The diner was closed. Moonstone's was closed. Everyone was either home or at the Mill.

Andie didn't want to admit she was hesitant to leave the party because of Trevor, but she'd been aware of him all day. He'd never come close to her, but he'd still pinged her radar constantly. Enough that she knew where he was and was careful to keep some distance.

Word was he was leaving after today's party. That Abigail had insisted he stay for this first event, to see the culmination of his—no, *their*—work.

She'd assumed too much and felt too much after a few conversations and some kisses. She had to get over him, and it would be easier to do when he wasn't around.

She was not going to regret his departure. She wasn't. And the only way to keep that promise to herself was if she didn't interact with him.

Enough of this. It was time to go. She'd received kudos from everyone on the work they'd done on the Mill. Couples were dancing, and romance was in the air. There was no reason to stay. Not for her.

She reached into her purse to get her coat-check tag. She turned, and this time it wasn't her radar pinging. Trevor was right there. She shivered and gripped her tag tightly.

"Uh, hi," she said.

She'd prepared a speech before she got here, in case she had the opportunity to talk to him. It was dignified and professional. But he hadn't come near, and now it was forgotten. Instead, she scanned him, checking his appearance. Did he look tired? Thinner?

She'd never seen him dressed in a suit, and it flattered him. Did he think she looked good, as well? What did it matter, if he was leaving? When he couldn't trust her?

He swallowed. "I hoped to have a word with you."

He'd had lots of time today if he'd really wanted that. She didn't need to listen to any words he had, since she'd forgotten all the ones she had prepared for him. But she couldn't keep up her indignation. This would be the last time she saw him.

She clenched her fingers into her palms so that she didn't reach for him. Despite everything, she didn't want him to hate or resent her. She was obviously stupid.

"Uh, now?"

She wasn't getting any smarter or more literate.

"If you don't mind? We could go upstairs?"

Rachel had changed out of her gown up there, in the rooms set up for that purpose, but they were empty now.

He wanted to talk in private.

She really didn't need to be nervous. There was nothing he could say to throw her off-balance. Not now. The job was done, and he was leaving.

Andie forced her feet to move toward the stairs. Her dress was cocktail length, so there was no problem climbing the steps. She looked over her shoulder, and no one on the main floor appeared to pay them any attention. She heard Trevor following her.

She led the way to the office in the back corner. It had been Abigail's old office, but after the renovations, it was now a smaller room. Just big enough for someone like Mariah to meet clients who wanted to plan events at the

Mill. Instead of a desk, there were a couple of chairs and a loveseat with a coffee table in between.

Andie sat in one of the chairs. Her knees were a little shaky. Trevor followed her in and sat on the edge of the loveseat across from her.

She was torn between the urge to fill the silence and another urge to keep her mouth firmly closed. She couldn't say anything stupid if she didn't speak, right?

"I'm sorry, Andie."

Her gaze shot to his. He looked serious. His eyes focused on her from behind his glasses.

She opened her mouth to speak, to tell him he'd already apologized, but he kept going.

"I'm obviously still not over everything that happened back in the city. But you didn't deserve to be hit by my issues. I did to you exactly what was done to me, and I'm embarrassed by that."

"But you were right in the end. It was Joey's fault." She hadn't planned to blurt that out.

"If I'd waited for that to be proven, I wouldn't feel like I betrayed you, betrayed the trust we'd built up. And he didn't do it maliciously or even to benefit himself at my expense. I knew you were out of town, but I didn't stay to be available if a problem came up. That's on me. Joey made a mistake, and he paid for it."

Andie swallowed. "Thank you. I appreciate that."

She did. That acknowledgement helped to soothe her professional pride.

He smiled, but it was a polite lacquer. She hurt, because the real smile was no longer on offer for her. He'd hurt more than her pride. He'd hurt her heart.

He rubbed his hands on his thighs, clearly restless. "I wanted to tell you that before I left. I wasn't sure you'd want to talk to me, so I hope you don't mind I tracked you down here."

No, she didn't mind.

"I don't hate you, Trevor. I was hurt, though. I thought we'd built up trust, and that's not easy. When you reacted like that, it felt personal." She needed to stop talking before she revealed too much.

"I'm sorry I broke that trust. That's why I'm leaving."

Andie frowned. "What?"

He shrugged. "Abigail told me she has to find someone else for the new projects around here."

"But you don't want to stay, not here in Cupid's Crossing? You have everything back in the city."

He lifted a hand, then dropped it. He shook his head. "Not everything. There's more here than I'd realized. But there's no future for an architect when the area's top contractor won't work with him."

Andie wanted to hit a replay button. He couldn't be saying what it sounded like he was saying, right?

"You want to stay? If we could work together, you'd want to stay?"

She tensed, scarcely able to draw a breath. He'd never mentioned staying. Why would he want to?

He didn't speak for a moment, and she felt her cheeks warm.

"I've been considering my options. Whether there's enough opportunities for me here, either, in Cupid's Crossing itself or in the general area around the town. It seems I'm more of a country mouse than I realized. But no one will want to partner with me after what I did."

Really? He'd considered staying here? What could that have meant for them? What could it mean now? Was she brave enough to find out?

"I guess it would depend on whether you would do something like that again. Everyone makes mistakes."

He leaned forward, staring at her intently. "I mean, I forgave Joey, so…"

Wait, she needed to think before saying anything more. Trevor was talking about cooperating on projects together. Nothing more.

"I didn't think you'd even consider that we could get past what I did."

Could she? Would she want to work with Trevor again? She thought of those weeks after they'd gotten past their initial problems, and things had been… Things had been great, actually.

"If I could be sure you trusted me." She couldn't go through that again.

Trevor shook his head. "I've learned my lesson from that. We were a team, and I hurt everyone by only considering myself. I'd felt alone for a long time, so I didn't understand that at first."

She tried to picture a professional future with Trevor going forward. Would they be able to make it a success? Could they get back to where things had been before she left for her vacation?

"Would you want to try? You always talked like the city was where you belonged."

"I did. It's true I never considered anything else. It's an adjustment, going from there to a small town. But I'm not good at getting to know people, and here, people get to know you whether you want them to or not."

A smile briefly warmed her lips. "You have a point there."

"I had no idea that I'd find a place that could accept me, all of me, just as I was. People that would accept me. Maybe a particular person that would."

He examined her face, and she waited. Had he just been talking to make her feel good? Had he made up his mind about his future?

"There's one other thing I damaged, something that doesn't involve Kozak Construction directly. I hurt you. I broke the trust you placed in me. Not as someone you worked with, but personally."

Her breath caught. It sounded like he had made some kind of decision.

"I think I would find it difficult to be here and not have that connection with you anymore."

He was still watching her. There was tension in his neck and shoulders and an anxious expression on his face.

"I, um, I mean, I would...find it hard, too."

"Would you? But is it possible to have it again?"

Andie tried to picture it in her head. Trevor staying here. Working here. Being with her here.

She felt her pulse beating slowly and thickly

through her veins. She was aware of every breath, as if time had slowed.

"I think it is possible." Her voice was small.

"You think so? Just think so?"

"I—" She swallowed. "I'd be willing to try."

He jerked as if his body wanted to move but had been stopped. "Can we work together and have something personally going on, as well?"

She raised her brows. "I can handle that, but I don't know if you can."

She watched the expressions play over his face. Worry, confusion, and then…he looked at her and smiled. Not just any smile. A warm, promising smile.

"Maybe you could give me some tips."

Andie stood and walked over to Trevor, reaching her hand down. He gripped it, and she felt warmth move through her. She tugged and brought him to his feet.

"Here's one," she said and kissed him.

BACK IN THE driveway of the Carter house, Gerald came around the limo and opened the door for Abigail. She let him help her to her feet and led the way to the front door of her home.

Once inside, Gerry took her coat and hung it with his in the hall closet, then he followed her into the living room.

"I'd say the launch of your romance initiative was a success."

Abigail smiled. She raised the decanter, and he nodded.

"I think you're right."

"Mariah tells me that you're going to turn this place into an inn."

Abigail passed him a glass and indicated that he should sit. She picked up her own glass and sat across from him. "I'm fairly certain I will."

His brows lowered. "I bought that property outside of town, the Slade place, for an inn and spa. Are we going to be competitors?"

Abigail smiled. "The town will need both places. We've already got a couple of weddings booked for this summer, and not everyone is willing to stay in a B and B."

Gerry leaned back, looking at her. "Are you going to be an innkeeper then?"

Abigail sat straight and shook her head. "No, I don't think I'm suited for that."

"I don't think you are, either. What are you going to do if your home becomes a commercial enterprise?"

She shrugged elegant shoulders. "I think I've done my part for Cupid's Crossing. With Mariah taking over, the town is in good hands."

"Don't think I've forgotten that you poached

her. She was supposed to be here for just a year before she came and worked for me."

Abigail upturned a hand. "But that was her decision."

"Abigail, you may fool many people, but you don't fool me."

"She and Nelson are in love. He'd never be happy in a city, and I think Mariah is quite content here."

He snorted. "Yes, she is. What are you going to do? Last winter at the Valentine's events, you talked about leaving."

She looked into the distance, staring more through than at the painting on the wall. "I think I'd like to travel."

"Travel?"

"I've worked hard. I'm ready to enjoy myself now, to be free of responsibilities."

He quirked up his mouth. "That sounds nice."

"Of course, I'd prefer doing it with a companion."

Gerry put his drink on the table. He leaned forward. "And do you have someone in mind?"

"Let's not be coy, Gerry. You haven't been coming to town just to check up on Mariah. It's time for you to give yourself a break, as well."

He grinned. "People don't tell me what to do, Abigail."

"I'm not people. And it's time you don't get your way on everything."

"I should just pack my bags and run away with you?"

Abigail raised elegant eyebrows. "Don't be silly, Gerry. I'm sure it will be about a year before either of us is ready to go. I've got this house to deal with, and you have your businesses. But I think I'd like to spend next winter somewhere warm."

"How long have you had this planned?"

She shook her head. "I'm not the devious planner you think I am. I'm just looking at our situation and being practical."

Gerry stood up and moved till he was in front of Abigail. "You know, the way I feel about you has never been practical."

Abigail stood up, allowing him to take her hand. "I should hope not."

EPILOGUE

It HAD BEEN a great year.

Andie had used her college fund to put a down payment on a small home in drastic need of updating, and she spent her free time renovating the house while living in it. It had been a challenge, but Trevor helped, both with the design and with the hands-on work. When the kitchen was being renovated, Andie almost lived at Trevor's. The proximity hadn't been a problem.

The Mill was a resounding success. There had been five weddings there over the summer. Mariah and Nelson were married, but not at the Mill. They'd had a small service in the park on Valentine's Day. Andie thought Nelson was happy about that.

Mariah and Nelson had just moved into the house on the farm that Trevor had designed for them, and that Kozak Construction had built.

Nelson had been concerned that the noise of the construction would bother the horses, but the crew had enjoyed spending time with the animals. One of Nelson's more recent rescues was now the property of—or more accurately, the pet of—one of the Kozak Construction crew.

Abigail was well into the process of converting her home into an inn, and Mariah's grandfather was building a small inn and spa on the old Slade property. Both projects were being handled by Trevor and Andie. They'd decided that when there was trust between them, working together while dating was not actually a problem.

Andie's mom was much better. She'd adapted to Andie moving to her own place, and even to Joey moving out of town. She'd become involved in the planning committees and taken on the bookkeeping for Kozak Construction again, freeing up time for Andie.

The first New Year's after Joey's accident, the family had gathered together one last time. They'd said a final farewell to their father. Andie's mom wasn't going to be attending any New Year's Eve parties, but this year, Andie wasn't spending the night with her family. She was at the Goat with Trevor.

For the first time in years, Andie was looking forward to the night. This past year had been the best she could remember, and she expected more of the same in this new year.

With Trevor.

Her house was almost ready to sell. They'd been discussing another project together but hadn't decided on one yet. Andie was leaning toward a family home. If all went well, maybe it would be one they could stay in. Together. And start a family.

It would be a big step for Trevor. She'd met his family, and they'd been polite, but they would never be close. Andie could see the difference in how they reacted to their two sons. With Trevor living in Cupid's Crossing, they could have a friendly relationship, though Andie did a lot of teeth gritting when they were around.

Trevor had found his true home in a small town well outside New York City. Her mother had practically adopted him anyway.

Trevor was in a strange mood today, though. He'd insisted on bringing his computer bag to the bar, which made no sense. They weren't supposed to be working. Maybe he had a new client he thought he might bump into.

He now ran his firm out of the Kozak Construction office, and while they didn't do every project together, they collaborated on most of them.

The bartender stopped in front of her with a soda for her and a beer for Trevor. Andie frowned. She didn't need to keep up that tradition, not now. The bartender moved on to another customer, and she sighed. She could drink one glass of soda and then get a beer. It was time to start something new.

She picked up the glass and turned to Trevor, but he was digging something out of his bag. She wished he could forget work for one day. She wanted to make this New Year's Eve something new, something happy, something to overshadow the previous ones.

A new start.

He pulled out a roll of paper and laid it on the bar top. She recognized the blue ink. These were blueprints. Another project to work on? Was this something they could do together?

If that was all this was, they could have discussed it at the office. She set down her drink, a little ticked now. This was supposed to be a special night. The anniversary of the first time they met.

He rolled off the elastic and carefully flattened the paper. She leaned over, curious in spite of herself, to see what he'd created, to see the vision in his head traced here so that she could build it in wood and stone and concrete.

It was a house. She scanned the lines, noting things like the elevation and the size. She ran a tentative finger over the letters and numbers he'd carefully inscribed, picturing in her mind what the finished structure would look like.

Two stories, four bedrooms. A fireplace of stone. Gorgeous. She couldn't imagine who in their small town could be building this home.

Oh.

Maybe it wasn't going to be built here. Somewhere else. Maybe this beautiful home, his next project, wasn't one she'd be working on. Was that why he hadn't showed it to her till now? How soon would he have to leave? And why did he have to do this now? This day had been a bad day for so many years. Did he think she wouldn't mind if he added more disappointment to it?

She'd hoped he'd be here in Cupid's Crossing to work on flipping a house with her.

She kept her face tilted downward, determined not to show any feelings, any hurt.

"It's beautiful. You've done an excellent job."

Her voice was steady, right? She wasn't revealing anything.

She heard his hand on the paper before she saw it. He was sliding something toward her, something that scratched across the paper. With an indrawn breath, she pulled together her tattered control and let her gaze move to where his hand rested.

He'd stopped on the kitchen, the heart of the home, and in his hand was a ring.

Her gaze shot up, meeting his. He wasn't smiling, and his fingers trembled.

"I love you, Andie. I wanted… I hoped, um, maybe we can build this place together? For us?"

Bubbles fizzier than any champagne moved through her body. She flung herself at him, wrapping her arms around his neck and almost knocking him off the stool.

"Yes, yes. There's nothing I want more."

She grabbed his cheeks, meeting the smile creasing his face. She pulled that face toward her, not caring who was watching, and kissed him.

Whistles around them finally brought her to her senses, and she pulled back, still ignoring the crowd. She had eyes for no one but him.

He grabbed her hand and slid the ring on. "It's not a big stone or very fancy. I didn't want it to be a hazard while you're working."

Andie didn't care about the size. "It's perfect. You're perfect."

"No, I'm not. But hang on to that thought as long as you can. We might argue a bit on this." He tapped the blueprints.

She rubbed her thumbs over his cheeks. "Doesn't matter. As long as we do it together."

He rested his forehead on hers. "I was so nervous. I hoped this would make the day better for you."

"It has. But I'll warn you, Mariah is going to be annoyed that you didn't make a big deal of it to put on the website."

His cheeks turned pink. "Um…" His gaze moved past her, and she turned her head to see what he was looking at.

A cheer went up from the crowd. Her mother, some of her siblings, most of her crew, Rachel and Ryker, Jaycee and Dave, Mariah and Nelson… Almost everyone she knew was here to celebrate with her, making this a day of happiness, no longer one of regret.

She gripped Trevor's hand in hers. "Have I told you I love you?"

"No, but I'll forgive you if you kiss me at midnight."

"It's a date."

* * * * *

Get 4 FREE REWARDS!

We'll send you 2 FREE Books plus 2 FREE Mystery Gifts.

Love Inspired books feature uplifting stories where faith helps guide you through life's challenges and discover the promise of a new beginning.

FREE
Value Over
$20

YES! Please send me 2 FREE Love Inspired Romance novels and my 2 FREE mystery gifts (gifts are worth about $10 retail). After receiving them, if I don't wish to receive any more books, I can return the shipping statement marked "cancel." If I don't cancel, I will receive 6 brand-new novels every month and be billed just $5.24 each for the regular-print edition or $5.99 each for the larger-print edition in the U.S., or $5.74 each for the regular-print edition or $6.24 each for the larger-print edition in Canada. That's a savings of at least 13% off the cover price. It's quite a bargain! Shipping and handling is just 50¢ per book in the U.S. and $1.25 per book in Canada.* I understand that accepting the 2 free books and gifts places me under no obligation to buy anything. I can always return a shipment and cancel at any time. The free books and gifts are mine to keep no matter what I decide.

Choose one: ☐ **Love Inspired Romance Regular-Print** (105/305 IDN GNWC) ☐ **Love Inspired Romance Larger-Print** (122/322 IDN GNWC)

Name (please print)

Address _____ Apt. #

City _____ State/Province _____ Zip/Postal Code

Email: Please check this box ☐ if you would like to receive newsletters and promotional emails from Harlequin Enterprises ULC and its affiliates. You can unsubscribe anytime.

Mail to the **Harlequin Reader Service:**
IN U.S.A.: P.O. Box 1341, Buffalo, NY 14240-8531
IN CANADA: P.O. Box 603, Fort Erie, Ontario L2A 5X3

Want to try 2 free books from another series! Call 1-800-873-8635 or visit www.ReaderService.com.

---

*Terms and prices subject to change without notice. Prices do not include sales taxes, which will be charged (if applicable) based on your state or country of residence. Canadian residents will be charged applicable taxes. Offer not valid in Quebec. This offer is limited to one order per household. Books received may not be as shown. Not valid for current subscribers to Love Inspired Romance books. All orders subject to approval. Credit or debit balances in a customer's account(s) may be offset by any other outstanding balance owed by or to the customer. Please allow 4 to 6 weeks for delivery. Offer available while quantities last.

Your Privacy—Your information is being collected by Harlequin Enterprises ULC, operating as Harlequin Reader Service. For a complete summary of the information we collect, how we use this information and to whom it is disclosed, please visit our privacy notice located at corporate.harlequin.com/privacy-notice. From time to time we may also exchange your personal information with reputable third parties. If you wish to opt out of this sharing of your personal information, please visit readerservice.com/consumerschoice or call 1-800-873-8635. **Notice to California Residents**—Under California law, you have specific rights to control and access your data. For more information on these rights and how to exercise them, visit corporate.harlequin.com/california-privacy.

LIR21R2

Get 4 FREE REWARDS!

We'll send you 2 FREE Books plus 2 FREE Mystery Gifts.

BRENDA JACKSON
Follow Your Heart

ROBYN CARR
The Country Guesthouse

RICK MOFINA
SEARCH FOR HER

B.J. DANIELS
FROM the SHADOWS

FREE
Value Over
$20

Both the **Romance** and **Suspense** collections feature compelling novels written by many of today's bestselling authors.

YES! Please send me 2 FREE novels from the Essential Romance or Essential Suspense Collection and my 2 FREE gifts (gifts are worth about $10 retail). After receiving them, if I don't wish to receive any more books, I can return the shipping statement marked "cancel." If I don't cancel, I will receive 4 brand-new novels every month and be billed just $7.24 each in the U.S. or $7.49 each in Canada. That's a savings of up to 28% off the cover price. It's quite a bargain! Shipping and handling is just 50¢ per book in the U.S. and $1.25 per book in Canada.* I understand that accepting the 2 free books and gifts places me under no obligation to buy anything. I can always return a shipment and cancel at any time. The free books and gifts are mine to keep no matter what I decide.

Choose one: ☐ **Essential Romance**   ☐ **Essential Suspense**
                     (194/394 MDN GQ6M)   (191/391 MDN GQ6M)

Name (please print)

Address   Apt. #

City   State/Province   Zip/Postal Code

Email: Please check this box ☐ if you would like to receive newsletters and promotional emails from Harlequin Enterprises ULC and its affiliates. You can unsubscribe anytime.

> ### Mail to the **Harlequin Reader Service:**
> **IN U.S.A.:** P.O. Box 1341, Buffalo, NY 14240-8531
> **IN CANADA:** P.O. Box 603, Fort Erie, Ontario L2A 5X3

Want to try 2 free books from another series! Call 1-800-873-8635 or visit www.ReaderService.com.

STRS21R2

#407 HER HOMETOWN HERO
Polk Island • by Jacquelin Thomas

Trey Rothchild returns home to Polk Island a marine veteran and an amputee. He barely recognizes the life he lives now—and he certainly can't make room in it for old friend Gia Harris, his beautiful physical therapist.

#408 THE SHERIFF'S VALENTINE
Stop the Wedding! • by Amy Vastine

Nothing can tear Sheriff Ben Harper away from his duties. Except perhaps thrill-seeking Shelby Young, who rolls back into town before his brother's wedding—bringing all kinds of trouble in her wake!

#409 MONTANA REUNION
by Jen Gilroy

When Beth Flanagan becomes guardian to her late friend's daughter, she heads back to the Montana camp where she spent her summers. Her teenage crush is now the rancher next door—a complication or a blessing in disguise?

#410 HOME FOR THE HOLIDAYS
Return to Christmas Island • by Amie Denman

Camille Peterson can handle running her family's candy business—she can't handle running into her ex and his adorable son. Maddox betrayed her years ago...but idyllic Christmas Island might just weave the magic of a second chance.

Visit ReaderService.com Today!

As a valued member of the Harlequin Reader Service, you'll find these benefits and more at ReaderService.com:

- Try 2 free books from any series
- Access risk-free special offers
- View your account history & manage payments
- Browse the latest Bonus Bucks catalog

Don't miss out!

If you want to stay up-to-date on the latest at the Harlequin Reader Service and enjoy more content, make sure you've signed up for our monthly News & Notes email newsletter. Sign up online at ReaderService.com or by calling Customer Service at 1-800-873-8635.

RS20